FINDING LOVE AT MERMAID TERRACE

FINDING LOVE AT MERMAID TERRACE

Kate Forster

An Aria Book

This edition first published in the United Kingdom in 2021 by Aria,
an imprint of Head of Zeus Ltd

A CIP catalogue record for this book is available from the
British Library.

ISBN (E): 9781788544375
ISBN (PB): 9781800246027

Cover design © Cherie Chapman

Typeset by Siliconchips Services Ltd UK
Printed and bound by CPI Group (UK) Ltd, Croydon, CR0 4YY

Aria
c/o Head of Zeus
First Floor East
5–8 Hardwick Street
London EC1R 4RG

www.ariafiction.com

To all the doctors and nurses who helped so many
through COVID-19.

Thank you.

Part One

Part One

Port Lowdy had ideas above its station. The sign at the top of St Martin's Road read *Welcome to the Coastal Town of Port Lowdy*. At best it was a large seaside village. Once famous for brown crabs and being the location of a film starring Dame Judi Dench, it was now so sleepy even the crabs took afternoon naps, no longer concerned with nets hauling them from their ocean floor slumber. Tourists came, not too many. There were enough visitors to help the village be lively in the summer and to make the residents feel smug in their decision to make Port Lowdy their forever home.

Tressa Buckland was one of the smug ones. She had been a holidaymaker with her family since she was born. Now she was a full-time Port Lowdian of two years and she loved everything about living there. The way it looked, with its messy, coloured houses along the shore and the cobbled streets amongst the village. There was a sense of routine in a village as old as this, a certain way things had always been done and though people came and went every summer, the routine stayed the same.

Tressa wasn't one to argue about changing the routine. The familiarity of the village was what made her want to be one of the smug ones who complained about the tourists but who knew the village relied on them to survive.

On a warmer than usual February morning, Tressa swung her backpack onto her shoulders, adjusted her helmet on top of her messy black curls that refused to be tamed, and hopped onto her pink bicycle.

At twenty-six, she was one of the few single people in the village under the age of sixty. Not that Tressa minded. She wasn't looking for a relationship; her art was her true love and that was enough for her.

Tressa never tired of her daily ride from her house – Mermaid Terrace, her pale turquoise cottage that sat on the edge of the esplanade overlooking the beach. It was one of four houses all painted different colours, and all with different names.

Tressa pedalled her bike along the esplanade, warming up quickly with the sun shining while a light breeze touched her face.

She had dreamed of living in Port Lowdy since she could remember, and she had always looked at the coloured terrace houses and imagined her life inside one of them. She longed to have it filled with things her mother did not approve of – like a cat, and plates that didn't match, and jam jars filled with flowers and paintbrushes soaking in water.

At the front of the terrace houses were a garden and a sea wall that overlooked a small patch of sand. If you walked across the sand bar at low tide, you could reach the rock pools where Tressa spent most of her time during the holidays as a child.

Her parents lived in St Ives, as did her older brother and

his wife, who had young twins, but Tressa had moved to Port Lowdy to escape them.

Mermaid Terrace was her heaven, a stone house with a bay window that looked out over the few fishing boats left over from a previous era. She had bought it with money her grandmother left her. She often wondered if her grandmother had understood how difficult it was to grow up under the mothering of Wendy Buckland. Her parents' house was so grand and so perfect that people stopped to take photos of it. Inside, it was impossible to put down a glass or a mug without a coaster appearing from somewhere. Tressa used to wonder if her mother had a holster of them ready to fling at anyone from ten yards like a cowboy, protecting the heavy furniture from unsightly water rings.

As she rode through the village, the freshly laundered tablecloths from the Black Swan pub snapped in the wind, bickering with each other. She waved at Marcel, the owner, who was sitting outside the pub drinking a coffee and reading the paper. Marcel made a lovely crab bisque with croutons, which was old-fashioned, but Port Lowdy was that sort of place. This suited Tressa. She painted old-fashioned pictures that weren't popular with the art market but they made her happy.

Penny Stanhope, the postmistress, waved as she turned over the Closed sign on the door. The post office also served as the bank, the local passport office, and the insurance office. Penny sold chutneys and jams made by some of the local women and questionable shell craft with googly eyes and the occasional diamante for pizazz. Port Lowdy didn't really do pizazz so the shell craft didn't sell but the jams were popular.

The bakery with its striped red awning was already open, the Cornish pasties just out of the oven and the scones rising for morning tea. There was a small garden with a white picket fence out the side of the bakery, where tourists could eat their Cornish cream tea under the apple trees and watch the passing foot traffic.

Tressa pedalled up the small hill and came to the front of the little office that was both the headquarters of *The Port Lowdy Occurrence* and the local car rental in the summer. She pushed open the door, trying to balance the bike and the heavy wood door. She took off her bicycle helmet and felt her curls spring outwards in protest after the short ride.

Tressa's black curls had a life of their own. Her brother didn't get them, in fact, no one knew where the curly hair gene had come from in the Buckland family. Everyone else was blonde and brown-eyed but Tressa had dark hair and blue eyes. As a child, she used to pore over the family tree in the old family Bible on the bookshelf. Her curls were from ancestors unknown, and it always gave Tressa a thrill to think of the relative who bequeathed the hair to her, generations later, like a charm. Her skill for drawing was also an unclaimed talent: no one could see where it came from in the family tree. Tressa cherished these differences because they made her special – and God knows it was hard to be special in her family.

Anything for a peaceful life, her boss George Fox said, and she agreed. George was the owner and editor of *The Port Lowdy Occurrence*. It was just the two of them working at the *Occurrence*, but the paper made enough to pay her wage and keep George in whisky, and it funded his passion for antiques. They were busy enough through advertising from the fishing and holiday community and George had business all over Cornwall, with the car rental in the summer and numerous other fingers in other Cornish pasties.

Tressa was grateful for her job because it allowed her to paint. She was an artist – a properly trained one at that, her mother would tell you if you asked, having gone to art school in Plymouth. Tressa sold her paintings and prints of the Cornish sea from a website under the pseudonym *The Cornish Mermaid*; the sales topped up her income to pay for living expenses and canvas and everything else was cream.

Her mother Wendy said that Tressa was the oldest twenty-six-year-old in the UK. She spent her money on not much else besides her art. All her friends were still drinking and dancing all night but Tressa was a loner, not so much by choice as by circumstance. She was shy and she had struggled to stay in contact with friends from school or university, all of whom seemed to be getting engaged or married now. A few of them even had babies. She sent little paintings off to her friends, celebrating their news, and drew cards for the babies and posted them to faraway places but no one wanted to come to Port Lowdy and stay at Mermaid Terrace. If Tressa ever pulled an all-nighter it was in front of her easel waiting for the moon to slide behind the clouds when it was the sun's turn to take over.

'How will you ever meet someone?' her mother asked. 'You'll never find anyone there. Come on home and find love. We will buy you a place, and you can rent out your house there and come back to it later on.' Wendy kept trying to coax her daughter to return to St Ives but Tressa didn't believe in finding love. Love wasn't lost, so why should she go looking for it? It would come if it was ready and if love never found her, she had her cat and her art and that was enough, she told herself. There was no one in Port Lowdy worth swinging hands with. She knew nearly everyone in the village and there were no eligible men under the age of sixty. Older men had never been her thing.

There was another artist she'd had a thing with for a while, who she used to see in St Ives, but it wasn't serious and they both knew it. She didn't want to live there and he didn't want to come to Port Lowdy. It was unspoken that their connection was merely physical and a mutual appreciation of art and nothing more. He was nice enough but not enough to want more from him.

The sound of her boss, George, talking on the phone welcomed Tressa to another day at work, as she put her bike into the storage room and then went into the kitchen to make them both a cup of tea. Her job at *The Port Lowdy Occurrence* had been a happy accident after his wife Caro left work to be more involved in with their grandchildren. It wasn't full-time but it gave her enough time to paint and stare out the attic window from her terrace house at the ever-changing colour of the sea.

'Can I see you, Tressie?'

'Sure,' said Tressa. 'Want your tea?'

'Yes and bring the digestive biscuits,' George said sombrely.

A morning digestive meant George was trying to solve a serious problem.

Tressa took the mugs to his desk and sat down facing him, the biscuits tucked under her arm, and she placed the morning tea between them.

'What's going on?' she asked. 'Am I being fired?' She was always waiting for the axe to drop on her life. She couldn't help it – that was the anxiety she lived with. Mostly, she kept it under control – but today, George looked worried and tired. She herself was usually the problem in most situations, her mother had once told her.

George blew on his tea. 'No, love, I have a business decision I need to chat to you about.'

'Okay,' said Tressa carefully.

'Caro's sick,' he said.

'Oh no! What's wrong?'

Tressa felt such dread at anything happening to George and Caro. They were her dear friends and meant so much to Port Lowdy. George and Caro Fox were the parents she wished she had. They were encouraging, peaceful, and the only ones who'd seen how hard it was for Tressa growing up with Wendy and David Buckland as her parents. Where her parents pushed her, George and Caro nurtured her. Starting as their local delivery girl over summer at thirteen, to now the advertising manager and photographer, Tressa had found her place in the Foxes' paper and family. Their children Anna and Blake were her friends over summer, and taught her to sail and snorkel and build fires on the beach. They were the siblings she was close to, not Jago, her older brother with whom she had nothing in common.

'Caro has to go to Plymouth for an operation. We'll have to stay there for a while,' he said slowly, as though he was still processing the news himself.

'What sort of operation?' she asked.

'It's cancer,' George said but he was white as he spoke, avoiding her eyes.

'Oh, George, shit sticks.' She felt tears welling. She stifled them by pushing her thumbnail into the palm of her hand. George needed her help, not her grief.

'I can't believe it,' he said.

'Is she okay? I mean, she's not okay but how is she feeling?' Tressa felt ill-equipped to ask the right questions. What she really wanted to know was if Caro was going to be okay. 'Did they say… how bad it is?' Somehow it seemed indelicate to ask what stage it was.

But George saved her the effort. 'Stage-three bowel cancer,' he said. His voice was lifeless as he spoke.

'Triple shit sticks,' she said and George gave a small snort of laughter.

'You sound like Caro. That was exactly her response.'

'Okay, what can I do to help?' she asked. 'What do you need at the house, at work? Do you need me to make food or something?'

She needed a task so she didn't feel so completely useless at such terrible news.

George was staring ahead of him, over Tressa's head, looking at the large whiteboard with its schedule of stories that they had planned to cover.

'You'll have to run the *Occurrence*,' he said. 'But hire someone to help you. It's too much for one person with summer coming up. The advertisers will need to be chased and the photos from the real estate companies compiled. And there are articles to be written about the new ferry and the art show at the school.' He paused. 'I was looking forward to those.'

Tressa put her hand on his across the desk. 'George, I'll

take care of it all, I promise.' She felt about twelve years old as she spoke.

George was thinking aloud. 'You'll need a journalist, maybe someone who is retired. You won't get anyone from around here. You'll have to advertise, and I'll pay for a room for them to stay here.'

Trying not to crumble at the fear in his voice, Tressa nodded.

'I can ask around for us but I have to get her to Plymouth tomorrow. The doctor called last night. I need to take her in right away.'

He looked ashen and Tressa worried he might be next for a health issue.

'I can handle this. I'll manage it all, I promise,' she said, trying to sound soothing while her stomach was twisting in knots.

'*The Port Lowdy Occurrence* hasn't missed an issue since 1781,' George said blankly.

'And it won't miss one under my guidance,' Tressa stated. 'You focus on Caro and I'll focus on the paper. Now head home and let me get on with it.'

He took a biscuit at last and dipped it in his tea.

'Can I finish my tea first, boss?' he said with a faint smile.

Tressa blinked away tears. 'Take as long as you need, George; I'm just going to just sit here and be with you if that's okay?'

'I couldn't think of anyone I would rather sit with at this moment,' he said and they finished their tea and the biscuits in silence.

2

Penny Stanhope adjusted the jam jars on the table by the door of the post office. These were a fresh batch from Rosemary March, who had been dabbling with new recipes after a trip to France. There was an orange marmalade with whisky and a plum and rum jam, both of which sounded delicious – but Penny knew she would have to hide them when Old Walter came in to post his weekly letter to the editor of *The Cornish Times*. The inhabitants of Port Lowdy were Old Walter's sober companions and everyone took the role very seriously. Walter was banned from the Black Swan and from the off-licence, and everyone in town knew to not let Walter buy the liquor-filled chocolates at the shops.

He used to get the bus to Truro and drink. Then Penny spoke to the bus driver, a man whose wife sold a tangy tomato chutney during the summer at the post office. She and the driver were old mates. So now Old Walter could no longer head over to Truro where all too often he ended up in a police cell sleeping it off.

'Morning, Penny,' she heard and looked up to see Tressa Buckland walking into the store.

'Hello to you, Tressa – lovely day for a bike ride.'

She liked Tressa. In fact, everyone liked Tressa. Tressa

was kind. She had given Penny a stack of old canvases for her little granddaughter who came to stay over the summer holidays, and then spent Saturday mornings with her teaching her how to paint kittens. Really, the paintings were just a mess of mad brushstrokes, but Tressa had claimed genius in the work, and Penny loved her for having been so enthusiastic. Her own father had done a fine job on her, his only child. So Penny knew what it was like to have someone tell you as a child that you weren't good enough.

Tressa unclipped her bike helmet and looked carefully through the jams by the door. She picked up a jar and read the label.

'Banana chutney? That sounds ambitious.'

'Rosemary has been trying new things,' said Penny diplomatically. 'The jams are lovely though; I can recommend her blackcurrant jam on a crumpet. Or the raspberry and kirsch if you like a little hint of alcohol.'

Tressa took the blackcurrant jam and went to the counter.

'I'm here to get the letters to the editor. George can't come today.'

'I know,' said Penny, 'I heard.' She was devastated to hear about Caro. Caro was an important part of Port Lowdy – and above all, she was a friend. Penny was aware that most of the children's books in the library had been paid for by Caro and George, and that she had refused to have their names added in bookplates.

Caro had supported Marcel when he first came to St Ives and worked as a chef at the pub. Eventually Caro and George bought it and made Marcel a shareholder. And it was Caro who had introduced Marcel to his wife. Together Pamela and Marcel had turned the Black Swan into such a success, and then they'd bought George and Caro out of the business.

News that Caro was sick had spread quickly over the village. Now here was Tressa picking up the mail by herself, and it made Caro's illness all the more real. George always came to the post office and Penny would always have a cup of tea with him and they would chat about the village, about his children and about Penny's own daughter and granddaughter. Sometimes they talked about Tressa, worried about what she was going to do in Port Lowdy for the rest of her life. Penny worried she would end up like Janet, Tressa's neighbour who since she'd retired rarely left the house. Who wore dressing gowns all day and stood by the letter box for mail that never came.

She opened the small door behind her and brought out a stack of letters and set them onto the counter.

'You have a lot of letters to the editor,' she said. 'I haven't seen this many at once since the one and only Miss Crab competition in the 1970s. Or this many letters for any one person, come to that.'

'Miss Crab?' Tressa started laughing. 'How awful – what a terrible crown to wear.'

Penny was confused. 'Oh it wasn't terrible. I was very proud to wear it.' She pointed to a faded photo behind the counter.

'Wait – you? How many Miss Crabs were there?' asked Tressa.

'Only the one: me. They stopped it after me.' As soon as the words were out of her mouth, Penny wished she hadn't spoken.

Tressa gestured at the photo, asking to have a closer look. 'Why have I never seen this before?' she asked.

Reluctantly Penny it handed it over, still wishing she hadn't said anything.

She'd only brought the photo down from the attic last night, after having a moment of nostalgia. It was coming up for twenty-five years since the night her life changed.

'You were gorgeous,' Tressa exclaimed. 'I mean you're still gorgeous but look at you.'

Penny looked at the photo in Tressa's hands. She wore a pale tangerine georgette dress and her crown was of golden crab claws.

'You look so beautiful,' said Tressa. But Penny didn't feel beautiful. She didn't feel beautiful then or now and she never knew what to do with compliments. They made her feel beholden to return them, or else brush them off – or else carry the weight of expectation with her ever after.

Silently she handed over the stack of envelopes of different sizes. People always liked to write to the *Occurrence*. They could have sent emails, but the readership was mainly older people and the internet connection in Port Lowdy was somewhat temperamental – especially when it rained, which kept the post office nice and busy.

'How is George?' Penny asked. 'It's a terrible thing.'

Tressa grew sombre. 'Holding up as best he can,' she said. 'They're heading up to Plymouth tomorrow.'

'Who'll run the paper with you?' Penny relied on the paper. People popped into the post office to pick up a copy and many of them bought other little items in the shop over the summer.

Tressa tucked the mail into her backpack.

'I'm hiring a journalist, just for the summer.'

'A proper journalist? How exciting. Although, don't tell George I said he wasn't a proper one, will you? He seems to be a man of many interests.'

Tressa nodded her head. 'I won't say a word.' Indeed, she looked like she was the keeper of many secrets.

'Is the journalist going to live in the village, or will they do that remote work thing that's so popular now?' Penny asked.

She wondered if there was potential love in the air. God knows there was no one here close to Tressa's age. Villages wasted girls like her – and girls like Penny, for that matter. Tressa deserved more time painting her pictures of the sea, which were lovely but, if Penny was honest, a bit samey.

'They'll have to live here,' said Tressa. 'We need them to attend the events over summer. But if they do come here, do you know anyone who might rent a room for a few months? The pub would be too expensive and loud for a six-month stay.'

'I might have one,' said Penny carefully. 'The extra money might come in handy.'

She thought about upstairs and the empty rooms and the silence at night. About how she would like to chat about the news or the weather with someone and have two mugs of tea steeping by the kettle.

'Oh, Penny, that'd be amazing,' said Tressa. 'Then I'll make sure I find someone perfect for both of us.' She pushed the jar of jam into her bag, pushing down the mail, and pointed to the photo of Penny still lying on the counter.

'And for the record, Penny, I reckon they stopped Miss

Crab because you were the most beautiful crab girl in all of Cornwall and they knew they would never have anyone as lovely again. You broke the crab shell when you won, Penny Stanhope.'

Tressa was gone in a blur of dark curls and energy, and Penny felt better than she had in weeks. Tressa Buckland was a tonic.

3

Caro Fox was doing the one thing she hated the most: lying in bed. This silly cancer was painful and annoying but she couldn't shake the sense it was too much for her to cope with.

If Caro had been a religious woman she would have prayed. But having not been in a church since her wedding day, she wondered if this was her punishment for being a non-believer. She had only married in the church because George's family had always married at St Cuthbert's since the thirteenth century. So who was she to go up against the thirteenth century? Not even Caro Fox could argue with that lineage.

So when the doorbell rang, she huffed from her bed, wishing she could tell them to come around the back. She loathed people who used the front door. Caro insisted people just let themselves in through the back door and as long as they wiped their feet, all would be well.

She smoothed out the sheets and blankets and wondered who it might be. News in a tiny village spread like the plague and since George's family were the oldest in Port Lowdy, there was a sense that at times they were considered the landed gentry. Perhaps it was the money more than the lineage, she thought at times, but still, it was a lot of pressure to be something they weren't. George had more deals on the run than Arthur Daley, and Caro couldn't arrange flowers if her life depended on it but was still invited to open new shops and new schools.

She absently wondered if she'd been able to arrange flowers, would that have saved her life now, but then she heard voices and then someone coming up the stairs. Perhaps it was a robber who planned to take her as a hostage and tie her up in a dingy shed somewhere? Anything would be better than lying in bed all day.

A gentle tap at her bedroom door told her she wouldn't be leaving for the shed after all, and then a mop of curls and two large eyes peered around the corner.

'Oh, you're awake,' said Tressa.

'I am indeed – come in,' said Caro, pleased to see her. Lovely Tressa who was like her own child and who never asked for anything other than friendship of her and George.

Tressa choose her words carefully. 'George told me you're not well.'

'I'm dying, actually. It's utter shit sticks.' Caro sat up in bed and tried to adjust the pillows. She and Tressa had coined the term shit sticks and used it profusely, loving the way it worked in any situation, enough to make a dent in the moment without causing offence.

Caro saw fear in her eyes and wished she hadn't said anything. But it was too late now. She might as well be honest.

'George didn't say you were dying,' Tressa said as she

stepped forward and adjusted the pillows for her. She sat down on the edge of the bed where Caro patted.

'George doesn't have my body,' she said. 'I know I'm dying. I've felt it for the last year. The doctors say they can operate but a body can only take so much.'

Seeing Tressa's frown, she patted the girl's hand. 'It's fine, really, Tressie.'

'Did the doctors say you're dying or is this just something you feel?'

'It's a feeling,' said Caro, 'but my feelings are always right.'

'You weren't right about the storm last winter when you handed out bottled water and cans of baked beans. You weren't right when you said that Penny would leave Port Lowdy. She will never leave here unless it's in a wooden box.'

Caro gasped and Tressa caught her slip. 'Sorry, that's a terrible thing to say.'

Caro made a face at Tressa and shrugged. 'I'm not always right but sometimes, when it matters, I am right.'

'I think you're just anxious,' said Tressa. 'The operation will go well and they'll get rid of the cancer and you'll be back here in no time.'

Caro patted Tressa's hand again. She was always an optimist about other people. It was a shame she wasn't so confident about herself but then again, with a mother like Wendy Buckland it was hard to be confident in life.

'You'll fall in love this year, that much I know,' said Caro. 'I feel it in my bones.'

Tressa shrugged. 'Men don't really visit here, and I don't

want to head into St Ives just to meet someone. Mum's always on at me about that or those dating apps but really, I don't think that's how I'm going to meet anyone decent.'

'I read a book about a serial killer on one of those sites. It's going to be made into a film with that girl from *Pride and Prejudice.*'

'You read too many crime novels,' Tressa said, glancing at the pile of books by Caro's bed.

'They're my escape. Just like your art, Tressie. Now tell me what plans George has for you and the *Occurrence.* How will you make it work?'

Tressa told her George's plan, which was really Caro's plan, but she didn't want Tressa to think less of her husband. He had been all discombobulated since they found out about her cancer.

It was a wretched thing for anyone to contend with. She wanted to change the subject.

'How are your parents?' Caro asked and watched closely.

A flicker of something she recognised as worry and anger crossed Tressa's face.

'The same. Mum's been at me about moving back to St Ives; said she and Dad would buy me a place there, and I could sell Mermaid Terrace and keep the money, and that I could paint in St Ives.' Tressa sighed. 'I don't know why they can't leave me alone. Mum said I was trying to prove something by living away from them, but I'm not. I just like it here more than anywhere else.'

'I understand,' said Caro, who didn't believe a word of it. Wendy Buckland was a dynamo of energy and a terrible mother. Ever since Tressa had first come to Port Lowdy with her family, Caro and George had watched the little girl be dismissed and ignored by her mother and tolerated by her father, who was far more interested in her brother Jago.

That was why they'd given Tressa a job. To get her away from her family when she was on holidays in Port Lowdy.

Then Tressa came back as an adult, with a fistful of money from her grandmother, enough to buy Mermaid Terrace and live a quiet life. She had been determined to buy only that house and she had made it happen. Tressa had made her own dream come true. It was a shame her mother couldn't be proud of her.

But Caro and George still worried about her. *The Port Lowdy Occurrence* would probably close after George retired and Tressa still wouldn't exhibit her art. Caro had encouraged her to approach some galleries in St Ives and Plymouth but Tressa said she wasn't ready. Caro wondered if she would ever be ready to come out of her shell.

Caro moved to get more comfortable and took a sharp breath in at the pain in her side. This cancer was not just in her bowel; she could tell. Everything inside her felt out of sorts, as though she'd had all her insides taken out and put back in the wrong order.

Tressa had jumped up from the bed. 'What can I get you? Pain relief? Tea? Hot water bottle? I feel a bit useless.'

Caro reached out and touched her arm. 'I'm fine, love, just a twinge. I might rest a bit until George comes home.'

Tressa leaned down and kissed Caro's cheek.

'I love you, Caro, but I promise, you're not dying.'

Caro smiled at her and gave her a little wave as Tressa left the room, closing the door behind her.

She closed her eyes and took a deep breath, even though it hurt her side. Tressa was wrong. Love was coming her way and even though she was sure she was dying, she hoped to God she could see Tressa happy and loved before she died.

4

Dan Byrne slammed his hand on the desk. 'You can disagree with my views but you cannot stop me saying what everyone thinks. This is called freedom of speech, Clive,' he stated loudly. A rare showing of Dublin sunshine disappeared as soon Dan's voice boomed through the office and just like that, rain started to fall.

Clive Halpern, his editor at the *Independent Times*, sighed. 'I don't disagree with you, Dan, but the owners of the paper disagree and they want you to step back from this.'

'This topic? They don't want me to write about the corruption in the hospital?'

Clive paused and Dan watched something flicker over his face.

'Just tell me,' he said, feeling some of his energy dissipate and sitting down on his chair. Being the angriest journalist in Ireland was tiring. Sometimes he just wanted to write about good things – but people didn't want good things. They wanted to be angry and anxious and have someone to blame; and he gave them the fuel for their emotional furnace.

But the one thing Dan Byrne hated was being told what

to write about. The billionaire owner of the paper usually gave him a wide berth but, clearly, he had hit a nerve when he wrote about the corruption in the biggest hospitals in Ireland involving a cover-up of malpractice from a senior surgeon.

'How was I to know the surgeon was a friend of the owner's?'

'You weren't – but you also wrote about items that were part of an NDA from the court.'

Dan looked out the window of his office. 'People died, Clive, and they covered it up and let him keep operating.'

The men were silent for a moment.

'They want me to let you go. And they want you to pay the surgeon two hundred and fifty thousand pounds or they will take you to court for twice that amount, and you know they will win.'

Dan turned to look at Clive.

'That's my flat,' he said. 'That's all I have.'

Clive sighed. 'I know, but maybe it's time to get a new job somewhere else, rethink the angriest man in Ireland thing you have going on.'

'You encouraged that persona,' said Dan, realising he sounded churlish.

'It sold papers; your column has always been popular but I can't fix this one. You've made a very powerful enemy; I don't think you'll get a job in Ireland for a while. Perhaps look in the UK, or Australia.'

Dan put his head in his hands. He was tired of everything, especially with this paper. It was his first job and he had worked up from the bottom as a cadet to having his photo in the masthead of his column: *Dan takes on the world*.

It was an egotistical title for the column but he did feel he had a responsibility to shine a light on the world's injustices. And there were so many of them, he worried he was running out of time. All he did was read the news from all over the world, fight with people online and do a weekly three-minute report on a television current affairs show about his latest column.

For the camera they always styled him like a messy, rumpled journalist, the hair and makeup girls teasing his hair out at awkward angles, and making him wear a tie, which he never normally did, but pulling it askew. It was all part of the act, he told himself; but sometimes he wondered if he himself wasn't the biggest story to uncover.

Angry, bedraggled journo actually irons his shirts and likes to listen to Easy FM and sing along to Lionel Richie.

Clive stood up and put his hand out to Dan. 'If I can help in any way, please let me know, Dan. I've always liked you and you're a fine writer. You have helped many people, you know?'

Dan looked at Clive's hand and realised he wasn't the enemy. Dan knew he was crossing lines when he wrote about the settlement with the families of the victims who'd died. But he didn't want the surgeon to work anywhere else or take more people's lives.

Losing his job and his flat was a small cost compared to those families, he reminded himself.

He took Clive's hand. 'Thanks, Clive.'

Clive had his hand on the door handle. 'The people from legal will be in touch, be out by 2 p.m. or security will be up,' he said in what sounded like a regretful voice, and then he left Dan alone in the office that he had worked so hard for.

Dan didn't love his flat but it was all he owned in the world. Oh, and his dog Richie – a beautiful golden retriever who liked tennis balls and sniffing people's crotches, which was proving a huge barrier to women he met in the park, walking their small terriers and pretty little fluff balls on legs.

Not that Dan was ever serious about the women he met, or even dated. He was too busy taking on the world to deal with the drama of a relationship. He liked the girls he went out with to be bright, independent and ambitious, so they didn't feel they needed to get married yet. He was thirty-six years old and just hitting the prime of his career: why would he want a relationship?

But now, as he opened the door to the flat and heard Richie running towards him, he wished he had someone to talk to about this. All his friends were journos and he knew they would enjoy his fall from grace, because they were all arseholes, just like him.

Richie ran up and Dan swung his work bag in front of him. 'No sniffing, you creeper,' he said to Richie and patted his head. 'Come on, boy, we need to find me a new job a long way away from Dublin.'

He poured himself a whisky and sat at the kitchen table. Then, after pulling his laptop from his bag, he went to the most popular site for jobs in his field.

He scrolled down and remembered Clive's words. *'I don't think you'll get a job in Ireland for a while.'*

He clicked UK and started to scroll. A police reporter in

Barking. A horse racing reporter in Cheltenham. A finance journalist in London – definitely not for him, he thought. So few jobs.

Richie sighed and sat on Dan's feet under the table.

'Big sigh, boy – I get it, I really do,' he said, as he took a slug of his whisky and kept scrolling. All he wanted to do was go away where no one knew him, where he could just live and write. Maybe he would write a book? That seemed like a feasible thing to do with his time. Maybe he could get a part-time job and have the time to write. He was unsure what the book would be about yet but still, it was the only idea he had right now. He could write a book about his childhood, but who wanted to read another misery memoir about a poor kid in Dublin who was bounced from foster home to foster home?

Maybe he could write a historical book – but maybe that was about wanting to rewrite his own history. But there was nothing better than starting to write something new. That staring at the screen while you formulated ideas, slowly stringing words together until they created a picture for the reader and then a story. It was a powerful pastime, one that could change lives, or ruin lives.

Dan clicked the part-time ads. Oh, how the mighty fall, he thought – and then he saw the ad.

Wanted, part-time journalist for a small local newspaper. Local news and a willingness to get to know Port Lowdy. Six-month contract and accommodation included.

He typed Port Lowdy into the search engine and peered at the map. A tiny village, on the English Channel. He clicked on the photos and saw a postcard village, like something from a BBC mystery show. It was so chocolate-boxish it almost set his teeth on edge but it was a long way from Dublin and they were offering a place to stay.

'Looks okay,' he said to Richie, whose tail wagged, hitting the floor with an approving series of thumps.

Dan thought about his approach. He couldn't say he was the angriest man in Ireland.

He thought about the local papers that were the soul of the villages in Ireland.

Dear Editor,
 I was excited to see the request for a journalist to assist with the production of your paper.'

He had to stop and look up the name of the paper.
'*The Port Lowdy Occurrence*,' he said aloud. Was that really the name? It sounded like something out of a Dickens novel.

The Port Lowdy Occurrence has a strong presence in your village and a long history, and I will ensure I am working to the ways of the paper. I am not trying to further my career through your paper. Instead, I am writing a book and am moving away from my very busy life reporting news in Ireland.
 I do have a dog named Richie, but he keeps his nose out of other people's business, mostly.

He laughed as he typed and then poured an extra splash of whisky into his glass.

'I am available to start immediately and would be most grateful if you would consider my letter of introduction and my enclosed résumé.

Regards,

Dan Byrne

Dan realised he didn't have a résumé.

Shit, he thought. He pulled up a template from the internet and started to type.

He needed to be credible but not overbearing. More local news than unearthing corruption scandals and the poisoning of important rivers. As he typed, he enjoyed creating a career that was the opposite of what he had. Flower shows, and the teacher of the year reports, plus some stories on saving owls in a local park. He thought of the most inoffensive content he could and put it down, stating he had worked as a freelance writer and editor for local papers all over Dublin.

It was as though he was creating another personality, and he hummed a snatch of 'Stuck on You' as he typed.

Finally, when he was satisfied. He pressed send and finished his whisky.

He didn't have a snowball's chance in hell of getting the job but at least he had done something positive.

Now he had to put his flat on the market and hand over the money to the wealthiest family in Ireland. It was enough to make you a communist!

5

Tressa walked downstairs as the light faded. She had painted for hours, watching the sun play on the water. She had once read that Turner, her favourite painter, had said on his deathbed, 'The sun is God.' This afternoon's sun has been a playful God, darting in and out from behind clouds, dancing on the waves and sending shots of light through the waves so the sea turned from green to sapphire to translucent and back again.

Trying to capture it in a painting was impossible but Tressa tried over and over again. If the sun was God, then the sea was her Holy Grail. Her hand ached as she washed them at the kitchen sink, letting the warm water soothe the tiny muscles that had been clasping the brush for hours. The suncatchers hanging by the window were sending prisms of light across the room and Ginger Pickles was trying to catch the dancing specks on the floorboards.

'Evening, Ginger Pickles.' Tressa greeted her orange tabby cat with a small curtsey, as she would be peeved for the rest of the evening if she wasn't given the appropriate respect and pageantry.

Ginger Pickles was the bitchiest cat Tressa had ever met. She was demanding and vain and, at times, mean, especially when she toyed with the field mice she caught from the garden – but she was also an excellent watch cat, making a particular sound when anyone was walking up the path to Tressa's house.

'Did Janet feed you tonight?' asked Tressa. Ginger Pickles waved the question away with her tail.

Mermaid Cottage was the last house before the esplanade turned and the cliffs ran along the side of the road and the sea on the other side. There was something about being next to the huge rock face that Tressa liked. It felt like an extra support against the winds from the sea and from the winds of change.

While her family home was groomed to perfection by her mother, Tressa ensured that Mermaid Terrace would never be perfect. There would always be something she was moving around and adjusting, from her collection of charity shop flowers hung haphazardly on the walls to the riot of unmatched colours that filled the small sitting room. There was her two-seater sofa covered in crocheted rugs that reminded her of her grandmother's house, and a winged armchair from a jumble sale in St Ives that she had convinced George to bring down in the back of his Range Rover. She had covered it in an apple-green upholstery fabric Rosemary March had given her in exchange for a drawing of her beloved poodles.

A floral pink Aubusson-style rug covered the floor; her mother had said it was hideous when she had first seen it. It was now Tressa's favourite thing in the room.

Books in the shelves. Old apple boxes from the farm a few miles down the road were stacked in a pyramid fashion on either side of the fireplace where paperbacks and artbooks sat spine by spine in no particular order. Tressa's living space was humble but lovely. It was a matter of money. She needed a few more things to make the house more comfortable, but it was fine for now and it was only the two of them – her and Ginger Pickles. The lamps she had rescued from her grandmother's house, and with some rewiring they were fine, more than fine really. An old crystal cabinet that she was filling with things she found on the beach, like old bits of china from shipwrecks and perfectly smooth piece of driftwood and sea glass in all colours. Blues and green and pinks and reds of all sizes, worn down by the sand and the waves until they lay exhausted and finally retired into Tressa's crystal cabinet.

She had painted the mismatched kitchen table chairs in different pastel colours and the old pine table had come with the house, as it was too big to manoeuvre out the door. Perhaps it had been built in situ, Tressa thought. Against one doorframe in the kitchen, children's heights had been measured long ago, over a period of sixteen years. Small pencil marks had the years written next to them, with initials in neat writing. It was an imperfect home, which was perfect for her.

Being in her parent's perfect home made her anxious but there was nothing in Mermaid Terrace that caused her anxiety to swell. In fact, there was nothing whatsoever in Port Lowdy to make her anxious. Not even when it was high summer and the beaches were filled and the pub was open late. Tressa enjoyed the few months of joy because she knew it would go back to sleepy Port Lowdy once the weather turned and the air became crisp in the evening.

As the sun lay down for the night, Tressa turned on the

lamps and closed the curtains. There was nothing cosier than Mermaid Terrace in the evening. The heater was on and she flicked on the television for background noise, as she poured herself a glass of wine. She wasn't much of a drinker but she liked a wine some evenings and today was not an ordinary day. She thought about George and Caro and hoped they were okay, safe and warm before they started their journey tomorrow towards – hopefully – Caro's healing. She sent Caro a quick text.

Letter to the editor requesting reinstatement of the Page 3 girl. Can we get George to pose? Put ad up for journo. Hopefully Piers Morgan doesn't apply. Mum loves him.

She knew the text would put a smile on Caro's face and that was all she could do to help right now. The sound of a text made her look and she saw an immediate reply from Caro.

That's cheered me up no end. George and I are deciding which of the Port Lowdy ladies would be willing to bare the body for one man's titillation, as it were. If Piers Morgan applies, we are closing the paper.

Tressa giggled and, settling in on her sofa, she opened her laptop and looked at her emails. Thirteen applications for the role already, which wasn't bad. She had thought there would be more but really, who wanted a part-time job for six months?

Skimming the first few letters, she didn't bother reading their résumés. They were mainly junior journalists with no experience who wanted to know if the job could be full-time, along with someone who wanted to know if they could learn how to be a journalist by being on the job.

Another person had applied for the wrong job and wrote a cover letter about their skill as a video content producer. Tressa didn't even know what that job was, but she was fairly sure they didn't need one at the *Occurrence*.

A few journalists were looking for a sea change but with an eye for something bigger than what the job offered. And then she found one that looked promising.

She read the letter and then read the CV. He seemed to have good experience and he was writing a book. She pictured a bearded older man with his faithful companion dog, ready to write down the stories of his colourful career. He would fit in well at the *Occurrence* and in the town.

She read through the rest but her mind couldn't pull itself away from Daniel Byrne. He would be terrific, she thought. She could learn from him and he would work well in the village. She picked up her phone and dialled Penny's number.

'Penny, I think I might have someone who will work for the paper, but they have a dog. Would that work for you upstairs at the post office?'

Penny paused. 'I'm more of a cat person,' she said.

'So am I! But I am sure the dog is well trained and quiet. He sounds like an older gentleman. The journalist, not the dog,' she clarified.

'If the dog is well trained, then it should be all right for a few months – but if the dog is unruly then he will have to leave,' Penny stated firmly.

'Of course,' said Tressa. 'I'll call this person tomorrow and get back to you as soon as I hear.'

Tressa looked at the CV and saw his referee: Clive Halper – an editor. That was good.

She quickly typed to Daniel Byrne.

Hello Daniel,

Thank you for your application. I was hoping you could give me some time for a phone interview tomorrow. We are in a tight spot here and need someone to start immediately. If this works for you, let me know what time and I will call you to discuss.

Best,

Tressa Buckland

She sat back on the sofa and called George.

'How is Caro?' she asked.

'Sleeping,' he said in a whisper.

'You need to be sleeping soon also,' she said. 'You won't be any good to her if you're not match fit, George.'

'I know but I can't stop thinking. We need to head to Plymouth tomorrow and I am so worried about the paper and you and Caro and everything. The kids are being wonderful but it's a huge thing to take in for all of us.'

Tressa listened.

'Did anyone apply for the job?' he asked.

'Yes, a few.'

'Anyone good?'

'I think so. I'm going to interview one tomorrow. He's

writing a book, so he could be perfect. Part-time and all that.'

'Sounds promising,' said George.

'Get some sleep, George. I have this completely in hand,' said Tressa, knowing she was sounding more confident than she felt. But George and Caro meant so much to her that she knew she didn't have a choice but to make this work, for them and for her. Because without her job she wouldn't be able to stay in Port Lowdy. She didn't make enough from her sporadic art sales to ever rely on the money and God knows she wouldn't ask her parents for anything because there was nothing given that didn't come with a caveat. This was everything to her and to George and God knows she had to make it work – no matter what.

Dan heard his email ping and he picked up his phone and saw the message. A phone interview tomorrow. What was he thinking when he applied? Two rounds of whisky and the adrenaline were to blame, he decided.

He could do better than this piss-poor job, he thought, just as a text came through.

Sorry about the job, mate. Do you know if Clive is looking for a replacement?

He went onto twitter and saw his name was trending.

People couldn't have been happier to read Dan Byrne had been fired and had to pay up. He's a prick who deserves even worse. Dan was aware he didn't have a strong fan base from some people that he had written about but still, it stung. His eyes scanned the glee at his downfall and he closed the app. He didn't need to read anymore to know people were enjoying his public humiliation.

Then he saw the next text, from Clive.

Their legal team has put a caveat on your flat. You will need to be out by the end of the week. Got anywhere to stay? You can bunk on the sofa here for a week but that's about it. Sorry, mate.

Dan felt sick in the pit of his stomach, like he did when he was a child and he didn't know what house he would be going to next. The flat was his biggest success. A child from foster homes buying his own home as an adult was an achievement worth more than anything else he had done in his life.

He re-read the email from the woman called Tressa and sighed. He didn't have anywhere else to go. No family, no friends who would put him and Richie up for a long period of time, and little to nothing in savings. He had his final pay-out coming from the paper but that was it and it was terrifying.

Typing quickly, he replied.

I can chat now if you like. I am sure you have a lot of applicants and have a lot of interviews to get out of the way.

Cheers,

Dan

He pressed send and closed his eyes, breathing slowly like he had learned, reminding himself he was safe, he was safe, he was safe.

Tressa felt on edge – perhaps she shouldn't have had the wine. She poured the remainder in her glass down the sink. Sometimes wine was not the relaxer it promised to be. Tressa wanted an omelette and a cup of tea and bed. Today had been too much for one day.

The thought of putting out the paper alone was frightening – but so was losing Caro. She thought about ringing her mother for someone to chat to but remembered it was Wednesday and Wednesdays were for belly dancing and Tressa shouldn't interrupt her activities.

Tressa often wondered if she was even Wendy's daughter, as the thought of attending a belly dancing class was about as appealing as breaking her own knees with her bike lock.

Perhaps she was more like her father, David, a doctor who preferred a long walk and reading a book in front of a fire. He was still working as a cardiologist in St Ives, where her brother, Jago, was a doctor also, though Jago was in family medicine. Tressa had clearly missed the medical gene, and the busy gene – instead she had a skill with the paintbrush and not the hairbrush, to judge by her unruly black curls.

In truth, Tressa found her family intimidating. She loved them but she never felt like herself around them. She was the quiet one who didn't want to debate over dinners about politics or the NHS. She wanted to talk about art and how the light fell on the boats on the port at a particular time and made them look like they were painted by impressionists. She wanted to talk about things that filled her soul, not about things that upset her. Perhaps this was why she hadn't met anyone yet who she wanted to share her life with; or perhaps it was that she didn't want to share her art with anyone. How could she paint for hours when someone wanted her time?

An email pinged and she checked it on her phone.

The journalist, Daniel Byrne, wanted to talk tonight. He was keen, she thought – but if he was good, it would be one less thing to worry about and George would feel better knowing the paper was in safe hands.

She made a cup of tea and put some bread in the toaster and messaged his phone number.

Can I call in ten minutes?

After buttering her toast, she put more of the jam from Penny's post office on top and ate it while thinking.

If this Daniel Byrne was pleasant and not about to take over the world then she might not even read the rest of the applications.

A text came back.

Looking forward to chatting with you. Dan

After she had finished her tea and toast, Tressa sat on the sofa and dialled the number, while Ginger Pickles came to her side, eavesdropping on the phone call.

He picked up immediately.

'Dan Byrne.' He had an accent, she noted.

'Hi, Dan, it's Tressa Buckland from *The Port Lowdy Occurrence*.'

'Hi, Tressa. How are you this evening?'

It was a low voice, younger than she had expected and with a strong Irish accent, which was to be expected since he lived in Dublin but it was melodious and had a hint of a smile in the tone.

'I'm fine, Daniel, thank you. How are you?' She tried to be professional but she had never interviewed someone before and she felt perhaps she probably should have looked up questions to ask before she'd called him. Too late now, she thought.

'Dan, call me Dan. Tressa is a lovely name. That means third, doesn't it? Are you the third child?'

Tressa paused for a moment. How did he know this? 'Yes, I'm the third child.'

'And your older siblings? Do they have traditional Cornish names?'

'Umm, well it's just my older brother now. My sister... died.'

She never spoke about Rosewyn only because she hadn't known her. Rosewyn felt like a dead grandparent at times and then at other times, she felt like a ghost who followed Tressa around for all of her life.

'Oh, that's terrible. I am sorry for mentioning it.' Dan sounded genuinely upset and Tressa thought this probably wasn't going as well as he had hoped.

'That's okay, you weren't to know.' Tressa felt Ginger Pickle's claws arch into her thigh and she flinched.

'Tell me why you think Port Lowdy would be a good choice for you?'

'The job sounds perfect, as I'm writing a book, so I can work and write and be away from the bustle of Dublin.'

'There is no bustle in Port Lowdy,' said Tressa, trying to uncurl Ginger Pickle's claws from her pants. 'You might be bored.'

'I don't think so – I'd like something peaceful, to be honest. It's been a bit hectic here for a while and I need to see new things, meet new people, you know?'

Tressa didn't know. She didn't like meeting new people on the whole and she certainly didn't want to see new things.

Ginger Pickles stared at Tressa with a look of spite, and curled her claws into her leg again.

'Ouch!' Tressa cried.

'Are you all right?' he asked.

'My cat just clawed me, sorry.' She shot a look at Ginger Pickles, who retreated, knowing she might not get her breakfast if she kept it up for much longer.

'Ah, cats do that. That's why I have a dog.'

'Yes you mentioned that – Richie?'

'Yes,' said Dan, laughing, and she found she liked the sound of the way it started small and then ended up in a loud guffaw.

'Tell me about your experience. You have an extensive résumé of covering local events. Are you good with people?'

'Excellent, people love me,' he said.

'They love you? That's a strong claim.' Something about his confidence annoyed her. She would never claim people loved her art. It wasn't for her to assume people's opinions about her work.

'They mostly love me,' he corrected himself. 'I mean what

is love anyway? Strong feelings that can easily be replaced by someone or something else.'

There was an edge in his voice.

'What is your book about?' she asked, changing the subject.

There was a pause. 'I don't know yet. I was hoping to get inspiration in Port Lowdy.'

'I really don't know how much you will be inspired here, unless you're interested in the latest batch of jams at the post office or trying to understand the rules of naming fishing boats.'

'Both sound perfectly fine topics to me.' He laughed and Ginger Pickles jumped onto the back of the sofa and started to tap Tressa's head repeatedly with her paw.

She swatted the cat away but Ginger Pickles returned to her task, her claws getting caught in Tressa's curls.

'Goddammit,' she said. 'Hang on. This cat is trying to tell me something or murder me.'

She put the phone down and untangled her hair from the cat, then stood up and picked up the phone.

'I'm sorry. That was very unprofessional of me. Now, where were we?'

Tressa tried to remember what they had been talking about and she looked at his résumé again on the computer screen.

'You mentioned you wrote obituaries. Covered anyone of note? Death is a big deal here; obits are always important news.'

'Just the usual. Politicians, musicians, priests, sporting icons.'

'Oh really? Like who?'

'No one you would know. All Irish identities.' He brushed her question away. 'Tell me: what are the rules for naming fishing boats?'

Tressa laughed. 'Do you really want to know? Because I can tell you – but I'm not sure if you're serious or not.' She had to think for a moment, trying to remember as she moved the laptop and lay on the sofa, looking up at the ceiling.

'A name with seven letters is good luck. Don't name it after an engaged woman or a married woman.'

'Are you engaged or married?' he asked.

'What? No, you can't ask that.'

'I'm not planning on getting engaged or married to you but Tressa would be a fine name for a boat.'

'It's not seven letters,' she said.

'I'll put an extra s in the name,' he said, and Tressa burst out laughing at him. This job interview wasn't going the way she had assumed it would. They kept talking about nothing to do with the job. At times it felt playful and silly and other times she felt he was avoiding questions.

'What else? What are the other rules for the choosing of names for boats?'

'Don't name it after one that sank; that's a given.'

'So the *Titanic Tressa* with three s's is off the cards?'

She laughed again. She couldn't stop herself. He was funny and nice and he sounded like just the thing she would like to be around over the next few months. She paused.

'You sound fine. I mean you might think it too small a paper but it's important to the people here. It's a much-loved paper.'

'I get it,' Dan said. 'All news is important to those who

44

receive it. Good news, bad news, interesting news and so on. Never underestimate the power of news. We could stop Poseidon's wrath on the wrong naming of a boat and save sailors' lives! You never know.'

Tressa rolled her eyes. Maybe he was a bit precious for *The Port Lowdy Occurrence*.

'And don't roll your eyes either, because you know what I am saying is true.'

Tressa looked at her phone to see if she was on video call. 'How did you know I rolled my eyes?'

'Because I could hear them rolling around, thinking *this Irish journo is off his nut*.'

'Yes, I was actually. And I really am getting the impression you're off your nut – but I need someone to start as soon as possible. When could you be here?'

'What's today? Monday? How does Wednesday sound?'

'Wednesday? Really? That would be amazing. We have an issue due out in ten days, which I should be okay in getting sorted, but anytime, really. I have a room for you organised with our postmistress, Penny Stanhope, above the post office.'

'Really?'

'Yes, is that okay?' Tressa was worried he was expecting something more glamorous but Port Lowdy didn't really do glam. It was more successful at cosy.

'No, it's fine; it just sounded like something out of a children's book. Living above the post office with the postmistress as the landlady. Can I lick the stamps and become an integral part of the postal service?'

There was that smile in his voice again. It was infectious.

'You cannot. Penny takes her role very seriously and she's

also very no-nonsense and wants to be sure your dog is well behaved.'

'Of course he is. Just like his owner.'

Tressa smiled. 'So call me when you arrive on Wednesday and I will meet you and Richie and we can get started.'

'I can't wait,' said Dan, and he sounded sincere when he said it.

Tressa put down the phone and turned to Ginger Pickles who was washing her paws as if she hadn't just assaulted Tressa.

'You won't be getting any treats for a week after that abuse,' she said to the cat, who looked nonplussed.

She texted George, who she knew would still be up, worrying about everything and more.

New journo starts Wednesday. He seems on the money and very capable. Rest up and message me tomorrow after you and Caro are at the hospital.

Thank goodness that was done, she thought. Although Tressa had never interviewed anyone before, she knew she hadn't done a traditional interview – but she figured he knew what he was supposed to do and it was only for six months after all. And if she didn't like him, she could ask him to leave. That would be pretty easy, wouldn't it?

Her head hurt from not only thinking but also from where Ginger Pickles had pulled her hair.

'I'm going to bed,' she announced to the cat, who stopped washing her paws and looked up at Tressa as if to say, *who cares.*

'I can't get any respect around here,' she said with a sigh and went to bed.

She woke at two in the morning with Ginger Pickles curled up next to her neck, as though nothing had happened.

Tressa went downstairs to get some water and saw her laptop and opened it. A quick google of Dan Byrne and then she would head back to bed.

She typed his name into the search engine. Dan Byrne. Journalist. Dublin.

And then the results came up: 23,000,000 results. *Can't be right*, she thought as she started to read. Were there two journalists in Dublin named Dan Byrne?

And then she saw a profile piece on Dan and his beloved dog Richie.

Oh. It was the same person, and he was handsome and he was young. Dammit.

She emailed the referee on his résumé, the man called Clive, and asked him to call her in the morning.

You had one thing to do, Tressa, and you messed it up already, she scolded herself. She should definitely have followed up with the referee and found out more about Dan and before offering him the job. She closed the machine and went back to bed where Ginger Pickles was now curled up on her pillow, like a selfish little minx.

6

On the Wednesday morning, Remi Durand arrived in Port Lowdy. He had been travelling for nineteen hours when he stepped off the bus from Plymouth, after travelling by ferry from France.

His body was sore from the travel, and his eyes hurt from the bright sunlight and from seeing so many bright colours and new things.

At twenty-eight, Remi looked older than his years. Not in his face but the way he held his body. He was rigid and stood straight. His movements were economical and he took small steps when he walked, used to exercising in a confined space. Dark-haired and with dark eyes, he wasn't a tall man but he was strong.

He looked around for a building called the Black Swan.

'Excuse me,' he asked a girl with black curls who was wheeling a bicycle. 'Can you tell me where the Black Swan is?' He hoped his English was passable.

The girl smiled at him in a friendly way and he was unsure how to respond. Did he smile back? Did he say, *I have been in prison and you won't want to smile at me again after you know what I did?*

She pointed ahead. 'It's up this hill and to the right. You won't miss it. She's a lovely pub. Are you staying there?'

'Yes, I am working for Marcel.'

She seemed thrilled at this news. 'For the summer? That's fantastic. The pub is so busy and Marcel and Pam can't do it all by themselves again. It nearly killed Marcel last year.'

'Pam?' he asked. What was a Pam?

'Pamela, his wife. They're fabulous. I can't wait to come and eat there now you're working with them.'

Her enthusiasm for his circumstances was confusing. Would she feel the same if she knew why he was really in Port Lowdy?

Remi nodded, not willing to say more.

'You must try the crab bisque – it's sensational.'

The girl wheeled her bicycle away and Remi looked up the hill. He had a backpack containing all he owned in the world, but he had a job. This was more than a lot of other prisoners had when they were released.

The village was small, smaller than he had imagined when he was told about working and living here.

It was so foreign to him. He only knew Paris and its busy, loud existence. Now he was looking at a little pier and fishing boats, and was standing on a cobbled street. He could hear the seagulls calling but that was all. It was so quiet. Not like Paris with the clubs and bars.

He shuddered thinking about that life.

Taking the curly-haired girl's advice, he made his way up the hill, where he saw a large old white building with painted signs of two black swans gently swinging in the breeze. There were tablecloths on the washing line and red geraniums in pots set out at the front of the doors. It looked nicer than he'd expected, and with the girl saying that they served a crab bisque, he was feeling more hopeful.

The door opened and a large man with a red beard emerged in an apron that could have doubled as a spinnaker.

'Remi?' he asked and Remi nodded, as the man pulled him into a hug.

'Welcome to Port Lowdy,' the man said.

'You're French,' said Remi.

'*Oui* but I am now Cornish. A Cornish crepe,' and he laughed as though he had said something outrageously funny.

The man, who was called Marcel, according to the letter Remi had received in Paris, owned the pub. He smelled of onions, garlic and seafood. It was the best scent Remi had smelled in a very long time.

'You will stay here with me and my wife Pam and we will teach you everything, *non*?'

Remi nodded.

A woman came towards them in a tight red dress, red lipstick and her hair done like she was from another time, perhaps the 1950s.

'Oh, look at you Frenchies,' said the woman and she looked over at Remi and smiled. 'You all right, pet? Had a rough trot, eh?' She had a voice like sandpaper and an accent that could have shucked an oyster but her eyes were kind and she smiled at him like she meant it.

Before he could answer her, she tapped Marcel on the arm. 'Your pastry is drying out.'

'*Merde*,' said Marcel.

'It's all right, I'm here. I'll take care of the young'un,' she said and she pushed open the red door for Marcel, who bustled in, and stood waiting for Remi to enter.

'Come on then, I bet you're knackered from all the travel. And hungry. Let me show you your room and then you can eat something and have a lie-down. Marcel has a lovely lasagna on the menu today. You like lasagna? Or I can get you a curry. Or even an omelette if your tummy is on the turn from the ferry?'

Remi stepped inside the pub and waited for his eyes to adjust to the light.

The pub had a low roof but was painted white inside. It was a large open room with a huge fireplace, like the sort that wealthy men would have warmed themselves in front of after a day of hunting.

The tables were scattered about and comfortable-looking chairs surrounded them, and the lighting was excellent. It was a beautiful room. There was a sense of homeliness about it but it was chic.

Remi remembered the discussions about lighting from when he was at the bar. There was much discussion about the lighting in the bar but in a restaurant, it was different – the lighting needed to be softer. He remembered that much but he didn't like to remember the time at the bar. That was before everything happened.

'This is very nice,' he said to Pam.

'Yes, it's lovely, and very busy in the summer. We also do fish and chips in the beer garden and takeaway packs.'

Pamela walked him through the restaurant and then through a door and up a back staircase.

There were doors along a hallway and they stopped at the one marked 21.

'Here you are,' she said and took a key out of her pocket of her tight red dress and opened the door. Twenty-one, he thought. The age he was when he went into prison. What a waste of his life. What a waste of the other man's life. No one wins when someone dies and the other one goes to prison.

Inside the room was a simple bedroom but it was nicer than anything he had ever had.

A double bed with a large navy bedhead, two bedside tables in white wood with lamps on them. A wardrobe, and a small table and chairs. A large comfortable striped armchair sat by the window.

'We just did it up – seaside, nautical theme,' she said. 'Not really my taste but the tourists love it.'

Remi smiled. 'I love it, too.'

'I'm sure you do, pet. A little bathroom here.' She opened a door and he saw a shower and toilet and basin, all in shiny white and blue tiles. God, this was luxury.

'You hungry?' Pamela asked him.

Remi shook his head. 'I'm very tired actually.'

Pamela made a sad face at him but she looked like she did genuinely feel sad for him. 'Oh, pet, I'm sure you're ruined. How about I send you up a tray and you can shower and sleep. Sound okay?'

At such unintended tenderness, Remi felt his throat swell and his eyes sting.

He hadn't cried in seven years; here was this woman, who didn't know him from Adam, offering him the most he had ever had.

He looked down at the floor. '*Oui, merci.*'

Pamela put the key on the table, turned and went to the door, opened it and stopped halfway through leaving.

'You know, a hot shower and good sob and you'll be right as rain, pet. Always helps me when I feel a bit run over by the world.'

She shut the door behind her, finishing the moment with a soft click, and Remi lay on the bed and wept. He really did feel run over by the world and he was grateful for Marcel and Pam. He was the first paroled prisoner they had taken in but apparently Marcel had spent time inside prison and knew how hard it was to make a life when you were finally released. Thankfully, the charity had set this up for him and he had a place to go. So many times he had heard of men leaving prison with nowhere to go and so often they came back to prison because it was safer than being out in the world with no family, job, or money.

But Remi wasn't given that opportunity, not even to try. He was sent to Cornwall and would never be able to return to Paris.

The man from the charity who helped prisoners like him had come and sat with him before his release in France.

'There aren't many jobs around at the moment. One in London as rubbish collector and one in Cornwall as a cook at a pub. The fellow there did some time, so he wants to help someone like you.'

Collecting rubbish in London sounded awful but where was Cornwall?

Whatever he had imagined would happen when he was released from prison, it wasn't what Port Lowdy offered: the unexpected kindness of Pam and Marcel, even though he was a murderer in the eyes of everyone he knew back in France.

Not that he cared about everyone else's view of him. Only Juliet mattered. But he would never be able to see Juliet again and that was what broke him. He always thought perhaps he would be walking down the street and he would see her and she would see him and they would reconnect. That had sustained him for seven years. Now he was thrown out of a country that didn't want him and living in a country that didn't know him. It was enough to make a grown man weep.

7

That same Wednesday that Remi had arrived, Tressa wheeled her bicycle towards the post office, where she was to meet Dan Byrne. She was early but he had said he would be driving down from Plymouth.

Her conversation with Clive, his previous boss, had been enlightening. Dan Byrne was the bad boy of Irish news, and he was self-destructive and cavalier but he was kind when he chose to be. She told Clive perhaps she had made a mistake in hiring Dan.

'He needed a break, and this might be good for him,' Clive said. 'There's nothing here for him. Maybe he needs to leave journalism and do something else. This might give him the space to think about it.'

Not that Tressa had any other options, since the other applicants were not even close to being right for the role. Dan was overqualified but it was clear from the lies on the résumé he knew what the paper needed.

She wondered if he would be bringing his car with him from Ireland or if he had a rental car.

After leaning her bike against the wall of the post office, she walked inside. A man who was way too good-looking was standing listening to Penny as she told him about the town.

Feeling awkward, Tressa looked through the jam flavours and spun the stand of postcards. A dog came out of nowhere and sat in front of her.

'Oh hello,' she said, patting the dog's head.

'Richie, are you being polite?' She heard the Irish accent and looked up.

'Daniel Byrne?' she asked.

'I am. Are you Tressa with three s's?'

'Just the two.' She paused a moment to take him in. Tall, well-built, dark hair, blue eyes, and a smiling mouth. He was wearing jeans and sneakers and a white T-shirt and looked far too good for someone in such a simple outfit.

'I'm waiting for the Tressa with three s's,' he said to Penny. 'She's the wrong one.'

Penny looked confused. 'There is only one Tressa – this one,' she said, pointing at her. 'She's the one and only Tressa in Port Lowdy.'

'Oh, well how lovely to meet you, one Tressa with two s's.' Dan put out his hand for her to shake and she noticed she still had paint on her fingernails.

'Dan got here early,' said Penny and Tressa was sure she was preening. 'He said he wanted to wander around and get the feel of Port Lowdy.'

Tressa raised an eyebrow. 'And how does it feel?'

'Too soon to tell. I'll need more time.'

'You only have six months to find out, don't forget.' She heard herself speaking to him in what could be considered a flirty tone. Maybe it was the Irish accent that made her playful. They had talked like this on the phone, and she had wondered why it was so easy to be silly with a man she didn't know.

'Dan has a car. He brought it over on the ferry with his lovely dog.' Penny sounded thrilled with the situation, which was a change for the usually dour postmistress.

Tressa felt as though she was standing on uneven ground in high heels, except she had her sensible flat shoes on. She touched her hair and realised she was still wearing her bike helmet.

If she took it off now she would look vain, but if she left it on, she would look more like a dork than she did right now. She casually unclipped the helmet and took it off as though nothing unusual was happening. Penny laughed, not unkindly, but rather tactlessly. 'Did you wash your hair and then put the bike hat on?'

Tressa touched her hair and realised that she had done that exact thing and then ridden the long way around the bay so she could enjoy the sunshine. The bottom half of her hair was dry but the top half was stuck to her skull, and she knew she looked ridiculous.

Why hadn't she made an effort to at least look nice for the new employee of the paper?

She ran her hand through her hair and smiled at Penny as best she could. 'It must look frightful.'

Penny shook her head. 'No, you always look lovely. Such a pretty girl you are. Now I was just going to show Dan to his room and then I thought you could give him a little tour of Port Lowdy and take him to your office.'

Tressa was glad Penny was taking charge. She couldn't seem to think straight.

'Let me take you upstairs and then he's all yours, Tressa.'

Tressa walked outside the shop and stood in the sun, fluffing her curls with her hands to give them some volume. Dan Byrne had nice forearms, she thought. She always looked at men's forearms and he had strong ones, with that lovely line of muscle showing he did something powerful with them besides writing.

Tressa felt something push her bottom and she spun around to see Richie panting at her.

'He has no manners, I'm sorry,' said Dan, coming out of the post office.

She shrugged. 'I've had worse from other males, so I'll be fine.'

Dan put on a pair of sunglasses and she felt herself frown at the sight of him. He looked even better with them on and she crossed her arms.

'You ready?' she said.

'Sure am, show me your Port Lowdy, Ms Buckland.'

She put her head inside the post office. 'Can I leave the bike at the front, Pen? I'll pick it up later.'

Penny waved her permission and Tressa clipped the helmet to the handlebars and turned to Dan.

'Let's go then,' she said and started off down the road.

Dan and Richie came rushing after her.

'Aren't you going to lock up your bike?' he asked.

'No, Penny will make sure it's safe.'

'You mean to tell me there is no theft here?'

'There is – mostly when the tourists or day trippers come. But on a Wednesday morning, early spring, my bicycle will be fine.'

'Wouldn't happen in Dublin.' He sighed.

'What did you think of Penny?' she asked. 'She's an odd bod sometimes. Can rub people up the wrong way.'

'Oh really? She seems fine to me, very suitable for the prim postmistress of a small English village.'

Tressa laughed. 'You know she was once Miss Crab, of the Port Lowdy crabs? What a title.'

'Miss what?' Dan started to laugh.

'It was a pageant that she won, celebrating Port Lowdy. I only just found about it but it's such a funny crown and name. I don't think Penny sees why it's funny.'

Dan stopped laughing. 'Maybe that was her big moment. We shouldn't be mean about it.'

'I'm not being mean. I just think it's a funny title. Penny is great, really, but sometimes she gets a bit judgemental.'

'That's a bit pot calling the kettle, isn't it?' he said and he was smiling but she felt ashamed. Why had she put Penny down? It was something her mother would do to make others feel small so she could feel bigger.

'I like Penny and she's good to me,' she said. 'She's a good person. I shouldn't have been critical of her.'

They walked in silence for a little while.

Tressa pointed down to the left.

'That's the library. They don't have a huge number of books of course but they get most of the papers from around here and from Ireland and Scotland. They also have *Le Monde* and *Le Figaro* if you like the French news. The chef up at the pub is French. He likes to read the papers at the library and swears loudly in French at stories he doesn't agree with. It's quite entertaining to watch. I learned a lot of new swear words actually. It's like a live reading of dirty

Duolingo. Oh and they have all the Agatha Christie books if you like some crime. George's wife Caro donates all her old crime novels to the library so you can read about all sorts of deadly characters.'

They kept walking, as a few villagers said hello to Tressa but ignored Dan and Richie.

'You seem to know everyone here,' said Dan.

Tressa nodded. 'Yes, I suppose I do. You'll know them soon enough. A journalist from Ireland who knows his way around a flower show? Well, they won't be able to hold themselves back,' she said, and she was sure she saw him wince.

She showed him the bakery, the doctor's surgery, and the best shops for grocery supplies; finally, they stopped the front of the Black Swan.

'I can show you the beach, if you like?'

'I would like,' he said, 'as would Richie.'

They walked down to the beach, and looked out over the shoreline. It was low tide and the ripples of glossy sand shone in the sunlight.

'Can I let Richie off?' he asked.

'Yep.' She walked down the steps and he followed her, unclipping the dog lead. Richie went speeding in circles, chasing gulls over the sand.

'We have a flower show next week to cover. You seem to have experience with those. Are you all right to handle it?' She gazed straight ahead at the dog.

'Oh yes, I love flower shows.'

'It's early peonies and petunias. Does that work?'

'I love all the P flowers.'

'What other P flowers are there?' she asked.

'Pansies,' he said, starting out with confidence.

The dog was barking at the water now. He didn't seem to be a very bright animal.

'What other P flowers have you come across in covering all your flower shows?'

Dan paused. 'Umm...'

She spun around to him. 'None! Because you're a big fibber!'

'A *fibber*? What's a fibber?'

'Someone who lies on their résumé to get a job that they are very overqualified for.'

Dan pushed his sunglasses up on top of his head. 'Listen...'

'I googled you. I know you got fired for writing about something you shouldn't have.'

Dan was silent for a moment. 'Should I go?'

Tressa laughed. 'No. Why? Of course I would google you, but I rang your old boss, Clive, who spoke highly of you and he said you need a break from hard news.'

Dan groaned and put his head in his hands. 'God, what a charity case I am.'

'Not at all. We need someone, I need someone, and I think it'll be fine. Honestly. You might even enjoy it.'

'You must think I'm a total eejit.' He scuffed the sand with his foot.

'I think you're full of shit and I can't wait for you to cover an actual flower show because we do have them here, you know.'

'I don't doubt it.'

'I also think it's brave of you to come here and we need the help,' she said. 'But I won't lie. I am looking forward to you covering some of the Port Lowdy events including the crime watch report and the outrage about the bus stop being built.'

Dan smiled at her. 'I will relish every story and treat them with the respect they deserve.'

She rolled her eyes at him. 'You like to lay it on thick. Is that the Irish patter?'

'No, I mean it,' he said, and he almost sounded like he did.

'All right, let's go to the pub for lunch.'

'Now?' Dan looked at his watch.

'Have you eaten?'

'No, but I thought you would want to get on with work,' he said.

'Work will wait, but my stomach won't.' It took Dan a solid ten minutes to get Richie to come to him when he called. He eventually bribed him with a mint from Tressa's purse. They walked slowly up the hill to the pub and Tressa pushed open the door. 'Any tables for a girl and two fellas?' she called, and Pamela walked out to greet them.

'You're the first in,' Pamela said. She turned to Dan.

'Pam, this is Dan, who is helping me with the *Occurrence* while George is away... and this is his friend Richie.'

Pamela smiled at Dan, and nodded to Richie. 'Table in the beer garden or inside?'

'You don't mind Richie being inside?' he asked.

'Not at all. We had Mrs Rouse and her parrot in last week and she got along famously with Walter's ferret. The parrot, that is.'

Tressa saw the look of incredulity on Dan's face and laughed.

'Well?' she asked.

'Outside would be nice, if that's okay with you?'

They went outside and sat at a table under the oak tree that was starting to show new leaves.

'Drink?' asked Tressa.

'Oh sure, what are you having?'

'Probably a pint.'

'Same, thanks.'

Tressa went inside where Pamela was working at the bar.

'He's very handsome,' Pamela observed.

'Is he? I didn't notice, not my type,' lied Tressa.

Pamela scoffed as she poured the drinks.

'Even a nun would have a little squirm if she was sitting opposite that man.'

Tressa blushed and took the drinks. 'Put this on the tab, will you?'

Pamela nodded.

'Oh, and we'll have the fisherman's basket with extra chips please.'

Outside, Dan was sitting with his head back, his arms crossed. Richie was lying with his feet on Dan's feet and Tressa stared at them both for a moment.

Yes, he was stupidly sexy, she thought, and put the pints down on the table with a little bang, causing some of the beer to splash.

'Careful there,' he said, 'that's liquid gold.'

'I ordered us the fisherman's basket, if that's okay?'

He nodded. 'Fine, thanks – but I'll get extra chips.'

'Already ordered,' she said and looked down at Richie. 'We can't leave him out; he's new in town.'

Dan pushed his sunglasses onto his head. 'Richie and I

thank you. No one ever thinks of him like a person, but he is to me.'

'I get it. I have a cat who is a person to me, even though she thinks I am subhuman.'

'What's her name?'

'Ginger Pickles.'

'Interesting name.'

'It's from a Beatrix Potter book. *The Tale of Ginger and Pickles*, who were the world's worst shopkeepers. They gave credit to all and sundry and then had to close their shop. Ginger was the cat and Pickles was a terrier. And their mouths watered whenever they had mice or rats in the shop as customers, but they knew that it would be bad for business to eat their patrons.'

Dan laughed. 'That is an excellent business strategy. Don't bite the hand that feeds you.'

She looked at him for a long time.

'What?' he asked.

'That's what you did in Dublin, isn't it? They sued you for your flat. Tough luck to lose your home over an argument.'

Dan looked downcast. She reached across the table and touched his arm.

'Dan, it's fine. Honest. I'm happy to go on if you are, and who knows, it might just all work out for us both. The main thing is to keep the paper going while George is away. Can you agree to do that?'

Dan nodded and looked at Tressa. 'You know, that's the first time I have felt okay since this all happened.'

Pamela came out and put their food on the table.

Tressa smiled at Dan.

'The sun is out, you have a new job, you have a pint, you

have the best fish and chips in Cornwall, and you're with Richie. What else is there? This is happiness right here.'

Dan sipped his drink. 'It's remarkable that you can say the right things to make me feel better. Twice. You're a good egg, Tressa Buckland. A good egg indeed.'

8

The Port Lowdy Occurrence was bigger than Dan expected. It had real stories, obviously written by George, and lots of fun little glimpses into the life and times of Port Lowdy. It was what a paper should be, telling people about changes in the village and the stories that might affect and entertain them. Naturally the paper was more profitable in the summer, from advertising, but there was a strong balance of stories in there on local events, and photos Tressa had taken, which were very good. She clearly had an eye.

'Your photos are great,' he said to her. 'You could do this full-time, like for the bigger papers.'

'Thanks, but I like painting. That's what makes me happiest. This job just supports that. I mean I like it but it's not my true love.'

He went through the schedule with Tressa and looked at the upcoming events that he was supposed to cover.

'We have the fishing boat naming ceremony next week. It will be something generic but they buy advertising from us in the summer for fresh crabs, so we need to cover it.'

'Oooh,' said Dan. 'That will be fun now I know everything there is to know about the naming of sea vessels.'

Tressa rolled her eyes at him but he ignored her. He liked learning new things and this was what he was here for, to learn – and also to sit back and find some peace in his head and heart.

Dan jotted notes in the notebook Tressa handed him when he sat at George's desk, with its old computer and keyboard with what looked like biscuit crumbs in the keys.

The desk was messy but he had seen worse, including his own desk back at the paper in Dublin.

Tressa worked fast, which he admired. She took him through the paper set-up. He would have to do his own copy-editing and subediting, which was perfect for him. He hated the stupid headlines his subs gave him in Ireland, always so sensationalistic and veering towards clickbait.

Tressa paused when they were going through the schedule.

'If you have any ideas, please feel free to bring them to the table. I mean I am sure you think this is a bit half-arsed but the paper matters to the people here,' she said, almost defensively.

Dan looked up in surprise. He would have expected her to be proprietary but she was anything but. She said she wanted his knowledge and experience and if he saw something he thought would be a good topic then he should write about it.

Everything about Tressa was surprising, from her easy-going nature, to her commitment to Port Lowdy. Also, she'd included Richie in the lunch order and for that he was grateful. Richie was his only family and it mattered to him that people recognised that.

'I'll have a think,' he said, watching the light on her curls.

Some of them were a dark auburn and some black, all springing out of their own accord.

She was prettier and younger than he'd expected but she wore no makeup except for red lipstick. She had a chic quality that only came from not dressing for anyone else but yourself. Dan had spent years dating women who were fixated on their looks and their style, but he doubted Tressa cared in that way. In her striped top and her jeans, she was casually elegant.

'Are they your natural curls?' he asked and realised he had said it aloud.

She touched her hair. 'Yes, all mine.'

'Sorry, that was weird.' He knew he had turned red.

'At least you didn't touch it. So many people come and just touch my hair like I'm a chia pet. That's weird.'

Dan laughed. 'I promise not to touch.'

'Thank you.'

They went through the rest of the paper. Dan had pages of notes in his book and he felt excited to start.

Maybe Tressa was right, maybe this would be the break he needed.

'Can I see your art?' he asked suddenly.

Christ, what was wrong with him? It was like he had turned into a child, blurting out whatever came to mind.

But Tressa didn't look fazed.

'Sure, but not today. Come for dinner with Richie. Tomorrow night?'

'Thanks,' he said, meaning it. He was lonely, even more now he didn't have his normal job to lose himself in.

When they finished work, Tressa walked him back to

the post office. The sun was getting lower and the sky was turning a lovely shade of pink.

'I can see why you love it here,' he said as they walked. 'It's like a made-up place. You said your cat was named after a Beatrix Potter animal, well, this village feels like a Beatrix Potter sort of a place.'

Tressa looked around with him. 'It still has pain and loss and tragedy; you just can't see it when the sun is shining so brightly and the sea is sparkling.'

Tressa's bicycle was exactly where she had left it and she pulled it away from the wall and jumped on easily.

'Goodbye to you, Dan Byrne, the angriest man in Ireland. I hope you will be the happiest man in Port Lowdy while you're here.'

She put her helmet on and then with a wave, she rode off towards the beach. He watched her until she disappeared into the distance, wishing she had stayed a little longer. She had a certain energy that made him feel calm, hopeful. It was a new feeling and possibly addictive. *Don't make a play for the only co-worker at the paper*, he reminded himself. Workplace romances were rarely a good idea.

Dan rang the bell for the post office and soon Penny had him upstairs, Richie was fed and Dan had a bowl of vegetable soup in front of him, which was perfect after such a heavy lunch.

The heater was on and BBC news was playing.

'This is lovely, Penny, really,' he said – and it was.

There were only a few times he had felt nurtured in his life. Once when he had a nice foster mother for a while who gave him tomato soup with toast soldiers and put a hot water bottle in his bed. And another time when he was in hospital when he was twelve and was having his appendix out. The nurse gave him extra ice cream and an extra blanket and she tucked him in the way he imagined a mother might.

Penny chatted about her day, which seemed extraordinarily boring, but she was enthralled with everything that had happened.

He remembered something one of his senior editors had said when he was working as a junior: 'Everyone has a story.' Dan listened to Penny and then he thought about the photo of her downstairs.

'Penny,' he asked, 'would you let me interview you?'

'About what? There has been a price rise on stamps but I don't know I have much else to say about the state of the British mail service.'

'No, about you, your life. I think it would be nice to do some stories on important people in Port Lowdy, and since you were once Miss Crab... I mean that's important.'

Penny took his empty bowl away. 'Nobody cares about that now,' she said.

'I think you would be surprised. People love reading about other people. Especially people they know.'

'Oh, I don't know...' Her voice trailed away.

But Dan was hearing interest in her tone. Gut instinct told him there was a story in the Miss Crab contest.

'You just answer some questions and if there is a story, I will tell you, and if there isn't then we can forget it. At the very least, I can get to know you.'

Penny frowned at him. 'I'm quite boring, you know.'

'I doubt that. Everyone is interesting, they just don't know it, and that's what makes them unique.'

Penny made them both tea and Dan fetched his notebook from his bedroom.

They sat in front of the heater in the armchairs and Dan started with one question. 'Tell me about being the one and only Miss Crab of Port Lowdy.'

It was the most thrilling moment of Penny's life. When they put the crown of claws on her head in front of everyone from Port Lowdy and the local area, she could feel the pride of her family.

All those girls who had said she wouldn't win and all those boys who'd called her names at school were now clapping as she paraded in her bathing suit. She had the best legs in Port Lowdy; in fact, the photographer from London told her that she could be a model. That she looked like an American actress called Sissy Spacek, but more beautiful.

After the ceremony, there was a celebration at the Black Swan and Penny drank far too many gin fizzes and danced with the photographer all night.

She spent three days with him. Even though her strict father had told her she wasn't allowed, she went anyway. Penny had never disobeyed her father before. But something in her made her lose all judgement or care. His name was Paul Murphy and he had come from Australia to London to be a fashion photographer. He was working for the local papers but soon he would be working for the fashion magazines like *19* and *Teen*. They had already asked to see his portfolio, he told her.

He promised to return after a photoshoot in Manchester but he never came back and Penny was left with a growing pregnancy and a bad reputation. People laughed at her in the street, and the council decided that Port Lowdy's Miss Crab competition would be no more because Penny had brought shame on the village, and on the Royal Mail service – or so her father told her. He didn't let her out of the post office for seven months and when she went to St Ives to have the baby, her father told her the paperwork was ready for a couple who couldn't have one of their own.

But Penny fought them tooth and nail in the hospital and told the doctors she would go to every paper in the country and tell them they forced her to give the child up. She screamed when her parents came into the room with the social worker until they finally left her with the baby.

When they returned home in silence, Penny's mother whispered to her that she was glad she kept her but she couldn't disagree with her husband; it wasn't right.

Penny said nothing to her mother but resolved to never be controlled by a man or give in to the opinions of others.

Eventually she earned her father's respect by raising little Tegan, as she called her. Tegan was a sunny child who turned Penny's father into a doting grandfather until his sudden death from a heart attack when Tegan was twelve. Penny's mother went not long after, a stroke – and then it was Penny running the post office and raising a teenager. She had no regrets. Port Lowdy had been good to her and Tegan was a single mother now to her own little girl, Primrose, or Primmy as they all called her, who loved

Penny more than Penny loved herself. She was grateful for the two of them.

But there were nights when she was so alone, she wondered if there was more to life than Port Lowdy. She felt like the oldest fifty-five-year-old in Cornwall. She was sure people thought she was over sixty, even closer to sixty-five, not that anyone really looked at her. She was just Penny Stanhope from the post office. Penny Stamp, the children used to call her at school. Lick a penny stamp, they used to say, and she would laugh along but she wanted to be more than the postmaster's daughter. Instead she became postmistress, with a child and no husband.

Sometimes she looked for Tegan's father on the internet but there were so many Paul Murphys she didn't know where to start, and besides, she didn't know anything else about him. They hadn't talked of themselves, only of their feelings, their hopes, and that he would be back. She had believed him. Tegan never asked much about him, assuming he was just another man taking advantage of a young girl.

Stupid woman, Penny told herself more often than she should.

Port Lowdy had been good to her, but it was easy to lose herself in the village and routine. There was a sense of complacency that was encouraged, living here, she tried to explain to Dan.

People didn't like change and perhaps that was okay to a point but Penny worried about the village. She worried about people who had stayed in their heads too long, like Tressa Buckland.

But she worried about everyone, she told Dan. The people

in the village who didn't get mail, who were expecting it, who left feeling abandoned and lonely.

The loneliness was exhausting for her some days. It ate away at you until you thought you had nothing of any value to give to anyone.

And when she finished talking, it was after midnight. This was the latest she had stayed up since Tegan had been sick as a child.

'I'm sorry, I talked too much,' she said to Dan, stepping over Richie to turn off the heater.

'You are an incredibly interesting and insightful person,' said Dan, closing his notebook.

'You just asked good questions,' she said, and she handed Dan a key. 'This is your house key. You can use the back stairs to let Richie in and out – and yourself, of course.'

Dan took the key.

'Thank you, Penny, for the room, the soup, the conversation, for your friendship.'

Penny laughed and shook her head at him. 'Oh, you are a charming Irishman, aren't you?'

'No, I mean it!'

'I know you do – that's what makes it so dangerous.' And she laughed to herself all the way to bed.

9

The Black Swan kitchen was busy when Remi joined for his first shift.

There was him, Marcel, and a dishwasher who Marcel called Melon, which Remi couldn't understand because he didn't look at all like a Melon.

Melon didn't seem to mind; he just stuck his headphones in his ears and washed the dishes in a rhythmic fashion along to the music. It was relaxing just watching him and the smells in the kitchen were soothing, without all that yelling from the prison dining hall or the guards screaming at him for a minor infraction.

'You can start with the salads and then you can move on to thickening the sauce for the shanks,' Marcel instructed. His tone was friendly, and Remi felt his body finally relax enough to ask a question.

'A shank?'

He wasn't sure what this was. His English hadn't really improved in prison. He had started to take courses but then the prison cut costs and the lessons stopped. He had talked to an American for a while who was in for a drugs charge, but he was soon sent back to America and Remi's English was forgotten.

'*Souris d'agneau,*' said Marcel in French.

'You're from Provence?' asked Remi, reverting to French without really noticing. The *souris d'agneau* was a classic French dish from Provence, where the sheep roamed the fields in the early spring and late autumn. In the summer months the lamb herds were transported to higher, cooler ground for grazing and the tender meat they yielded was exceptional.

'*Oui,*' answered Marcel. 'Now – here is the cold room, where you can gather the ingredients for the salad.'

Then he pointed to the board above the work bench and said in English, 'Monkfish and mussel curry, with jasmine rice. Slow-roasted shanks and garlic mash. Spinach and feta pie with Greek salad. They're the specials,' said Marcel proudly.

Remi nodded. His mind was trying to catch up.

'You start with the salads. Greek and garden,' said Marcel and Remi pushed open the cold room door and took out the ingredients for the salad.

Chopping tomatoes and cucumber, he marvelled at the sharpness of the knife. The knives in prison were as dull as some of the inmates and guards. It took so much longer to slice anything. But he had watched videos in the training courses the prison service offered, and learned how to use a knife properly. He had tried his technique while in the prison kitchen but now finally he felt the knife do what it was supposed to do.

He was able to sweep through the chopping easily and with flair. After tearing apart the lettuce for the garden salad, he moved on to making large bottles of dressing for the garden salad.

Then he turned to Marcel. 'I am done.'

Marcel looked up from the stove and glanced at Remi's work.

'Not bad,' he said. 'Come thicken the sauce for the shanks.'

Marcel showed him what he needed and Remi worked quickly, having been accustomed to the pace of the prison kitchen where hundreds of men needed to be fed.

He met every task with a positive attitude and did his best, which was what he was taught growing up in his grandmother's kitchen in Seine-Saint-Denis.

Marcel was a reasonable boss; he laughed too hard at his own jokes but he was generous with the serves to the tables and went to meet the guests throughout the meal.

He was exactly as Remi was told he would be when he left prison. The man from the charity had said, 'There is a chef named Marcel Foulard, who wants to help someone like you. He will train you, and he will help you with a new job after you have finished with him.'

Remi hadn't asked why Marcel wanted to help him. But the five-dotted tattoo, like that of the number five on a dice, placed between his index finger and thumb, told its own story.

Some prisoners had it. The meaning was *un homme entre quatre murs*. A man between four walls of the prison cell. Marcel was thirty years older than Remi, and only the older prisoners seemed to have them nowadays – but Remi knew it was usually reserved for those who had done long sentences.

But thanks to the unwritten rule, he wouldn't ask about Marcel's time in prison and Marcel wouldn't ask about his.

Though come to think of it, he very likely already knew all the details, from the charity that had set up the placement.

After the dinner service was finished, Pamela came and divided up the tips and split them between Melon, Remi, and the three wait staff.

'Well earned,' she said loudly, 'nothing but compliments all round tonight.' Then she leaned in to Remi and whispered in his ear. 'The sauce for the *souris d'agneau* was highly commended but don't tell Marcel. He'll be jealous.'

Remi smiled at Pamela who gave him a wink. Her false eyelashes tinged in glitter sparkled in the light.

He stood holding the money in his hand, wondering where he should hide it in his room.

One by one the wait staff left, and then Melon; now it was just Remi and Marcel and Pamela.

'Cognac?' Marcel asked, and Remi nodded.

How long since he had had a cognac? Probably seven years, eight months, and two weeks… give or take a day.

He didn't like to think about that last night at the bar when the life he had known had suddenly ended. As the thought of it approached he pushed that night from his head and followed Marcel into the restaurant. They sat at one of the big square tables, and Pamela brought them two glasses and a bottle of brandy.

'You did okay,' said Marcel, pouring the liquid generously into the glasses and then lifted his to Remi.

'Santé.'

'Santé,' replied Remi and he took a small sip.

The flavours filled his nose and mouth: vanilla, cherry, coffee, almond, rose, fig, orange zest. He closed his eyes for a moment and savoured the liquid in his mouth.

'You forgot, hey?' he heard Marcel ask.

'I forgot so much but taste... taste is the best thing to rediscover,' said Remi.

They sat quietly, both tired, but it was companionable and peaceful, something Remi had also forgotten. Who had he even been, before prison? He could hardly remember – but right now, this felt like something he was meant to be.

'*Merci mille fois*,' Remi started to say but Marcel waved his hand away.

'*Après la pluie, le beau temps*,' he said gruffly and Remi smiled.

After rain, good weather, he repeated in English, in his head.

God knows there had been enough rain. He was ready for the sunny weather of Port Lowdy.

The next morning, Remi woke early, as his body was used to. The sounds of doors opening at 6 a.m. and then the guards calling for wake-up used to permeate his mornings. Now he woke of his own accord, but heard nothing. He lay in the bed with his eyes closed, his ears straining to hear something familiar.

Finally, he stepped out of bed and went to the window and lifted the blind.

His window looked over the village and down to the little bay. The sun was rising and Port Lowdy looked asleep. He pulled on his only clean set of clothes, washed his face and cleaned his teeth, and went quietly down the stairs. There were only a few guests staying at the pub but he was very aware of being a good tenant for Marcel and Pamela.

Unlocking the door downstairs, he stepped outside and the cold early March air touched his face, waking him better than any coffee could.

The water called him, which was strange as he had never really loved the water. Like most kids growing up in the poor parts of Paris, he was not a confident swimmer – but there was something that called to him today.

He walked to the stone wall and looked down at the beach. The tide was out, leaving ripples across the sand, glistening in the strengthening morning light.

A dog was running across the sand with something in his mouth while a man ran behind him, calling out the name 'Richie'.

Remi watched as the man ran in circles after his dog. He walked down the stone steps to the beach and across the sand and gave a whistle. It pierced the morning stillness but the dog stopped and ran towards Remi and skidded to a stop. '*Assis*,' he commanded, and the dog sat in front of him.

In his mouth the dog was holding a very dead sea bass and the stench was intense.

'*Donne*,' he commanded and took the tail of the fish. The dog reluctantly let go.

The owner ran up to Remi, panting. 'Oh my God, how did you do that? He's not really used to having free time on a beach, let alone a dead fish. He's usually very good but I think the Cornish air has got to him.'

Remi laughed and threw the fish as far as he could. It skipped a few times across the sand, eventually laying to rest in the shallows with a ceremonial splash.

'He is the best dog ever until there are seagulls or dead

animals around.' The man glared at Richie the dog. 'He either wants to chase them or eat them or both.'

Remi laughed again. The fresh sea air felt so good and somehow everything felt easy. 'I had a dog as a boy who was like him. He chased squirrels in Paris.'

'That sounds very glamorous compared to Richie's current fascination with seagulls.'

Richie had flung himself down on the sand and was rolling around giving little self-soothing snorts.

'Are you on holiday from Paris?' asked the man.

'No, I work at the pub,' Remi said, hearing the words he said but still feeling they were a lie.

'I just had lunch there yesterday. I'm Dan. Dan Byrne. I'm new in town.'

'Remi Durand,' he answered and shook the man's hand. 'I'm new too.'

'Then we should have lunch,' said Dan. 'I have no friends here and you probably don't either.'

Remi paused for a moment. This Dan Byrne seemed friendly enough but a friend seemed a bit much after one brief meeting. In prison, friendships were strictly transactional. Something for something and rarely something for nothing. Everything would have to be repaid in the end.

'I work a lot,' said Remi. 'But stop in for a drink sometime. I finish late. Bye.'

He turned and walked back to the pub, wondering if Dan Byrne would ever come for the drink if he found out what Remi had done and why he was here.

10

Tressa unlocked the office door and turned on the heater. She had been up since 5 a.m., painting the sunrise in watercolours from the room of Mermaid Terrace. Sunrises were notoriously hard to capture. The fleeting moment was less than three minutes long – three minutes to collect all the colours and the mood. She had prepared various shades of cadmium orange and lemon, ready to record the moment, but then Ginger Pickles pushed over a jar of paintbrushes soaking in water, which nearly soaked her sketchbook.

She'd given up on the sunrise and continued with her series of seascapes instead. Now she turned the kettle on and waited for the water to boil.

She'd thought a lot about Dan last night, after their first day. He seemed pleasant and not at all like the angry man she had read about online. The reputation didn't match the man she had lunched with. But she was wary of him, just in case he lost his temper over a story. Although to be quite fair, she wasn't sure there was a story at Port Lowdy for the angriest man in Ireland to uncover.

What troubled her more than his reputation was his looks. He was the sort of man she would have admired if she had met him at a party. Perhaps they would have flirted and danced. Maybe he would have kissed her in the darkness of the hallway.

At that moment, the door opened and the dog came bounding in with Dan following.

'Morning,' he said gruffly and threw his bag onto his desk. Tressa turned away from him, hiding the rising blush on her face.

'Cup of tea?' she asked, clearing her throat after she spoke.

'Ta,' said Dan. 'Sorry I'm late. Richie had an incident with a sea bass on the beach and a French guy had to help me with him, and the fish. It was incredibly embarrassing.'

'Oh no,' said Tressa. What sort of a conversation opener was this? She felt as if she was in a dream.

'Anyway, I'm going to head up to the pub at lunch and catch up with him. He seemed like he might have a story. We could do a profile on the new French chef.'

'We could,' she said. 'But he might not be interested.'

'Everyone wants to tell their story,' said Dan. 'You just have to ask the right questions to get people to open up.'

Richie came and pushed his face between Tressa's thighs.

'Come here, Richie,' growled Dan. 'He has issues with personal boundaries.'

She brought their teas to the desk and sat opposite Dan at George's desk. She warmed her hands on the pretty floral mug. Caro had bought them for the office last year, to replace the odd set they had, many with cracks and chips.

Thinking of Caro and George made her want to cry and she sipped her tea, trying to stop the tears from starting.

'You all right?' asked Dan.

'Yes, just burned my tongue on the tea.'

'There's a superstition in Ireland that if you lick the underside of a lizard, it will cure your burns.'

'Um, no thanks,' said Tressa. 'Is that a real superstition or are you pulling my leg? Irish humour and all.'

'No, it's a real Irish superstition.' He laughed.

'What's another one?'

'Never play cards with a man who has a cloven foot.'

'Oh come on, that's not real!' she exclaimed.

''Tis, so. Cos it could be the Devil himself, and you'll never win cards against the Devil.'

'That's ridiculous,' she said, shaking her head at him. 'Come on, we have to plan the next issue in more detail.'

'About that, you mentioned I should bring any ideas I had.' Dan pulled a battered notebook from his bag.

'Yes,' replied Tressa carefully. She picked up a pen and her own notebook and started to sketch. She always sketched when she was nervous. Even the simple act of holding a pencil or pen calmed her.

'I want to do a profile piece on Penny.'

'Penny Stamp?'

He frowned at her. 'Don't call her that. She doesn't like it.'

Tressa felt affronted at his correction. She would never call Penny that to her face, but everyone in Port Lowdy used it.

Dan opened his notebook. 'Penny Stanhope, yes. I interviewed her last night and she's a remarkable woman.'

'Really?' Tressa tried to reconcile Dan's review with her own experience. Penny was kind and always friendly but she wouldn't have called her remarkable. 'Remarkable how?' she challenged him.

'Let me read you what I wrote. It's a rough version but it's a start.'

'I don't know that people want to read about Penny,' she protested.

'People want to read about everyone, especially about people they know. Why do you think Penny isn't of any interest? Isn't that your bias, because you don't know enough about her? You haven't bothered to know her?'

Tressa said nothing but she knew he was right. She hadn't ever asked much about Penny. All these years and she only learned about her being the one and only Miss Crab recently.

'I get a final editorial decision and veto, so if I think it's not print-worthy then I will say so.' She knew she sounded peeved but she couldn't help herself. In twenty-four hours, Dan had made a new friend, had a lunch date, learned Penny's life story, and invited himself over to dinner at her place tonight.

He was not just the angriest man in Ireland, he was now the most popular man in Cornwall, it seemed.

'Go on then, read me what you've written so far,' she said and turned the page of her notebook where she had been drawing Richie gnawing on a hairy human leg. Dan's presumably, she thought.

Dan cleared his throat, which she thought was a bit show-offy but she said nothing.

And then he started to tell Penny's story.

As he wove through the incidents of Penny's life so far, of the photographer who stole her heart and her future, Tressa felt her eyes well up several times at all Penny had had to face. She laughed when Dan told Penny's story of the little girl trying to post her baby brother to her gran in Plymouth, and felt ashamed when she heard about the aching loneliness Penny felt at times in the village.

It was beautifully written by Dan, filled with warmth and respect. And he gave Penny and Port Lowdy a side Tressa had never seen before.

When he finished she was silent.

'Thoughts?' he asked finally. Was there a sense of trepidation in his voice?

Tressa put down her notebook and pen. 'It's beautiful,' she said truthfully. 'It's moving and sensitive and special.'

She paused.

'But?' he said. 'I am sensing a but.'

'But is it relevant to Port Lowdy? I mean, we cover the local events; we aren't like a Humans of Port Lowdy paper. It might be a bit much.'

Dan sat back in his chair. 'Do you really think that? Or do you just not like it because it's different to what you usually do?'

Or because she herself hadn't written it. Hadn't even thought of it. 'No,' she said quickly, 'I think it's great but I don't think it's right for *The Port Lowdy Occurrence*.'

'Why?' he challenged.

'Because I know what the readers want.'

There was a current in the air and she wasn't sure whether she liked it.

'You know what the readers want?' He was mocking her. 'That's grand then. You should head to London. You could save journalism from itself.'

Tressa narrowed her eyes at him. 'I am simply stating that—'

'That you underestimated your readers and that you're a bit of a snob.'

'Excuse me?'

Dan tipped back on the chair, balancing on the back two legs.

'I'll ring George and get his final say,' said Dan.

'No! I'm acting editor.' Tressa heard her voice rise. 'I have the final say.'

'You're not the editor, you're the photographer.'

Tressa glared at him. 'So who's the snob now?'

'Okay.' Dan put away his notebook and shrugged. 'No skin off my nose.'

But he wasn't happy – she could tell by the way his jaw tightened and the muscles flickered. He was keeping his mouth shut, which was clearly an internal struggle.

They sat and worked through the planned events and what Dan would write and what Tressa had to photograph and the advertising, and when they finished, Dan looked at his watch.

'Righto, I'm off to meet Remi,' he said, and he picked up his bag and whistled to Richie and walked out the door, leaving Tressa sitting at the desk.

Whatever goodwill she'd had towards him dissipated as the door closed behind him. He was rude and angry and self-important, she thought, as she picked up the empty mugs and took them into the kitchen. And he just walked out and left the cups for her to wash, like a good little secretary.

Hiring Dan Byrne was a mistake. She went to her bag and pulled out her phone to ring George.

But just as she was about to dial, a text came through from him.

Dan told me about the Penny profile. Genius. I think he should do a few characters in the village, tell their stories. Good for business as they will buy more papers to send to family and so on. Excellent work, Tressa. Dan said it was your idea. Well done. Caro okay, surgery tomorrow morning. She's resting and sends her love.

Tressa growled at the phone. Bloody Dan Byrne and his Irish charm. God, the next six months were going to be hell, and she wondered if she was playing cards with a man with a cloven foot or working at a newspaper with the Devil himself.

11

Tressa finished up for the day, left the office and went home to paint, but on the way, she sent Dan a text.

> George texted me. Well played. Dinner invite is rescinded.
> I don't dine with men with cloven feet.

She was feeling petty but she had every right to, she thought. He'd tried to soften the blow by passing the idea off to George as her own. It was insulting.

Riding her bicycle along the esplanade, she saw clouds building in the distance, and she pedalled a little faster. Not because she was worried about being caught in the rain but because she wanted to capture the rain and those clouds in her watercolour sketchbook.

A few drops of rain hit her face as she opened the gate, and Ginger Pickles sat in the bay window, assessing the clouds, and then Tressa's arrival.

'Hey, Ginger P!' She opened the door and wheeled the bike into the small verandah area.

Tressa had put in shelves along the glass-walled verandah, and they held her seashell collection, ordered raggedly from large to small, some found on the beach, some bought in charity shops, or from garage sales. She loved that they used to be homes to little sea creatures, just like Mermaid Terrace was to her now.

Her phone rang and she took it from her bag and checked it wasn't Dan.

'Hi, Mum,' she answered as she walked through the front door. She patted Ginger Pickles's head as she passed the window.

'How are things? I haven't heard from you in a while.' Wendy sounded peeved. 'I did mention I was having my spider veins lasered, didn't I?'

Tressa counted back the days and realised she hadn't spoken to her mother in over a week.

'It's okay,' Wendy continued, with a martyred sigh. 'No need to worry, Jago picked me up.'

'Sorry, Mum, there's a lot going on.' She paused. 'Caro's in hospital. She's really ill. Cancer.'

'Oh no, I didn't know. They should have told me. I could have helped. Is George with her? What does he need? Did you mention I can help?' And there it was. The amazing transformation from peeved, neglected mother to concerned doctor's wife and dear friend of the Foxes.

'Yes,' said Tressa, 'they're in Plymouth. She's having surgery.'

'Who's the surgeon?' Wendy asked.

'I don't know. Should I know?'

'Well, I would have asked – but you weren't to know. I'll call them.'

Tressa sighed as she kicked off her shoes. There were one thousand ways she disappointed her mother, and now she had found one thousand and one.

Wendy was still talking. 'Now how are you? Who is doing the paper with you if George is with Caro?'

Happy to have a change in topic, Tressa spoke honestly to her mother. 'The most annoying person in the world. Honestly, Mum, he's only been here a little over twenty-four hours and he's already turning Port Lowdy upside down.'

'Port Lowdy could do with a little shake-up,' said Wendy. 'It can be very stifling.'

Tressa bristled at her mother's review. 'It's changed since you used to holiday here, Mum,' she lied defensively.

'So what is this annoying person's name?' Wendy wanted to know.

'Dan Byrne, he's a journalist from Ireland who got fired for being too outspoken. I only hired him because there wasn't really anyone else and I wanted someone to start right away. Now I regret it, deeply.'

'Dan Byrne, the one who did the story on that dodgy doctor and the corruption at Royal Dublin? Oh, he's marvellous. Your father followed that story closely. He saved a lot of lives with that exposé.'

Of course her mother and father would know of him. God, it was so infuriating. Why did Dan have to be so... She tried to think of a word to describe him. Why did Dan have to be so Dan?

And how her mother was singing his praises – naturally her parents thought he was God's gift to free speech and to Port Lowdy.

Tressa interrupted her mother's commentary on the virtues of Dan Byrne's work.

'And he got fired for it and he has had to put his flat on

the market to pay back the owner of the paper. I mean he's not a saint, Mum.'

'I think that's poor form from the owners of the paper. He saved the hospital a lot of money from being sued if more people died under that surgeon's hands. And to take away the livelihood of that man – it's unconscionable.'

Tressa was silent. She knew her mother was right and she was being childish. If she was honest with herself she would say that she was being churlish because it was all so easy for Dan. The way he got Penny to open up and tell him about her life in a way Tressa hadn't bothered to uncover. She felt ashamed that Dan had found out so much detail about Penny's story, but she was more ashamed that she herself hadn't bothered to try. She was a snob, and had thought Penny was a little silly – until she read what Dan wrote.

'I have to go, Mum. I have a friend coming over for dinner,' she lied. Wendy's disloyalty wasn't new but when it was right it stung even more.

'Is it Dan? Is he single? Bring him up to St Ives to meet Dad and me. We would love that. Jago and Kelly can come with the twins. I'll do a frittata.'

Inaudibly, Tressa rolled her eyes. 'I don't have time to frittata around, Mum. I have to go. Call George. He might need something at the hospital. Maybe the surgeon is crap and Dan can write an exposé on him.'

Wendy ignored the dig and said goodbye and rang off immediately as Tressa knew she would. Wendy loved to help and to be needed. It was the unfulfilled healer in her, which often came with the territory being the spouse of someone in medicine.

Tressa went upstairs and changed into her painting

clothes, an oversized flannel shirt and jeans, and her red felt slippers. She was cosy and ready to paint the storm that was coming but she would need tea.

She ran downstairs and turned on the kettle and watched Ginger Pickles curl into a small ball on the red armchair. Rain was definitely coming, she thought. This was her cat's one tell about the weather.

Tea in hand, in her favourite mug that read **Not Paint Water** on the front, she went upstairs just as the first crack of thunder came above her. Storms thrilled Tressa like nothing else. The lightning, the rain, the thunder, the electricity in the air made her curls tighter and her eyes sparkle.

Storms reminded her that she wasn't in charge of anything in life, that life was unpredictable, and above all they gave her a valid reason to just stay home and paint.

Sipping the tea, she sat in front of her easel and propped up the watercolour sketchbook. She would paint with oils later but this would be to quickly get the movement of the storm as it came across the bay.

Mixing the colours of blues and greens and grey, she lost herself in the sky outside, until the rain came pelting down and it was so dark she couldn't see anything.

'Shame,' she said to herself, as she went downstairs with her empty mug.

Ginger Pickles was sitting in the kitchen under the table and Tressa realised she was late with her dinner.

'I am very sorry, Madam, I am onto the food now,' she said, hoping the cat wouldn't launch at her feet. The clock in the kitchen said it was close to six already. How was it she lost so much time when she painted? It was as though she went to another place where time moved at double speed.

Ginger Pickles came out from under the table as Tressa pulled a can of food from the cupboard and opened it, pouring the contents into her faded Bunnykins bowl.

'There you go,' said Tressa, and she washed her hands in the sink.

No word from Dan. She checked her phone in her back pocket. She had at least expected a response to her text, but he was rude, so she shouldn't be surprised. Just as she turned on the lamps and drew the curtains, Ginger Pickles let out a terrible howl and she looked out the window and saw him leaving Janet's house.

'Oh God. No,' she said aloud, as she watched him push open the gate to Mermaid Terrace. He came to the door and knocked on the glass.

'Shit sticks,' she said to Ginger Pickles, who was still eating.

Tressa opened the door and a very wet Dan stood on the doorstep, holding takeaway bags.

'I came to make you dinner, as an act of contrition that will hopefully result in forgiveness.'

'Why were you at my neighbor's house?'

'I wasn't sure which one was yours. So, I knocked on them all. Of course, yours was the last one.'

Tress threw her hands up at him. 'Really? No. Please. Go to Penny's and offer her dinner.'

'I can't. I have a fish curry and she doesn't like curry or fish, which seems at odds with her being once named Miss Crab.'

'*I* might not like fish curry,' Tressa said, crossing her arms.

'You do; you mentioned the excellent fish curry at the

Black Swan, so I brought it to you. But if you don't I can go back to your neighbors house. She seemed far more hospitable.

The scent of the fish curry was tempting and Dan really was soaking wet. She stepped aside and gestured for him to enter the house.

In the kitchen he put down the parcels of food on the table.

'Can I borrow something dry?' he asked.

'God, you're a lot of work,' she grumbled. But she went upstairs and brought him back a towel and another large flannel shirt – one she used for painting. But unlike the one she was now wearing, it was clean.

Dan pulled his wet T-shirt off in the kitchen and Tressa turned her back hastily. That glimpse of his torso left her even more cross. His body matched his looks. Every single thing about him was annoying, she decided.

But the smells from the paper bags on the table were more tempting than Dan's chest. She realised she hadn't eaten any lunch.

'I owe you an apology,' she heard him say, and she turned to face him.

'Hey,' he said, 'we're twins.' He put his arm out against hers. 'We match.'

Tressa went to the bags and took out the containers.

'Can I apologise, please?' He put his hand on hers and she put the container of rice down on the table.

'Go on then, get it over with,' she said with a sigh.

'That's the spirit.' He was laughing, damn him.

Tressa crossed her arms and waited.

'I was out of line by ringing George today, and causing

you to rescind your dinner invitation. Nice word by the way. I plan on using it often.'

'I am sure it will come in handy when people get to see what a pain you are and start rescinding all their offers to you,' she said. 'Jobs, dinners, and more.'

'Touché. Anyway, I was being immature and pissy, trying to be the important new person. I should have been more respectful of you and your role at the paper. I was being a total eejit and I'm sorry.'

Tressa was surprised. People were usually crap at apologies, but he wasn't bad. It sounded like he meant it and he looked sincere.

She decided to meet him halfway.

'I should've been more open to the story about Penny. I was being pissy because you had such a good idea and you're such a great writer. I'm sorry for being so rude and rescinding your dinner invite.' She was surprised at her own honesty. But she had the feeling Dan Byrne would see through any insincerity or humouring.

She extended her hand to him and he shook it firmly.

'Let's start again,' she said, and he smiled at her.

Shit sticks, he was so handsome and he'd bought her favourite dinner and he gave a really good apology.

Ginger Pickles jumped up on the table and sat staring at him.

'Hello, Ginger Pickles. Catch any rats or mice today?' he asked and her cat betrayed her by purring like a sports car.

Damn you, Ginger Pickles, you put the 'diss' in disloyal, she thought, and she settled down to her favourite meal with her least favourite person.

12

The final dish was washed by Dan and placed carefully into the dish rack, watched by Tressa.

'I feel like you'll give me a score for the state of the dishes once I'm done,' he said, glancing over his shoulder at her.

She shrugged. 'I might hold up a sign with your number. It depends on if you were able to rid them of that soapy aftertaste that some people leave on hand-washed dishes.'

'Never, we all know you have to rinse them in hot water. Do you mix with animals? Who leaves a soapy taste? Is that a Cornish thing?'

But Tressa didn't crack a smile. She was a tough audience. Usually if he turned up at a woman's house with takeaway and an apology she would swoon; but Tressa seemed bored by his presence and his conversation. As though she was doing him a favour by letting him be here... which she was, but it would have been nice to have some positive feedback.

Was he flirting with her? he wondered. He was definitely trying to gain her approval in some way.

'Your neighbour was pleasant,' he said, mining deeper for conversation.

'Janet? She's nice,' Tressa answered. 'Maybe a little lonely. She overfeeds Ginger Pickles.'

'Perhaps I should have stayed there for dinner with her; she might have been more enthused than you have been.' He wiped his hands on the tea towel and hung it back up on the rail next to the oven.

'Janet doesn't like fish,' Tressa said, and she crossed her legs.

Dan laughed and then so did Tressa.

'Can I see your art?' he blurted out. Tressa made him lose all his usual skills at conversation. He considered himself a high-quality conversationalist, being able to ask questions and draw out information from others until suddenly they had told them all their deepest, darkest secrets. But here Tressa, and even Remi at lunch, gave him nothing.

Remi had been pleasant. He asked Dan lots of questions about his work in Dublin, they talked about food, about Paris, but Dan had the feeling there was a gap in Remi's story somehow.

He turned his attention back to Tressa. 'Come on, take me upstairs and show me your etchings,' he said and pretended to twirl a moustache.

Tressa frowned at him. Then she made a face. 'God you're a ham,' she said and sighed as she stood up. 'Okay you can look but I am not asking for any sort of criticism. You can just look and keep your opinions to yourself, as I really don't want to hear it today from you. Is that a deal?'

Dan nodded. 'I wasn't going to offer my opinion because I don't know anything about art – but I just want to see what you do.'

Tressa pulled her hair down from its bun and scratched her scalp. 'All right, let's go.'

He followed her up two flights of stairs to a small room and she opened the door. He had to stoop to keep from hitting his head.

If the rest of the house was minimal, this room was maximalist, with paintings lining the wall, two easels, a chaise longue covered with blankets and cushions, and an old paint-stained Persian rug on the floor. There was a kettle and small fridge, and a stereo and sketchbooks of all sizes.

'My God, this is like something from a movie set,' he said, looking around. 'It's fantastic – wow.'

He moved around the room, looking at the paintings on the wall of so many different seascapes. They were all so contrasting – from the raging ocean to the pale calm waters of summer.

'These are amazing,' he said aloud.

'No commentary, remember,' she said.

'That was to myself, not to you, so please don't interrupt my conversation with myself.'

Hearing her laugh, he felt pleased.

On a stool were a collection of notebooks and he picked one up that had a sketch of the Black Swan in pen and ink on the open page.

'Oh, now this is marvellous,' he said, as he turned the page and saw all of Port Lowdy in drawings.

There was the post office, with Tressa's bicycle parked out the front. The pier with people milling about, eating ice cream, a dog on the beach, seagulls perched on the lights along the water.

There were the terrace houses, in colour, with Ginger Pickles sitting in the window of Tressa's house. Small sketches of kites from cliffs over the village and blossoming trees that lined laneways, pots of geraniums perched on steps leading up to houses with blue doors.

'Now these, these are exquisite,' he said. 'We have to use them in the paper.'

Tressa shook her head. 'No, no, I don't show that stuff. It's just me messing about.'

'You should,' said Dan. He put the book down and picked up another and found sketches of people in them. Portraits of people he presumed to be her family and friends.

'Who's this?' he turned the pad to her.

'My brother, Jago,' she said.

He found he was relieved at hearing it was her brother. For some reason he felt jealous when he saw the sketch of the man.

'Your mam?' He turned the page towards her.

She nodded.

'Dad,' he said and he turned the page.

'Hey, that's me! With Richie. Gosh he's handsome, isn't he?'

'He is,' said Tressa. 'Richie, I mean.'

'Obviously.' Dan looked up and smiled at her. 'Richie is the handsomest of dogs. The human equivalent is Brad Pitt but still, he's more handsome than him, I think.'

'If you say so,' she said, and then her phone rang and she took it from her back pocket.

'I have to take this. It's George,' she said. She left the room and he heard her in the hallway talking.

Dan half listened to Tressa talking to George. They

seemed to be talking about George's wife and not the paper, so he assumed he still had a job for the moment.

God, Tressa's art was fantastic. Why didn't she show anyone? He couldn't understand why people would hide their talents from the world. If she thought she wasn't good enough then she was wrong. All of a sudden he had the powerful urge to show the world Tressa's work. He pulled his own phone from his pocket. Opening the sketchbook of the drawings of the village he took high-definition photographs of them all. He worked quickly, feeling the familiar thrill of discovering something – a feeling that usually, in his career to date, had been negative, but Tressa's drawings were joyful.

Hearing her finishing the call, he slipped his phone into his pocket.

'All okay?' he asked as she came back into the studio.

'I guess. I worry for them. But his kids are with him, and my parents will go and see them.'

'Your parents know George and his wife?'

'We used to holiday here and I started at the paper as a summer job. Then I moved here and stayed to help George.'

Tressa started to walk down the hallway, so Dan followed, realising his tour of the studio was over.

'So I am pretty tired. Thanks for the dinner though. It was nice and I didn't have to cook,' said Tressa as they came back downstairs.

'So no coffee or whisky?' he asked, knowing he was being cheeky. But Tressa wasn't having any of his usual tricks.

'I don't drink coffee after midday and I hate whisky,' she said as she left the room and came back with his T-shirt, now dried.

'You're breaking my heart, Tressa Buckland. Not liking whisky? This is terrible news for our relationship.'

Tressa looked puzzled. 'What relationship?'

'Working, strictly business. I would never expect an artistic genius like you to lower yourself to a mere newspaperman like me. I am sure you wine and dine with those who speak of palettes and sunrises and whose fingers are like brushstrokes.'

Tressa rolled her eyes at him. 'Do you think you are being a lyrical Irishman? Because you sound like a bit of a wanker actually.'

Dan roared with laughter. 'That isn't the first time I have been called a wanker. People have said I am more full of blarney than the stone itself.'

She sighed. 'You can go now. I'm tired.'

'And you sound like the Queen of England herself.'

Pulling off the shirt, he slipped on his own T-shirt and handed the shirt to Tressa.

'Thank you for the shirt,' he said.

'Thank you for the dinner and the apology.' She smiled.

Dan gave Ginger Pickles a pat on the head as he passed her sitting on the back of the armchair. The little animal purred happily in response to his touch.

'At least she likes me,' he quipped as Tressa opened the door for him.

'She's as fickle as a pickle, just like her name, so don't assume she likes you more than any of the gentlemen callers I have coming over with fish curries to try and steal my art or my heart.'

Dan paused at the door. How could she know he had

taken photos of her sketches? He calmed himself as she laughed and pushed him out the door.

'Goodnight, Dan.'

'Goodnight, Tressa,' he said as the cool night air snapped him into reality after the warm comfort of Mermaid Terrace.

13

The weeks passed in a blur for Tressa as she and Dan attended a bonsai exhibition in the next village, a series of parked cars lost their side mirrors near the library, and a mysterious skeleton turned up on the cove, further around from Port Lowdy.

'People are saying it's a mermaid,' said Dan, as Tressa took photos of the gross-looking thing on the sand.

'People are stupid,' answered Tressa.

'You have no romance about you. What if it was?'

She pushed her hair away from her face. 'Aren't you the hardened journalist who only deals with facts? When did you ever believe in mermaid stories?'

'I don't but it's a nice headline for a story. We can do something on the mermaid of Cornwall and the fact this is a seal skeleton but before people knew better they assumed. That's where the news is important. We clear up assumptions.'

'Mermaids are fake news,' said Tressa, as she took her last photo.

'They are but I am still going to write about them and this sad seal who probably lost his battle with a shark.'

They walked up the beach to the path and back to Dan's car.

Richie was sitting in the back seat, with his head out the window.

'He wants an ice cream,' he said to Tressa.

'Does he? Or do you?' She felt like she was dealing with a toddler. A very charming and likeable toddler but he was still annoying.

'I wouldn't mind one. Can I shout you a cone?'

'Sure,' said Tressa and she put the camera into her bag as they got back into the car. 'There are good ones at the Lowdy Creamery in the village.'

'Done,' said Dan, as he put the car into gear and they drove along the coastal road. Dan turned on the stereo and the sound of Lionel Richie came through the car. He burst into the chorus of 'Dancing on the Ceiling' and pressed a button so the window went down, and the sea air rushed through the car and Tressa's curls covered her face.

'I didn't take you for a Lionel Richie fan,' she yelled over the music.

But Dan shook his head at her and sang louder so she gave up on trying to discuss his passion for this song.

By the time they returned to Port Lowdy, Dan was singing 'Hello', and Tressa reluctantly hummed along and heard herself singing the chorus. *Damn you, Dan Byrne, you have me singing Lionel Richie.*

Dan parked the car and turned to Tressa. 'I like you even more now that you sing along in the car with me, and to Lionel Richie. I think we are going to be best friends.' He jumped out of the car and opened the door for Richie to follow him.

Tressa felt like her head was spinning, as she shut the car door behind her.

'How many cups of coffee have you had today?' she asked as they walked towards the ice cream shop.

'None,' he answered. 'Just enjoying myself. Nothing to worry about, nothing to be angry about – it's quite a new thing for me. Let me have it because who knows how long it will be before my dark mood returns.'

Dan pushed open the door of the ice cream shop and gestured for Tressa to step through first.

'Can I help you?' asked the girl behind the counter.

Dan walked along the counter, checking the flavours.

'Lavender? What sort of ice cream is lavender flavour?' he asked.

'Would you like to try some?' asked the girl.

'No thank you, I'll leave it for the bees.'

Tressa watched him peer at the ice cream. No amount of handsome charm could make up for his cavalier energy.

'I will have a single cone of vanilla ice cream and a waffle cone of chocolate mint and peanut brittle.' He turned to Tressa. 'You? What do you want?'

'I'll have a single cone of rum and raisin.'

'You won't drink whisky but you'll eat rum ice cream? You're a mystery, Tressa Buckland.'

He paid for the ice cream and handed Tressa her cone, then walked out to Richie holding two cones and held one for Richie to lick, which he did messily.

Tressa watched Richie enthusiastically lick the offering. 'I don't think dogs are meant to eat ice cream.'

'We're not meant to eat ice cream either but it's a nice treat for humans and for fur humans.'

When Richie had finished eating his cone, they walked down to the beach, licking their ice creams.

Richie ran onto the beach and chased seagulls who had the better of him while Dan sat on the wall and Tressa sat next to him.

'It's lovely, isn't it?' Tressa said.

'It is, but don't you get bored of living here?' Dan asked.

'No. Why would I?'

'Because I think it would be very routine. You know everyone; you know what happens every season. You work in the newspaper but there is no real news to report on because nothing actually happens.'

'It does so. There was a mermaid on the beach today.' But his words hit a nerve because sometimes, she thought about these things also.

Dan finished his ice cream and wiped his hands on the napkin that was wrapped around the cone.

'And what about you?' she asked. 'Why are you here since it's so boring?'

'Because I have nowhere else to go and my flat is about to be sold and no one in Ireland will hire me.'

For some reason this annoyed Tressa and she stood up and walked to the bin and threw the rest of her cone away.

'Hey, Richie would have eaten that,' he said but Tressa kept walking towards the office.

'What did I say?' he asked as he chased after her.

'Nothing,' she answered but she was offended that he didn't want to be here. She was offended on behalf of Port Lowdy and she was angry because he had triggered something inside her that she knew to be true.

Port Lowdy could be very unremarkable to the outsider but there were days when the sun hit the water and the children ran on the sand and lovers proposed on the rocks and Ginger Pickles lay stretched out on the tiles of the front step and everything was right in the world.

Tressa opened the door to the office, went to her computer, plugged her camera into the machine, and started to download the photos.

Richie entered the office and sat under her desk, while Dan came puffing behind.

'You have an angry walk,' he said, leaning over the desk, trying to catch his breath.

'I do not.'

'You do. It's all tight and fast, like this.' He proceeded to do an impression of Tressa that reminded her of Wendy.

'God, you look like my mother when she's asking to speak to the manager.'

Dan threw his hands up. 'See? You inherited your mother's angry walk. Most women do.'

'That's sexist.'

'Not really. Most men inherit their father's balding pattern. It's just DNA.'

Dan sat at his desk and she heard his laptop turn on.

'I think Remi has a story,' he said.

'Unless Remi tells you his story, then it's none of your business,' answered Tressa.

'It is; it's everyone's business. Remi might have something extremely fascinating to share and he doesn't know it yet.'

Tressa said nothing, as she started to file the photos into the folders on the server.

'When we had lunch, he seemed to have no idea about things like *Game of Thrones*, or Snapchat. He's your age, right? Late twenties. He should know about those things.'

'I don't use Snapchat and I haven't watched an episode of *Game of Thrones*. Does that make me mysterious?'

'No, because you're a painter and that's your thing. And you've at least heard of those things. But Remi – I want to get to know him better.'

Tressa spun around on her chair.

'You said you wanted to be his friend, so be his friend. Don't look for drama when there isn't any because you're projecting your boredom about being here and your resentment that you're not winning a Pulitzer for your exposé on Mrs Caddy taking off all the side mirrors on the cars near the library while driving in her new car.'

'So it was Mrs Caddy?' He slammed his hand down on the desk. 'I knew it.'

Tressa went back to her work. Richie put his head on her lap, while he was under the desk, and she scratched his head.

'Your dad has more issues than *The Port Lowdy Occurrence*, and we have been in print since 1781,' she said and she heard Dan burst into laughter behind her.

'You're funny – that's why we're friends,' he said and Tressa turned to him and looked him in the eye.

'We are colleagues. We aren't friends. I don't want to be your friend if you do to me what you are planning to do to Remi. Snooping about his life and trying to find plot holes. So let's just get this issue finished and to the printer and then we can have a break from each other for a week.'

Dan looked hurt and she wondered if she had been too harsh. But he needed to be told. The last thing she wanted was for him to start snooping around her life. God knows she had moved to Port Lowdy for a reason only she knew and she wanted it to stay that way.

14

Two weeks later, Penny Stanhope lifted up the bundle of papers by the front door of the post office and carried them inside, placing them on the rack. She cut the plastic wrapping off them and then took the top one, went behind the counter and laid it on the wooden surface.

There was the photo Tressa had taken of her, holding the Miss Crab photo. **Postmistress Reveals Past. Turn to Pages 5 & 6,** instructed the text under the photo.

She looked old, she thought, as she turned to the page mentioned and started to read.

It was as though she was reading about someone else. Someone wiser and braver and infinitely more interesting than she felt.

The photo of her as Miss Crab was bigger on the inside spread and there were large quotes from Penny in bold text.

'I have forgiven Port Lowdy, but I can't forgive him.'

She closed the paper and dialled Tegan's number.

'Tegan, it's Mum. I want you to know that I'm in the paper today. No, *The Port Lowdy Occurrence*. It's a bit of a thing, you see, and I think we should talk now in case anyone asks you about it.'

*

'Goodbye, Ginger Pickles,' Tressa called out as she shut the door to her terrace. She had fed her but she would probably be skulking around Janet's for extra breakfast soon enough.

'Morning, Tressa,' she heard and looked up to see Janet in the doorway of her own terrace, in her blue dressing gown.

'Hi, Janet, I was just thinking Ginger will be over later for more food, so just to let you know she's been fed – so nothing too much, if you don't mind.'

'Oh, I don't mind. I like having her over. She's company,' said Janet. Tressa wheeled her bike down the path, shaking her head.

She really wished that Janet would get her own cat instead of having a part-time connection with Ginger Pickles. It wasn't that she minded Janet looking after her cat, but she wanted Janet to have more than occasional company.

'I loved your drawings today,' said Janet, as Tressa opened her gate.

'Pardon?'

'In the paper. The sketches of Port Lowdy – they're gorgeous. I mean, I have seen a lot of tourist tat of paintings and the like – but yours are special. You know the place. You can see the heart and soul of where we live.'

Her head spinning, Tressa jumped on her bicycle and rode away from Janet towards the village. That lying, snooping bastard, she thought as she rode towards the post office.

She was unsure if she had ever pedalled as fast, making it to the post office in record time.

Penny had already opened the shop, and there were a few locals crowded around the counter while Penny held court.

'Tressa,' she called, 'isn't this marvellous?' She waved the paper at Tressa, who grabbed a copy as she passed her.

'Dan upstairs?' she asked before even waiting for an answer. At the back of the shop she went through to the back stairs and ran up them two at a time.

Richie met her as she opened the door, but she pushed him away as she stormed into the kitchen.

Dan wasn't there.

'Dan?' she yelled.

'In here,' he yelled back and she opened the door and realised it was the bathroom. Dan was behind a shower curtain that was printed like a giant airmail envelope.

Tressa ripped open the newspaper and found the page of her drawings. 'You took photos of my art without my permission and you put them in the paper. I signed off on the edition and this wasn't in there. Who the hell do you think you are?' she shouted.

Dan put his head around the curtain. 'Good morning, Tressa,' he said. 'Let me finish up here and then we can get tea and I will make you a full Irish.'

'I don't want a full Irish, I don't want a part Irish, I don't want any Irish.'

'You sound like Dr Seuss,' he said and she heard the water turn off.

'I'll wait in the kitchen.' She left the bathroom.

She spread the paper out on the table and looked at her work in print.

The Magic of Port Lowdy in Art

Tressa Buckland, Port Lowdy's resident artist, has drawn Port Lowdy in a series of delightful and charming sketches, capturing the spirit of Port Lowdy with her insightful art.

Tressa has several pieces for sale and is planning a solo exhibition later in the year.

You can contact Tressa through *The Port Lowdy Occurrence* for further details on her work.

Dan walked out of the bathroom wearing a towel.

'An exhibition? Pieces for sale? What the hell, Dan?'

Dan switched the kettle on and took a fry pan from a cupboard. 'Scrambled or fried?'

'You invaded my privacy and you printed my work without my permission. I could sue you.'

'Get in line,' he said. 'But be warned all I have is my shitty Subaru and Richie, and both of them have dodgy exhausts, quite smelly with the wrong fuel.'

'You don't get how awful this is, how sad this looks to have my crappy sketches in the local paper. It's bloody amateur hour. Being in the Miss Crab edition to boot.'

Dan turned to her. 'You're a snob.'

'I am not,' she said.

'You are, you think your work is too good for *The Port Lowdy Occurrence* and that Penny's story is a joke. Yet I don't see you pushing yourself out there as an artist. And you should, because you're good. Those sketches are fantastic; they live and breathe this place. Much better than those paintings of the sea you seem to have an obsession with.'

'Oh seriously, you are so out of line. I see why you were fired and you're alone and with only your dog for company.'

'So what's your excuse?' Dan put down the fry pan and leaned against the cupboard.

'What do you mean?'

'You're alone, with a cat for company, working for a paper that will probably fold once George retires, unless someone buys it, which they won't because no one cares about Port Lowdy except the people who are in it and they're all old. Ever noticed you are one of the few people in your twenties around here? You have to have a plan.'

Tressa listened. Part of what he said made sense; in fact, these were the things that kept her awake at night sometimes.

'But this isn't your plan to make. This is my life, Dan. I hardly know you and you have betrayed me with no awareness of why I don't want my art to be out in the world. You're a bulldozer and you think your good-looking charm will make you immune to the fallout. But it doesn't.'

She stalked out of the kitchen and towards the stairs that went out to the street.

'You are talented; your work should be out in the world,' he said, following her.

'My life is none of your business, Dan. None.'

She opened the door and walked down the stairs and out into the street, feeling the tears welling in her eyes. They spilled over and turned into racking sobs as she managed to find her bicycle and walked it down the street towards Mermaid Terrace.

15

The phone ringing woke Tressa up from her nap on the sofa. She picked up the phone and saw it was her mother.

She deliberated whether to answer it or not but knowing Wendy's doggedness, she chose to get the call over and done with.

'Hi, Mum,' she said.

'Darling, we're so proud of you. Jago showed us the drawings you did. They're online. Isn't that wonderful?'

Tressa closed her eyes. Of course they would be online; she had forgotten about the online edition. God, this just got worse.

'I am so pleased you put your work out there, darling. I am proud of you. Everyone needs to see how wonderful it is and now they can. It's good you have moved on from that stage, darling, and now can put your name to your work. I mean no one even thinks about that now, do they?'

Tressa sat up and sighed. *Except you, Mum, you're the one who mentioned it*, she thought, but didn't have the energy to try and explain.

'Thanks, Mum,' she said. 'Hey, Mum, I have someone at my door. I'll call you later, okay?'

Before Wendy could answer, Tressa had ended the call and put her phone down on the table.

Of course Wendy would bring up her first exhibition. Sometimes Tressa wondered if Wendy struggled with her daughter's failure as an artist more than Tressa did. It was difficult to follow a sister who was apparently the most charming, delightful child, who was the light of her mother's eyes and whom Jago doted on.

She had died at age seven from a brain tumour. Jago was ten and bereft – as were Wendy and David – so they had another baby.

Perhaps they were hoping to clone Rosewyn, but instead they got Tressa. Even her name was unremarkable. Tressa meaning third. She was just the third one, since they lost the second.

For her whole life she had seen Rosewyn as the competition. Her mother talked about her as though she was still alive. She and Jago never clicked, not with ten years between them. He remembered Rosewyn too well to have Tressa replace her memory.

And her father buried himself in work.

Perhaps they thought having another baby was a mistake. Often in their family home, she felt so out of place. She wasn't academically inclined like Jago, and she wasn't one for activities like her mother encouraged.

But when they came to Port Lowdy, things were different. Everyone knew her as Tressa the girl who could draw anything, and George saw her photos when she was a teenager and gave her a job at the paper. The family dined outside in the garden and would have walks on the beach in the evening, and sometimes, they played Monopoly or Scrabble until Jago went away to university.

Rosewyn had never been to Port Lowdy – they only started going when Tressa was born – so it felt safe from her mother mentioning that Rosewyn might have swum in the sea or how everyone loved Rosewyn at the ice cream store.

No, Port Lowdy was Tressa's special place, and it was no wonder she returned after what happened after art school.

A howl from Ginger Pickles and a knock at the door made her jump and she saw Dan standing outside. She stood up and looked at him through the window for a long moment and then turned and walked upstairs to her studio.

'I don't know how I could have got it so wrong,' said Dan to Clive down the phone, sitting on the stone wall overlooking the beach.

'I can. You just push your way into things,' his former boss reminded him. 'You have good intentions but no subtlety.'

Dan rubbed his forehead. The look on Tressa's face when he arrived at her door had made him feel sick, and he realised he really cared about what she thought. Perhaps more than anyone else in a very long time.

'I thought I was helping her, you know, her career – she's genuinely talented,' he said.

'Maybe that's her choice to make,' said Clive. 'You don't know what is right for everyone. You might think you do but what worked for you going through life isn't for everyone else.'

'What do you mean?'

'You had a shite upbringing, Dan, and you managed to escape the cycle using your smarts and your ability to fight with your words but you can't do it for other people unless they ask you for your help. Maybe she was happy with where she was. Did you ask her?'

'No,' said Dan.

'You never do,' Clive said.

Dan said goodbye and ended his call.

Clive had been his most loyal supporter in his career and he knew a lot of the details about Dan's life but not all. No one knew all the details of being raised in group homes for most of his life. There was the occasional foster family but sometimes it was better being in the home than exposed to some of the people who claimed to love children so much they would take them into their homes.

Maybe being in Port Lowdy was a mistake, he thought, and he whistled for Richie to come to him to head back to the post office.

Penny rushed upstairs to where Dan sat at the kitchen table, typing at his laptop.

'You'll never guess,' she said.

'No, I probably won't,' said Dan. 'So you might as well tell me.'

'*Everyday Faces, the TV show* called me, and they want to do a little interview'

Penny could hardly believe it; they wanted Tegan and

Primrose on the show too. It would be filmed in Port Lowdy and they would see the photos and the costume crown and talk about her life.

'That's nice,' said Dan, not looking up from his laptop.

'You all right, Dan?'

He nodded. 'Fine, just working on something.'

'Writing your book, are you? Tressa said you were writing a book.'

Dan looked at her now. 'Have you spoken to her?'

'Not today. Why?'

He looked at the screen again. 'Nothing.'

Penny looked at his face and saw his jaw was tight and she wondered, just wondered, what had happened between him and Tressa.

Her phone rang in her pocket. 'More calls! I have never been so popular, Dan, all thanks to you.'

She ran down the stairs to the post office, where more locals were waiting to chat. What was this about being lonely? she thought to herself. Today she couldn't keep up with everyone wanting to talk about the past and the present.

It was as though Penny was finally part of Port Lowdy.

George sat by Caro's bedside as she slept. The surgery had been successful but she was sleeping a lot. Normal, said the nurses, but George wasn't used to Caro not chatting away as they read the paper together in the morning. He quietly opened his copy of *The Port Lowdy Occurrence* and started to read. When he was finished he closed the paper and sat back in his chair.

It was better than anything he had ever produced. The article on Penny, the art by Tressa. Dan had better headlines and even his article on the washed-up seal on the beach and the way he had intertwined it with the myths of Cornish mermaids was genius. There was a new life in the paper; even Tressa's photographs had a fresh sense of creativity to them and George wondered if Dan had pushed her to take different approaches to the subjects. Dan Byrne was just what *The Port Lowdy Occurrence* needed and George wondered how he could get him to stay.

16

There was an understanding between people who had been to prison to not ask questions about each other's time inside or what led them to being in prison – and with that came the understanding that sometimes things were harder to get used to once you were released. For Remi and Marcel, they both saw the effect of their time in prison in different ways.

Remi saw Marcel's emotional distance and the tough exterior that had protected him for years, perhaps only broken down when he met Pam, whose nurturing could make a hedgehog lower his spines and curl into a little ball of love.

Marcel saw Remi's compact movements from living in a confined space and working in one in the prison kitchen. No eye contact and a lowered head when Marcel barked orders at him in the kitchen was another sign, but what Remi had, that Marcel also had, was ambition. *Ambition is the only thing that will get you through*, Marcel had often said to Pamela and he repeated it to her again when they received the call from the charity to take Remi on as a trainee cook.

'He wants his own place one day. That's what he was

working towards in Paris, before he went inside. This is something I can work with.'

Too many times Marcel had seen ex-prisoners leave with no confidence, no ambition and no reason to stay straight. Remi was different and he knew it from the moment he met him.

For Remi, Pamela and Marcel were lovely employers and were becoming even better friends.

When dinner service was over, they would have a drink in the restaurant with Melon, whose real name Remi still didn't know. They would listen to stories from Marcel about cooking for rich men and gambling with poor men. Pamela usually had her feet in his lap and he would massage them as he spoke, his knuckles digging deep into the balls of her feet.

And Remi would remember Juliet. She was ticklish and hated her feet being touched but she loved her hair to be brushed and played with, and when he lifted the hair from her neck and kissed her lightly where the tiny hairs sprung out...

Thinking about her was both a pleasure and pain. In prison he had tried not to think about her but she wouldn't be ignored, coming to him in his dreams, sitting on his bed and asking him why he didn't call her. Why he didn't write to her.

And he would wake and stare at the grey ceiling and wonder if she ever thought of him at all.

Tonight, Dan was with them, drinking heavily while arguing with Marcel about who was the best fly-half in the World Cup.

Remi watched Dan waving his hands about. His Irish

accent was even thicker when he was drunk and arguing. The raised voices triggered something in Remi and he stood up. 'I am going to bed. Goodnight,' he said.

'Yeah, I'm heading off,' said Melon, pushing his chair out also.

Dan and Marcel didn't hear them as they left.

'You all right, love?' asked Pamela as he went through the kitchen where she was making a cup of tea.

'Yes, just tired,' he said.

'Don't worry about the yelling. Marcel is loud at the best of times.'

Remi nodded. He didn't feel like being in his room. He had spent too much time in four walls. He needed air.

He left the pub and walked down towards the beach. The village was quiet, the beach empty. The moon was waning and the stars were bright, the sound of gentle waves soothing as he stood on the stone wall looking out into the darkness.

'Hello,' he heard and he turned around to see the girl with curly hair standing under a street lamp.

'Hello,' he said.

'You're Remi, aren't you?'

'Why?' he answered slowly.

'I met you when you arrived. I pointed you in the direction of the pub. I'm Tressa. Penny from the post office told me you were working with Marcel.'

Remi nodded. '*Oui*, I am.'

'The beach is lovely, even at night,' she said and he realised she was standing next to him.

'You did the drawings in the paper,' Remi said to her.

'Yes, they aren't very good – just sketches. They shouldn't

have been in there.' She sounded upset but he would never pry into anyone's life unless they wanted him to know more.

'They are fantastic,' he said. 'Do you draw people also?'

'Sometimes, if they're nice people.' She laughed. 'Did you want a portrait done of yourself?'

Remi shook his head. 'No, of someone I know. But I only have a photo of them – it's very old.'

The breeze picked up and blew Tressa's curls over her face. 'My bloody hair,' she said and he laughed.

'I knew a girl who had long hair. It was annoying to her sometimes too. But not all the *bouclé* like you.'

'Yes, I have far too many *bouclé*, indeed.' She burst into laughter and Remi found himself laughing also.

She had swiftly changed his mood and he didn't know how she'd done it, but she had.

'If you have the photo, I can look at it tomorrow if you like? Come to my place and we can have a coffee and I will have a look.'

Remi smiled. 'Merci, Tressa.'

'*De rien*,' she answered.

'You speak French?'

'A little but I would like to improve. Maybe I can do your drawing and you can give me a French conversation lesson?'

'Okay,' he said and put out his hand for her to shake, which she did.

It had been a long time since he'd held a girl's hand and the smoothness of her skin surprised him.

'Sorry,' he said, realising he had been holding her hand too long.

'It's fine.' They stood side by side on the stone wall.

'I have been in prison,' he said suddenly, unsure why he was telling her. He just felt he had to. 'I came here because Marcel gave me a job, because he understands.'

'Okay,' said Tressa.

'But I'm not a bad person. I did something I regret, and I live with it every day, but I don't think I remember how to be in the world, especially a new country. France deported me, because my mother was English.'

A cloud went past the moon as he spoke, momentarily dulling the world.

'I feel like a different person now but I don't know who I am. People think I should be something or they have expectations of who I am based on who I was but why can't people change? I know I have but I don't know who I am now.'

'I understand,' she said, and Remi knew that she did understand, at a visceral level. 'Do you want to come and have a cup of tea now? I live along the esplanade. We can talk or not talk about it but I would like to be your friend if you want one.'

Remi nodded at her and smiled, feeling tears in his eyes. This girl was so gentle and real, and he thought about Juliet.

'I love someone in Paris,' he said.

'She is lucky.'

'We haven't spoken for seven years.'

Tressa took his hand. 'Let's drink tea and eat digestive biscuits and talk about it.'

'What is a digestive biscuit?' Remi thought it sounded horrific.

'The best tea companion biscuit in the world; now, come

on,' she said and they walked along the esplanade, still holding hands.

Dan walked down to the beach, looking for Remi when he saw Tressa standing next to him holding his hand.

'Jesus, that was quick,' he mumbled to himself.

He watched them talk and laugh and then walk in the direction of Tressa's house and he felt the pit of his stomach drop.

Oh dammit, he had a crush on Tressa Buckland and he was jealous of her and Remi. He didn't even know they knew each other and now Remi was walking to her place holding her hand. A workplace crush on the first woman he'd spent any time with, in a long time? While living in a tiny village? God, where was the Dan Byrne he thought he was? He was turning into a romantic fool and he didn't like it one bit.

17

Remi fell asleep on the sofa before three in the morning, so Tressa put a crocheted blanket over him and went upstairs to bed.

She didn't know why he trusted her enough to tell her everything, but he did, and her heart cracked into thousands of pieces. She cried as he told her how he was left to rot in prison. Made an example of, in the courts, with poor legal representation and no family support, Remi never had a chance.

Marcel had given him a chance – but was it a broad enough ledge for him to launch from later?

He would never get a bank loan, with his history, and he would struggle to buy a property or even get a job unless he had someone backing him all the way.

Remi was a good man who deserved better than the hand he was played.

When she woke at midday Remi was gone, with the blanket left folded and the heater turned off. On the table was a plate of madeleines, covered in icing sugar, spilling off the plate and onto the table like confetti, and in the sugar was the word *Merci*, written with a finger.

Tressa picked one up and took a bite. Lemon. Perfection, she thought as she put the kettle on. Ginger Pickles wandered in and circled her feet.

'Morning, Miss,' she said and she took her bowl and filled it with food.

Her phone rang. It was Dan's number.

She put it down again and poured her tea. She had let the tea steep, like her anger against Dan.

When her phone rang again she saw a local number she didn't recognise.

'Hi, this is Tressa.'

'Tressa, wonderful. This is Barbara Crawford from Crawford Gallery in St Ives. I saw your sketches in the Port Lowdy paper and I was wondering if you would be interested in coming up to see me and showing me some more of your work. The article mentioned you were having an exhibition somewhere but perhaps you might find my gallery more suitable. There is a real market for work like yours and I think you would also have some larger pieces?'

Tress sat down at the table. Her tea spilled over onto the wood surface.

'I do have some oils,' she heard herself say.

'Wonderful. Do you think you can come and see me?'

'I can. When?'

'How about next Monday? Does two work?'

'Yes, thank you. See you then.'

Tress put down the phone and looked at the word in the icing sugar – *Merci*.

She needed to speak to Dan.

*

Dan pushed open the door of the office where Tressa was already seated at George's desk. Richie betrayed him immediately by going straight to Tressa and putting his head on her lap.

'Hey,' she said and gave him a small smile.

He walked in and sat in George's chair.

'Your text said you needed to talk to me. Before you fire me, I'm resigning to George today, so forget about the lecture.'

Tress shook her head. 'No, I wasn't going to fire you, I wanted to say thank you.'

'For what?' He raised his eyebrows at her.

She paused. 'A gallery rang me today. A really good one in St Ives.'

'That's nice for you,' he said. He noticed a red flush on her neck.

'It's nice, but it's also stressful.'

'Art is pain.' He folded his arms.

Tressa looked puzzled. 'I don't know about that. It's just harder for me sometimes. And I really lost it when you published the images without my permission.'

'And why is it harder for you?' he asked, homing in on the easier part. 'What makes you so special? Most artists would love to have galleries call them and to see their art printed in publications.'

Tressa bit her lip and then she sighed.

'I have a disorder.' She paused again. 'And it's hard for me to put my work out there.'

Dan felt his stomach fall away. He went to speak but she put her hand up.

'No, I have to tell you before I lose my courage.' A long pause.

'I went to art school, a good art school. And I was told I was the most talented artist in my year, which is a huge amount of pressure, let alone for anyone with anxiety. I mean I had always been anxious as a kid, but I was told I was just oversensitive. Overdramatic and so on. Dismissed by my parents, but that's another story. By the time I got to art school it was blossoming into a fully blown disorder.'

Dan listened.

'And then there was the final show. I was supposed to present my best works, the ones that reflected the mark I wanted to make in the world. It was at the Tate in St Ives, a big and important night. This was the culmination of everything, all those years. You know?'

Dan nodded. He could see the importance of it on her face.

'My parents came. They were proud of me for the first time, probably the last time.' She laughed wryly. 'And I fucked it up.'

He saw tears forming in her eyes.

'How did you fuck it up?' he asked, keeping his voice low.

'Because I couldn't get my work up. I didn't submit anything in the end because I was so anxious that all my work was terrible, that it wasn't what people were expecting, or whatever story I told myself. I just didn't mount anything in the show. My parents came, friends came, and there were the blank walls where my work should have been. My name was on the walls and there was nothing. I had all the works there ready to hang but I couldn't put anything up. Part of the rules of the final show is that the students must hang their own work. My arms wouldn't let me pick up the art to hang. I couldn't make a decision on where to put them. It was overwhelming to the point I thought I was about to be physically sick. I lost my peripheral vision, my ears were ringing, I was sweating and couldn't catch my breath.'

Richie whined anxiously. His head was in her lap and Dan watched as she stroked the dog's head, unaware of the comfort the animal was giving her as she spoke.

'And my mother, God, she was furious. I told her I couldn't do it, and she slapped me in the face and told me I was ridiculous. That I—'

'She slapped you in the face?' Dan was incredulous. He had seen some bad parenting. But Tressa's mother was the worst sort of parent: one who thought she was a good mother. Why was it always the ones who thought they were best mothers, who were the worst?

Tressa went on, 'She said I was a disappointment. And that my dead sister would have done something, anything to be alive and have her chance to show her art and be part of life, so why didn't I just step up to my life and get over whatever made-up illness I was trying to create.'

'Jesus,' Dan said quietly.

Tressa shrugged. 'She's an unhappy person and I forgave her. But it doesn't mean I want to be near her or my dad much. They add to my anxiety.'

He nodded.

'But you put my work out there without my permission.

And you betrayed my trust. I showed you something in private and you threw it out to the world as though it meant nothing.'

'That's not true. I knew how much it meant. That's why I wanted people to see it,' Dan argued.

'You were careless with something that meant more to me than anything else in my life.'

'But – a gallery called you.' He recrossed his arms.

'Not the point, Dan. Try and put your ego in the drawer for a moment and work out why this was a betrayal. Have you ever been betrayed? Trusted someone and then had it be used against you?'

Well, yes. Dan knew that feeling. Every time he went into a new foster home, his fear and anger were used against him. He remember Clive's words, claiming that he didn't make any effort to know what people were feeling, or dealing with. He had made an assumption about Tressa and he was wrong. He sat back, crumpling at the realisation he had crossed a line with so little thought, so little empathy.

'I get it. I fecked it up. I'm sorry. I really am, Tressa,' he said, meaning it.

She was silent. But she stared at him in a way that made him feel truly seen and he didn't like what she was viewing. The worst, most impetuous part of himself.

'How can I make it up to you?'

'Don't lie to me again. Don't keep secrets from me that have to do with my life here. You are a blow-in, but I live here.'

The phrase 'blow-in' irked him but it was true. Did he want to belong in Port Lowdy? Or was it something more?

Tressa swallowed. 'But this time it feels different, you

know? I mean I sell my work under a pseudonym but this time it will be my name on the gallery wall and it feels okay. I don't know why, but there isn't the pressure. I don't know. I mean, it just feels different.'

She smiled at Dan and he smiled back.

'You are extraordinarily talented, you know?'

She smiled again, broader this time. 'Thank you.' He watched her fine hands fondling the dog's head in her lap.

'You know… I interviewed a famous film director once, and he said something to me that I'd forgotten until now.'

'Oh?'

Dan waited, trying to collect his thoughts.

'He said that artistic people are more sensitive because they are more aware of the world. They see into the shadows and because of this, they know where the monsters lie. Being observant all the time is exhausting. You can read the little nuances of people. I bet people tell you things they haven't told others?'

Tressa nodded. 'They do.'

'It's such a big responsibility to imagine art and then create it, and yet it's such a gift.'

A tear fell down her face. 'That's the most truthful explanation of what I feel that I have ever heard. Thank you.'

Dan wanted to wipe the tear away from her chin but he sat still, not wanting to scare her or cross any more boundaries.

'I need you to know I am deeply sorry, Tressa. I wanted the world to see what I saw but I was wrong to do it. I know what it's like to have power taken away, have your choices taken away. I should've known better and I am actually shocked to learn I was such an eejit.'

'I know. You said your apology.'

But Dan shook his head at her. 'I need to earn your trust back. I would never knowingly try and hurt you. And even though this is total shite, I have seen myself in a different way and I need to sort myself out.'

'Don't leave,' she said suddenly.

'I don't know that this is the place for me. I seem to get in the way,' he said.

'Don't leave, please – at least do the six months. I would like your help with the gallery visit; maybe we can drive to St Ives together and you can come and meet my family?'

'Your family?' This was sudden.

'It's always good to have a buffer.' She smiled.

'What about Remi?' he heard himself say.

'Remi? Did he tell you he stayed over and slept here? God, what a sad story that is. He really needs friends, good true friends. He was absolutely ruined in Paris by his old friends.'

Remi had stayed over? Dan nodded as though he knew the story, a trick that always worked when he needed people to tell him more than he knew.

'So sad,' he said, shaking his head sadly.

'He had already left when I got up. He slept on the sofa. Ginger Pickles betrayed me and slept with him because she's a floozy, but he made me madeleines and said thank you in icing sugar and it was so lovely. It felt nice to have a friend, and I hope you and I can be real friends also. Even though you're a pain, you mean well.'

Dan laughed, and he felt his insides twist. Whatever he was feeling was new to him; he knew Tressa Buckland had put a spell on him and he had no idea how to break it, or even if he wanted to.

18

The arrival of the television crew in Port Lowdy created a stir not seen since Dame Judi Dench wore a bonnet and stayed at the Black Swan with the cast and crew of that film made so long ago. The weather was on the improve as March finished up and moved into April, and though the wind was still chilly, the sun was higher in the sky, promising a glorious summer ahead.

The crew would be in Port Lowdy for two nights, interviewing Penny and the locals, discussing the village life and her life. The series was called *Everyday Faces*, which Penny thought was spot on for her, as she did have an everyday face, even though Paul Murphy so long ago had told her otherwise. The television crew seemed very nice and the host was even nicer, handsome too – but Penny had learned her lesson years back. She would never again get involved with a handsome man who was near a camera, television or otherwise.

'Will you come and watch me be interviewed?' she asked Dan who was feeding Richie toast.

'I would, but I promised I would help Tressa with something,' he said.

Penny made a little face at him but he didn't see her – which was just as well, as Dan had been touchy over the past few days whenever she mentioned Tressa.

Tressa was her normal self until Dan was around, she noticed, when she would touch her hair a lot, which Penny knew was a telltale sign of something brewing between them.

Not that they showed any obvious interest in each other but Penny knew the signs. A lifetime of reading romance novels and watching romance films made her an expert, she thought.

But it was all research, with no real practice in her own life.

Tegan was driving down to be interviewed, which Penny was pleased about. She wanted any excuse to see her daughter and her granddaughter and she wanted to see she had made the best out of something that others had considered to be her downfall.

At that moment her phone rang. It was Tegan.

'Hello, pet,' She listened as Tegan explained she would have to stay the night and could Dan stay at the pub for a few nights?

Finishing the call, she asked Dan, who agreed, thank goodness. Within minutes she had the bed stripped and new sheets tucked in for Tegan and Primrose. She felt excited for the interview and the few days ahead. She wanted to thank Dan but he was already gone. Dan had turned her days around since he came to Port Lowdy, and she wondered how she could ever repay him.

*

Dan wandered down to the pub with Richie, where Pamela was hanging out white tablecloths on the line around the back of the building.

'Got any room at the inn, for a weary traveller?' he called out. 'Penny has her daughter and her wean coming down to stay and I'm out on my arse.'

Pamela stopped shaking out the tablecloth she was holding up and shook her head as she called out. 'All the rooms are gone, lovey – the telly people are here.'

Hmm. He wandered back to the post office and unlocked his car, telling Richie to get in the back.

'Come on, boy, time to fetch Tressa.'

He had promised to drive her to St Ives to see the woman at the gallery, and she'd said they would pop in to meet her parents, which he was oddly nervous about.

Tressa was at the front of the house, talking to Janet over the fence when he parked the car.

'Well, good morning to you both,' he said, parking in front of Mermaid Terrace.

'Hello, Dan,' said Janet cheerfully.

Tressa smiled at him and he felt his stomach spin around. This was ridiculous, he told himself.

He was thirty-six years old and had a crush on a girl he barely knew.

Maybe it was because there were no other young women in the village, at least none that he had seen who were not close to menopause. Tressa wore a beautiful emerald-green dress that made her hair even shinier and she had a silver pendant around her neck with a large blue stone in it.

Janet waved at him. 'Isn't she so clever, Dan? And now off to a gallery no less, what an exciting time. She's been working so hard for weeks getting ready,' she gushed. 'I've been feeding Ginger Pickles for her.' He noticed she was wearing her dressing gown; in fact, she always wore her dressing gown the few times he had met her when at Tressa's.

Janet went inside her terrace and Dan followed Tressa into hers.

'She is always feeding Ginger,' said Tressa with a sigh. 'And now she's getting fat.'

'Janet or the cat?' asked Dan, momentarily confused.

'The cat. I have no idea what Janet looks like shape-wise as she's always in a dressing gown. She's depressed. It's sad. I wish I could help her.'

Dan felt a sudden urge to kiss Tressa for being so kind and thoughtful but instead put his hands into the pockets of his jeans. He had been staying out of her way over the past week, knowing she was busy with getting her work ready for the gallery, and he missed her. Not because she was the only person he really connected with in Port Lowdy but because she was great company. Still, she had texted him, called him, invited him to dinner, and showed him her works in the studio. He thought she was merely being kind, but each time she connected with him he felt the delicious thrill of having a crush on someone.

'I will be your artistic Sherpa. So what am I carrying to the car?' he asked.

'I have the oil paintings I want to show her here,' she said, gesturing to the sofa, 'and the sketchbook ones are here, plus I've added a few new portraits. I need to wrap the paintings in bubble wrap though.'

They worked together, wrapping the art carefully, and

Dan tried not to stare at her in her lovely outfit as she concentrated on her task. Finally, they were done. Dan picked up the book and flicked through, seeing a new sketch of the terrace and one of a girl he hadn't seen before.

'Who's this?' He held up the sketch for Tressa to see.

'That's Juliet,' said Tressa, with a shake of her head. 'Remi's Juliet.'

'Ah,' said Dan. Who was Juliet? He sensed there was a story. He always got that tingle on his arms when he was close to a good story.

Tressa spoke as though Dan knew more about Remi than she did, and he didn't correct her. He knew something had happened to the man but Tressa hadn't divulged and Remi hadn't spoken to him much other than to nod and say hello as he was working at the pub.

Maybe on the drive Tressa would spill what happened. Long drives had that effect on people – all the passing scenery, the close comfort of the car, the lack of stimuli.

In fact, Dan couldn't wait to spend any length of time with Tressa. She was already the favourite part of his day.

'You ready?' Tressa asked him and he picked up an armful of art and went outside.

'Lay the paintings down in the boot of the car,' she said. 'Hey, Richie,' she said to the dog whose nose was hanging out the window. She kissed him on his hairy snout. Dan wished she would kiss him instead.

Carefully he stowed her artworks in the car and went around to open the car door for Tressa.

'Oh, you're such a gentleman.' She laughed. 'Lucky I know what you're really like.'

Dan wondered what she thought he was really like.

Probably thought him overbearing and rude, like the rest of the Northern Hemisphere. Reputation was a hard thing to repair, as he had learned over time, watching many people's reputations splinter into fragments after he had written an exposé on them. It seemed now the story was on him. He'd seen the headlines about him losing his job, and losing his flat in Dublin, and he had seen the gleeful Twitter posts crowing over his professional demise.

All of this worried him less when he was around Tressa. In fact, he didn't think of it at all. Her constant teasing and needling him and calling him out on his ego was refreshing, and the way she asked his opinions about world events, and pushed his beliefs and asked questions, made him think deeper and harder about himself and about his responsibilities as a journalist.

Had he always been fair? Had he pushed his own views too hard?

'Sorry I am such an idiot sometimes,' he blurted out as they drove towards the motorway to St Ives.

'Okay? What brought that on?' Tressa asked.

'I was just thinking about how much of a big mouth I have been since I came here and how I need to pull my head in.'

She didn't answer; instead she watched the passing scenery.

'I think it's because I would push my way into things in Dublin and I would write about things and back then, there wouldn't be personal consequences.'

'How so?' Tressa asked, turning her head to look at him now.

God, she was lovely and Dan tried to answer as honestly

as he could. He wasn't good at introspection but he felt Tressa deserved nothing less.

'Because I didn't have to work with anyone in Dublin. I worked alone. And if I did a hatchet job on someone, it was usually deserved, so I never felt there were any real repercussions.'

'Until there were,' said Tressa.

'Every day I think about what a massively shite thing I did when I took those photos of your art. In your own personal studio, which you had shared at my request. I'm actually embarrassed when I think about it. Who does that?'

'We have covered this, Dan. Don't chew on the bone anymore; there's no meat left.'

Tressa had forgiven him for encroaching on her privacy and she had forgiven him for going behind her back with George.

Dan was silent for a while as they drove. He turned the music on and Lionel Richie flooded out his speakers.

Tressa raised an eyebrow but Dan ignored her. He turned up the song, singing, 'Say you, say me' louder and louder until finally Tressa reached out and turned it down.

'You're a good writer,' said Tressa.

'Thank you.'

'And I think you could write something amazing one day, a book like you mentioned when you applied for the job. But fiction – I think there is a ripe imagination in there when you're not yelling about the state of the world. You could write a new world in your book.'

Dan held the steering wheel tightly.

'I've had second thoughts about that. There are already so many books out there,' he said. 'They don't need another one, from me.'

'Yes, there are lots of books but not yours, so you should write it.'

'Just like that?' He laughed.

'Just like that.'

He watched her cross her legs in the passenger seat and felt his body respond.

'What if I don't sell it?'

'At least you'll have written it,' she said. 'Sometimes that's enough. Just to get the idea out of your head and stop it annoying you, pestering you to be written. It's like that with my paintings.'

'And yet we are off to see a gallery about these pestering paintings.'

Tressa laughed. 'I like the way you say that with your accent – "pestering paintings",' she said, imitating him.

'Is that an Irish accent? You sound like a pirate.'

Tressa howled with laughter and he had never felt more successful at anything than at the sounds of her loud cackle filling the front seat of his car.

19

Tressa sat in Dan's car. Her hands were shaking but she couldn't stop smiling.

'She loved them; she loved it all,' she said.

'Tell me everything she said, from the moment you walked into the gallery.'

'I'm starving. Can we get an early lunch and then I'll tell you everything?' She sounded excited. Dan started the car and listened as Tressa gave directions to a cafe she liked.

'Park here, and we can get tea and eggs on toast.'

'Yes, Madam,' said Dan and he paid the meter while Tressa went inside to find a table. Dan let Richie out for a run on the grass and then popped him back in the car with the window down.

'Back soon,' he promised Richie, with a pat on his head to seal the deal.

Finally, he was sitting opposite her and they had pots of tea in front of them and orders had been made. Scrambled eggs on toast for Tressa and eggs Benedict for Dan.

'Now tell all – it obviously went well for you,' Dan said.

'She was so nice and she loved everything.' Tressa could hardly believe it herself.

'And is she giving you a show?'

Tressa shook her head. 'She offered me one but I don't feel ready yet. Instead she is taking some pieces to put them into the gallery and see if they get interest, and then we can discuss a show, maybe later in the year.'

'That's fantastic,' said Dan. 'Although I'm not surprised – you are so talented, Tressa.'

She smiled at him. 'Thank you. And thank you for being a total sneaky shit and printing my work without me knowing. I would never have had the courage or the ego to do it.'

Dan laughed. 'I may not have many things but I do have courage and ego enough for both of us.'

Tressa liked the way he said 'us'. It made her feel special.

'Do you have a girlfriend in Dublin?' she heard herself ask. *Try and be subtle, Tressa*, she reminded herself. She wasn't even sure she liked Dan that way but he was handsome and funny and successful, at least until he'd been sacked and lost the whole life he'd built up.

'No,' he said, 'no girlfriend. Not really the relationship kind.'

Before Tressa could ask why, the waitress had appeared with their food.

'What about you?' asked Dan, as he ground black pepper all over his eggs. 'Do you have a fella?'

She shook her head. 'Not since university really, not interested. I like my own space too much.'

But as she said it she felt like she was telling a lie. She had like Dan's company. He made everything fun and as though the colour of her world was brighter somehow. Everything felt different. The days were filled with surprises, with him insisting she accompany him on all the stories for the paper.

Not that she minded so much, as he was great company, but she had less time for painting since Dan had come to Port Lowdy and he seemed to be in her head a lot.

'Speaking of your space, can I sleep on your sofa for two nights? Penny's kicked me out for her daughter and the wean and the hotel is full up with the telly people.'

Tressa paused, thinking about the sofa.

'Of course, it's fine if you can't. I can sleep in the car with Richie,' he said and she realised he was serious.

'No, you can sleep on the sofa. I don't know how Ginger Pickles will go with Richie but we can see.'

'I can keep Richie outside?' Dan suggested.

'No, no, they need to learn to get along,' she said. 'At least for the time you're at my place.'

'Absolutely,' he said.

They ate in comfortable silence for a while.

'Why do you like Lionel Richie so much?'

'Because he's a good singer,' said Dan. 'You should give him a try.'

'No, really. Why?'

Dan looked thoughtful for a moment. 'Lionel Richie defied the odds in his life. I like that the most about him.'

'How?' she asked.

'He grew up in Alabama when it was segregated, and he pushed ahead. He got onto his tennis team at high school. Tennis was a white man's sport and there he was, just serving aces. He kept pushing into a world that wanted him to be one thing and he defied it. He remained true to himself and stayed focused and not only did he break through the ceiling, he also fecking danced on it.'

'Wow,' said Tressa, 'you really are a fan. You know... my

mum loves him, so you two will have something to talk about later.' She was teasing him but Dan wasn't biting.

'Oh? Grand, I look forward to it. Let's go, I need to check on Richie,' he said and he went over to the counter to pay.

Tressa sat watching him. *He's not the relationship kind – he's already told you*, she thought. And anyway he wasn't staying in Port Lowdy for long. *Just friends – that's enough, more than enough*, she told herself, even when he opened the door of the cafe for her, and when he opened the car door for her and checked it was shut and hopped in the car and asked her if she wanted to listen to something besides Lionel Richie. *Yes, just friends*, she reiterated as she glanced at his forearms while he drove to her parents' house, and when he parked out the front of the house and looked at her and asked if she needed a code word so he could get her out of there, because he could tell she was anxious and he didn't want her to feel crap on such a special day.

And that was it; Tressa was done for. *Just friends my arse*, she heard in her head as they walked the path to the front door.

20

Remi was standing smoking a cigarette when a man came out of the pub and walked round to the side where he was and lit a cigarette also.

'You work here?' the man asked.

'Yes, second chef.'

'The food was very good,' the fellow said. 'As good as anything I've had in London or Paris.'

The mention of Paris made Remi's head snap up.

'You're French?'

'*Oui*,' said Remi, 'yes.'

The man blew a long stream of smoke out into the night air. 'How long have you been here?'

'Only a few weeks,' he answered.

'Why here? You could be working in Paris, couldn't you?'

Remi thought quickly. He hadn't been asked this question yet. Everyone in Port Lowdy assumed he had chosen to be here because it was Port Lowdy, why would you live anywhere else? This question from this stranger was fair and reasonable, but he simply didn't have an answer.

'I don't like Paris,' he lied.

'Fair enough,' said the man, 'not for everyone,' but he looked at Remi longer than Remi felt comfortable with.

'Your face seems familiar,' the fellow said at length. 'I lived in Paris six years ago – perhaps you worked at one of the places I ate at? Les Nomades? Figaro?'

He named restaurants that Remi knew but had never worked at, only passed them by as he walked to the bar wondering when his turn to own his own restaurant would come.

Remi stabbed out his cigarette against the wall of the pub and stood holding the butt in his hand.

'No, I never worked there,' he said. 'I have to go and clean. Goodnight.'

On his way inside he threw the butt into the rubbish and washed his hands.

The odds of being recognised here were slim to none, or so he'd thought. If he left tonight, or tomorrow – where would he go?

He had started to wipe down the benches when the man put his head around the door of the kitchen.

'I remember!' he said and Remi looked up, noting that Melon had his earbuds in and Marcel wasn't around. He waited for the truth to come out.

'You used to work the bar at Bouillon Chartier,' the man crowed triumphantly.

Remi laughed with sheer relief. 'You have a good memory. I did work there for a year,' he said.

'And I drank there for a year.' The man laughed and Remi could picture him telling his fellow diners about his clever memory and remembering the young man from Paris who served him steak frites and carafes of the latest *vin du mois*.

As he wiped down the benches, he heard himself sigh with relief. He had never worked at Bouillon Chartier but he would say he did until the end of time if it meant people didn't know his past, and about Juliet.

Juliet worked with him behind the bar. She was pretty and young and laughed at all of Remi's jokes and for the first time in his twenty-two years, he wanted to spend every moment with someone – with her. They would talk on their breaks, where Remi blew smoke rings to impress her, and she used to try and catch them like a child with bubbles in a park.

She was smart, working at the bar while also attending university, studying at the Paris School of Fashion, and she could push back at the customers who were rude or too pushy. Sometimes she and Remi caught each other's eye at the bar and laughed at the crowds; and more often they just worked, without needing words to know what the other needed.

It was clear they liked each other and their friends at work teased them about it relentlessly, until finally Remi said to her that they should go out on a date, just to keep everyone happy and then they could shut up about it.

They decided to go dancing when they'd finished their shift.

There was nothing unusual about the night his life changed. They were busy, but Fridays were always busy. The crowds were thirsty and Remi couldn't take his break when Juliet waved her hand at him, gesturing she was heading out to the alleyway to smoke.

He made a thumbs down, and she made a face and moved through the bar towards the back area for staff.

Remi kept working, watching the clock, wishing he could be outside with Juliet. After ten minutes he hadn't seen her return through the door and go back on the floor. He tried to catch a glimpse of her red top and dark hair tied back with a red ribbon but he just couldn't see her.

Telling the other bartender he would be back in a moment, he pushed through the crowd and went outside.

In the silence of the alleyway he heard Juliet call out and he ran to the sound of her voice.

The man had her up against the wall, his hand at her throat, and was trying to kiss her.

He couldn't remember what happened next. The man was on his back. The sound his head made hitting the ground was sickening and then he didn't move.

Remi hadn't meant to push him so hard. He tried to say so. Juliet was hysterical, sobbing and grabbing at him, while her knees kept buckling under her. He held her up until the police came and the ambulance who declared what he already knew: the man was dead.

Perhaps if he'd had more money, or a better background, or if Juliet wasn't considered an unreliable witness because she couldn't remember anything from sheer trauma, or if the victim hadn't been the son of a well-known businessman – maybe Remi might have been able to get a lesser sentence. But nothing worked out that way, and he was sentenced to ten years, and served seven. Finally he got released on good behaviour, probably because the prison was overpopulated and he had never caused any issues during his time.

After Remi was arrested Juliet went home to her parents in Biarritz, abandoning her course. She gave a statement about the assault but didn't give evidence at the court case.

Remi's lawyers told him that his victim's family had been influencing the case. They didn't want their son's reputation tarnished by an attempted rape charge.

So many victims, he often thought.

Juliet tried to see him but he thought it better she moved on with her life, so he refused her visits. She didn't need a jailbird for a boyfriend. She wrote to him for a while but he never wrote back. Though he kept the letters.

Not a single friend from the bar came to see him, and no one from his family. His father and grandfather had died when he was inside and he didn't ask to attend their funerals. He didn't care now. He was numb for seven years until he stood on the wall of Port Lowdy and watched a dog chasing after a seagull.

The absurdity of the dog lolloping after something he would never catch made him laugh until he cried. He felt like the dog, and Juliet was the seagull. He would never catch her now and all he had was the drawing Tressa had made of her from the photo he showed her. It was close but not close enough, yet he still looked at it every night, remembering her laugh and her smile.

Perhaps they would have gone dancing that night, and he would have kissed her and they would have ended up in his bed, limbs tangled together, gossiping afterwards about people at work. And she might have moved in and improved his clothing choices. She would have finally got rid of that green bomber jacket of his she always made fun of, and bought him something nice from a cool boutique in Marais instead. They would have gone to meet her family by the seaside and he would have taken her to meet his grandmother, who would have approved immediately and then nagged him about when they would be married. The endless dreams of possibility of what could have happened between them had been what sustained him during his time in prison – but now they felt empty in such a full world.

What hurt him most was how unfair the system had been. To be jailed for so long for trying to protect someone he cared about, to be essentially forgotten, and then removed from the only country he knew because France didn't want him anymore, though he was a better person than the man who died. How was that fair?

Marcel had told him there was no such thing as fair but there had to be justice, didn't there?

God knows he didn't get justice in court or in life, but what power did he have now? He had no friends in France or England. Nor did he have any family.

21

Dan sat in the speckless living room of David and Wendy Buckland's impressive home. Everything was so neat and ordered, he wondered if any living really happened in that room. Perfectly plumped silk cushions on the spotless cream sofas, and a plate of small biscuits so perfectly arranged that they seemed to be for looking at, not for eating. He adjusted the cup and saucer in his hand, wishing the tea wasn't quite so milky.

Wendy Buckland was also spotless but so thin and dressed in such formal clothes, he thought for a moment when she first met him at the door that she had another appointment, perhaps with a local duchess.

She made too much of a fuss when Dan came in, then scowled at Richie. 'Does he want to go outside?' she asked, but he realised it was more of a request than a real question.

'He would love to,' he said and turned to Tressa. She had slumped her shoulders and her head hung down. Her hair had been pulled back into a low ponytail and her hands were in the pockets of her jacket.

'Hello, dear.' Wendy kissed Tressa on the cheek.

'Hi, Mum.'

'Lippy on the teeth, sweetie,' Wendy said and she mimed cleaning her teeth with her finger.

Dan watched the interchange with interest. Tressa had lost all her energy and Wendy seemed on edge, as though waiting for an accusation or an argument.

'Come through,' Wendy invited brightly, and the two of them sat on the sofa in the lifeless living room and balanced tea on their knees while David Buckland grilled Dan about his story on the hospital in Ireland and why on earth he wanted to live in Port Lowdy.

Wendy asked Tressa questions about George and Caro but nothing about her job, or her art. It made Dan furious. They didn't even ask about the gallery visit.

Ignoring David's question about healthcare in Ireland, he looked at Wendy. 'Did you know Tressa was seeing a gallery today? They are going to show some of her pieces. She's very talented. Such a wonderful opportunity for more people to see her work, don't you think?'

Wendy frowned. She looked first at David and then at Tressa. 'You didn't tell us that? That's wonderful, darling, really. Are you having a show?'

Tressa shook her head. 'No, she took a few pieces on consignment and will see how they go and then maybe I can build up to a show.'

'How wonderful,' David said. 'Which gallery?'

Dan thought he sounded genuinely proud and it made him like the man a little.

'St Ives, on Fore Street,' said Tressa.

Dan watched Wendy look surprised. It seemed she even had to pause for a moment before speaking. 'Oh, really?

But that's actually a lovely place. I'm very proud of you,' said Wendy and Dan watched Tressa barely acknowledge her mother's words, giving a sort of moderated nod of her head.

'Tressa was quite cross with me when I put her art in the paper. But she really does deserve a wider audience for her work.'

'Oh we definitely agree, don't we, David?' Wendy said but Dan thought she sounded tense, as though she was performing the role of the perfect mother saying all the right things at all the right moments.

He took a biscuit and took a bite. On the marble mantelpiece were photos of Tressa, and presumably her siblings. There were only two of Tressa and three of her brother and five of her dead sister. Not great, he thought, and looked around the room for at least some of Tressa's art but it was all boring, pale prints of flowers in colours that matched the walls.

'Do you have any of Tressa's art hanging anywhere?' asked Dan. 'I'd love to see how her style has changed.'

'There isn't any,' said Tressa, putting the cup and saucer down. 'They don't work with Mum's aesthetic.'

'That's not true – we have some in the guest room. You said they made you embarrassed to see them on the walls.'

Dan watched David's face flinch at his wife's words and he felt Tressa's body tense on the sofa. 'I don't remember saying that,' she snapped at her mother.

'It was when you were starting art school.'

'A long time ago...' Tressa's voice drifted off.

'I saw in the paper that one of the fellows you went to

art school with just had a show at a new gallery in London. He's friends with James Middleton now. Quite the coup.'

This woman was outrageous, he thought. Putting her daughter down so slyly, mentioning some geezer she went to college with who was out doing bigger and better things with his career. He was about to speak his mind when Wendy spoke again.

'But I would like to have some of your paintings on display, Tressa. Dad took my favourite one of the geraniums in front of the blue house to his office at work, which was rude of him; he knew I loved it.'

Tressa looked surprised. 'I didn't know you had that one at work, Dad.'

'Patients love it,' he said. 'They say it's very soothing to look at, all that sunshine.'

Dan noticed that he didn't say he loved the painting, only that the patients did. These parents were awful, he thought.

'We need to go, Tressa,' he said, remembering how it felt to be dismissed as a child. No matter how old you were, it hurt. A parent's meanness, not being able to recognise a talent that didn't come from them, and that they couldn't own. It hurt more than a red-hot brand to the skin, he thought.

'Oh,' cried her mother, 'why?'

'Yes, we have a dinner date and Richie and I are staying the night,' he said and he pulled Tressa up by the hand.

'How exciting,' said Wendy. 'I didn't know you two were involved.' Somehow she pronounced quotation marks around the word 'involved'.

Tressa looked at Dan and laughed, and he smiled back at her and raised an eyebrow.

'Time to get Richie and hit the road,' he said. And he led Tressa by the hand on the way to the back garden.

Richie was in the middle of doing his business and Dan waited for a moment until he finished. He'd leave that for David or Wendy to clean.

Tressa was still holding his hand when they went to the front door and then down the stairs and along the path. Her parents followed, nattering about the dog and about the weather.

'Righto, off we go,' he said and Tressa let go of his hand and kissed her parents goodbye.

Dan shook their hands, pretending not to notice Wendy went in for a kiss, and soon he had beeped the horn twice as he turned the car outside their house and drove towards Port Lowdy.

Tressa was silent for a while then she pushed play on the car stereo and 'Stuck on You' started to play. She turned it up.

As Dan sang along, he glanced at her and saw tears falling. She was quiet. He reached over and took her hand again, holding it as they drove in silence.

As they rounded the corner towards Port Lowdy, Tressa screamed, 'Stop the car.'

Dan skidded to a halt so fast Richie nearly landed in his lap.

'Wait,' she said and she jumped from the car as he turned off the engine.

'Stay here,' he commanded Richie. Tressa was crouching

over something on the ground by the road. He leaned down and looked.

'It's a kitten.' Such a tiny thing. Barely covered in hair, its eyes were closed and it mewed as it clawed the air around it.

'I think its mother must have moved it and dropped it.'

'Leave it,' he said. 'She might come back for it.'

'I don't think she will – it will die here,' Tressa said and she carefully picked it up, cupping it in her hands. 'We have to take it to the vet in Port Lowdy. I have her number in my phone.'

She was already walking to the car, tenderly holding the small animal.

Dan opened the door and Tressa got in. 'Can you put my seatbelt on me?' she asked.

He pulled the belt over her and clipped it into the holder. This was the closest he had been to her physically. But her attention was on the kitten. The way she held it so delicately made his heart break a little.

'It's so small,' he whispered. 'Perhaps the vet will say there's no hope.'

Tressa looked up at him. 'There is always hope. Some milk – the vet will have the special formula – and we can keep it warm. And love, lots of love – that will help. That's the thing.'

Dan felt his heart swell and his eyes sting with tears. Jesus, he hadn't cried since he was ten and here was this kitten breaking his heart, or was it the words that Tressa spoke?

He was eight when he was taken from his parents and put into his first foster home. He longed for love. Instead he was moved from carer to carer, some better than others but all lacking the love and all claiming Dan was too angry to stay with them long term.

Who wouldn't be angry about being the son of two shite alcoholics and then being shoved from pillar to post?

'Are you driving or what?' Tressa looked up at him and he snapped out of his thoughts and rushed around to the driver's side.

Richie snuffled over Tressa's shoulder a while but then he put his head out the window once more, more interested in the seagulls in the distance than the tiny dot in her hands. Tressa made a phone call to the vet, the kitten in her lap mewing endlessly.

'She can see us straight away,' she said to Dan, who pressed the accelerator harder at the urgency in her voice.

Dan took Richie for a walk and a stretch while Tressa was inside with the vet. When she came out, she was holding a box and a bag and they met at the car.

'It's about four weeks old, and it will survive, if we care for it,' she said.

'We? I can't raise a kitten, I haven't been properly raised myself. I'm barely housetrained. Richie has better manners than me.'

Tressa opened the car door and sat inside with the box on her lap. Inside it was a yellow towel and the little cat. Dan drove them back to Mermaid Terrace, and as he parked, Janet came outside to check the mailbox, and waved at them.

'Janet,' said Tressa. She carried the box over to Janet and set it on the fence.

Dan watched as Janet leaned over the box and clasped her neck in shock. Her expression was infinitely sad. Tressa waved at him to come over to them, so he slipped on Richie's lead and smiled at Janet.

'Seen the wee thing then?'

'Janet's going to look after it for us until it gets stronger,' said Tressa.

'That'd be grand, Janet – what a lucky little fella Ivan is to have you as his mam.'

'Ivan?' Tressa and Janet asked at the same time.

Dan laughed, and spoke the rhyme.

'As I was going to St. Ives,
I met a man with seven wives,
Each wife had seven sacks,
Each sack had seven cats,
Each cat had seven kits:
Kits, cats, sacks, and wives,
How many were there going to St. Ives?'

'Except we were coming back from St Ives, and I didn't see a man or his seven wives and it's a female,' Tressa pointed out.

'Then Ivy is a lucky lassie,' he said, smiling.

Janet was so earnest, she looked like she had won the lottery as she picked up the box.

'Ivy it is then,' said Janet. 'Leave the milk with me and I will start a chart for feeding. Now off you go. I can't leave her out here being cold. I need to warm up a wheat bag for her.'

Janet bustled away inside and Tressa clapped her hands as the door closed.

'You seem happy with yourself,' said Dan.

'I have been trying to get to Janet to take a new cat in since hers died. She's always been against it. Now it's like she's been waiting for this one all along.'

'Sometimes it's worth waiting for the right one,' he said and then glanced sideways at Tressa. Would she think he was being obvious? Tressa didn't seem to hear as they walked inside the house.

22

Penny closed her eyes tightly while a woman brushed makeup on to her face. The process was taking longer than she would have imagined, even if she was meeting the queen. The television crew had booked out the Black Swan. Penny had given them a village tour while Rosemary March looked after the post office and had listened as the crew exclaimed about the quaintness, the atmosphere, the cute pier, and the charming beach. She wasn't sure a beach could be charming but she took their word for it, since they seemed to know more than her about what made for a good location.

Penny wanted to wear a new top that Tegan had bought her but the camera man said it didn't look good on television because of the stripes. Now she had on something else, a blouse that was too tight around her arms and shoulders and made her feel more self-conscious than she already was.

'It will be okay, Mum,' Tegan said, but Penny wasn't sure it was going to be okay. She shouldn't have said yes: everyone would be laughing at her. She would be old Penny Stamp again, stupid silly Miss Crab who got knocked up and had nothing to offer besides postcards of Port Lowdy and some locally made banana chutney.

A dousing of hairspray finished her off and she was taken into the post office, where they made her pretend to sell stamps to a crew member and then tidy up the shop, which was already tidy, while they filmed her.

Then finally they were sitting in Penny's living room, which had been taken over with lights and cables and cameras. They had moved all her furniture around and had taken a mirror off the wall and closed the curtains on one of the windows.

'It's just for setting up, Mum,' Tegan told her, standing watching with Primrose in her arms.

'I wish I had said no,' she whispered to Tegan, or perhaps to the whole room. Was she wearing a mic? She wanted to sit down and have a cup of tea and read Primrose a story and hear about Tegan's new job at the council in Truro.

Before either could say any more, the director drew her into the centre of the room and sat her on one of the large armchairs that Dan usually sat in at night.

People fussed about her with lights and holding things up to her face and then finally, the host came into the room and sat on one of the kitchen chairs they had put in front of her.

'Penny, Mike Sutherland, pleased to meet you,' he said in his trademark deep voice and he put out his hand for her to shake. It was one thing to hear his voice and see him from her television but to have him in her home was paralysing.

She tried to speak. Her mouth was opening and shutting like a fish out of water.

'Lost your nerve, Penny?' He was jovial. 'You'd better find it soon. We're about to shoot.'

'I don't think this is a good idea.' She found her voice at

last. 'I think that this is going to be a boring story and I'll look stupid. You're probably wasting your time.'

'Don't be silly, Penny, your story is as interesting as anybody's, probably more so,' Mike said soothingly. 'Now just answer my questions and we will be on our way. Think of it as a nice long chat with an old friend.'

And so it was. He was so skilled at making Penny feel comfortable, asking about her childhood, asking about her parents, life in the village growing up. He asked question after question until Penny felt herself relaxing and her mind opening up to the past. Memories long since forgotten returned with Mike's gentle coaxing.

'So tell me about the man you met when you were eighteen,' Mike asked.

Penny paused. How could she explain who Paul Murphy was, and what he meant to her?

She had believed every word he had said and she was the fool – not that she regretted Tegan and now little Primrose. They gave her life some value. At least she could say that it wasn't all wasted.

She tried to explain about him, but Mike kept asking her questions about being abandoned, and being left vulnerable. 'You must have been scared?' he prompted her.

'I was scared,' she admitted. 'But – there is a certain thing about growing a person inside you. You become brave; you have to be.'

'And you never heard from Paul after he left you?'

'No, I tried to call the newspaper he worked for but he had left. I suppose I was naive but most girls were at that time and with a lack of confidence, I didn't ask for more than I thought I was worth.'

That was something Dan had said to her about her story and she knew he was right. She didn't think she was worth more than what she received from Paul, or from what she received from the small-minded villagers of twenty years ago.

Penny glanced at Tegan who smiled at her mother. All of a sudden Penny found her nerve. She felt such pride at all she had achieved in her life. It might be a small life but she had done it alone and it was enough to say she paid her bills on time, and she raised a daughter who had a career and a lovely child who Penny doted on. She kept a post office that was the hub of the village. And she knew so much about everyone in town, yet never told a soul. Who could claim such success and say it wasn't worth anything?

'I am proud of my life,' she said to the interviewer. 'It may not be much to some but I have I built everything myself, alone – and that is something more women should be celebrated for.'

His smile broadened and deepened, and he nodded. 'Hashtag Pennypower,' he said and laughed at his own joke. Penny joined in even though she wasn't sure if it was a compliment or not. Tegan was smiling off camera so presumably it was good.

After the interview, the plan was for Penny to walk them around Port Lowdy and chat about the village. They'd meet some locals. Penny felt like the Lord Mayor of Port Lowdy without the robes. Finally she was no longer the girl who'd made a mistake but a woman who had risen above it and turned it into a life that worked for her.

As she showed the television crew around the familiar village, she remembered more than she had in a long time.

How long had it been since she had walked around the village just for pleasure? Too many years hiding in the post office, the rearranging of the jams and waiting for Tegan to return as her only entertainment.

Why hadn't she gone on a holiday, or gone to visit her daughter and granddaughter? She could have hired Rosemary March to care for the post office while she was gone. Rosemary helped over Christmas and did a wonderful job, sorting and serving.

But it wasn't too late, she realised, as she chatted to Marcel and Pamela at the pub and waved at the young Frenchman who was working for them. The film crew captured all of it but she had lost her self-consciousness. She could travel to Paris, she had always wanted to go there, or she could even travel to Australia, where Paul Murphy was from. Not that she expected to see him but Australia was as far away as any place she could think of at that moment.

'I love this village,' she said to the camera. 'It's been good to me, but there is a world beyond here, and perhaps I might see it now that I'm a telly star.' She laughed. The interviewer laughed with her and they walked down the pier, where she saw Dan and Tressa driving by.

'That's Dan Byrne. He's a famous journalist from Ireland – even he's living here now. It seems everyone loves Port Lowdy. Once they visit they never want to leave.'

'Dan Byrne from the *Independent Times*?' he asked sharply.

'The very same,' Penny said proudly.

'Why is he here?' The interviewer glanced at the woman with the clipboard, who instantly started writing.

'Well, he was fired – that's common knowledge. He's

running the paper here now. That's who did the interview, but he put it under Tressa's name. I don't think he wants the spotlight on him here.'

The man laughed, and his laugh made her uneasy. 'Dan Byrne not wanting the spotlight? I don't think that's possible.'

The woman laughed along with him and she definitely sounded cruel. Penny wondered if she had said too much. The interviewer didn't say any more about Dan and she was afraid to mention it to him. No point if it was just a chat, she told herself, and took them right down to the end of the pier to see the new boat and tell them how they were planning to name it *Lady Penny*. Now that was a story.

23

'I don't know why I bothered seeing them,' Tressa said. They had left Janet with Ivy the kitten and they were back inside Mermaid Terrace. She switched on the kettle. 'Nothing changes.'

Dan showed her the painting and sketchbooks that the gallery hadn't taken. 'Do you want these upstairs?'

Tressa nodded, opening the back door for Richie to head outside into the small yard.

Peace filled her heart as she leaned against the doorframe and watched him sniff and potter about the little garden. The simple fact of being home in Mermaid Terrace soothed her after seeing her parents. As a child all she had wanted was a space away from everyone. Now her house was a place far away from her mother's judgements and her father's disappointment.

'Your mother is a lot to take in,' said Dan as he sat at the table. 'She's very pretentious.'

'She is, isn't she?' said Tressa, feeling validated that Dan had seen that part of Wendy.

He raised his eyebrows at her. 'Yes! But she seems really insecure, and your dad seems like he can't say anything that doesn't align with her views or goals.'

Tressa thought for a moment. 'I don't know about insecure. She's always been super confident, always having an opinion on everything.'

He shrugged. 'Classic insecure behaviour. I should know, I do it all the time.'

Tressa stared at him, and then laughed. 'You're the least insecure person I've ever met.'

'It has taken enormous practice to cover it up. Deep down I'm always waiting to be found out.'

'Found out about what?'

'Anything and everything.' He laughed.

Tressa brought the teacups to the table. 'Why did you let them think we were seeing each other?' This had surprised her. She had thought about it a lot on the drive home. His comment was not serious, but she couldn't help thinking about it. God, what if they were together and he spent the night with her and they made coffee in the morning and eggs, and kissed as the toast was browning. She'd never realised until now she wanted something like that.

'To give them something to talk about,' he said, 'to keep your mother entertained, to create a diversion.'

'I won't hear the end of it now.' Tressa sighed. She was surprised by her own feeling of disappointment.

Richie wandered back in and flopped under the table and Tressa felt his head on her feet. Ginger Pickles leapt down from the top of the fridge and came circling Dan's legs. 'Our animals have changed loyalties, it seems,' said Tressa. 'And Ginger isn't even bothered by Richie. I'm really surprised.'

'Simplicity and complexity need each other,' he said and

Tressa looked under the table, where Ginger sat looking at Richie, who had his eyes closed peacefully.

'I think we know who is what.' She laughed.

'They can take it in turns,' said Dan. 'But they know they have each other's back when the world feels a little too intense.'

Tressa smiled at him. There was a tension in the air and she liked it. A fizz of something delicious. The pause between them felt like a decision – or perhaps that was only from her. He looked so handsome at her table and she wondered what it would be like to sit on his lap and kiss him until they couldn't catch their breath.

Tressa pulled herself from her fantasy and tried to keep the conversation polite.

'Thank you for coming to my parents' today, and thank you for supporting me. Even if they don't get it, it mattered that you did and that you tried. It was kind. You're a good friend.'

Dan seemed to turn red at her words, and he shrugged. 'My pleasure. I am glad the gallery worked out – that's the most important thing, not your parents.'

They sat a while in silence. She needed to move, otherwise she would kiss him and then it would be more awkward than it had been between them. She could already imagine the gentle rebuff and the excuses about working together and him not staying and so on. But she didn't want his promises, she wanted to kiss him.

'Want to go for a walk?' she said, too brightly. 'Stretch the legs and take Richie? We can go along the cliffs and I can show you France if the sun is out.'

'Really?' Dan pushed his chair back noisily, making Ginger Pickles bolt back to her perch on the refrigerator.

Tressa laughed. 'No, but it did get you off your bum, so come on, let's walk off the car trip.'

'Okay, don't get your knickers in a twist,' he said and Tressa blushed and laughed. She felt better but she didn't know why. Usually a trip to see her parents would have her in a funk for days but Dan was right: the important part of the day was the gallery. Somehow today she finally felt like a real artist.

She remembered her hand in his and wished he would hold it again as they walked along the path and up the stairs to the cliffs.

Shoving her hands into the pockets of her jacket so she didn't feel tempted to hold his hand, she saw him do the same.

Gosh, being in love was awful, she thought, if this was love. It definitely felt like love. All she wanted to do was touch him. It made her almost angry as they strolled along the cliff, Richie barking at seagulls and Dan stopping periodically to peer over the edge or gaze ahead, looking for France.

'You okay? You're quiet,' asked Dan as they turned to walk back to the house.

'Fine, just thinking,' she said.

'About?'

'None of your business,' she said half-jokingly.

'Is it about me?' he teased her and nudged her shoulder with his.

'No, Captain Narcissist, it's not about you,' she lied.

'Why not? I was thinking about you,' he said and she pushed his shoulder with hers in return.

'You're a liar,' she said and Dan stopped to face her.

'I think about you a lot, Tressa.'

'About how I am wasting my life by living here and not showing anyone my art?' She was teasing.

Dan looked out at the view of the village below. 'I don't know, it's pretty special. I think I get why you stay here. It's almost made up in some ways. Magical as though it's been bypassed by the rest of the world.'

'We have Wi-Fi, you know? And you can get a takeaway coffee at the cafe that isn't complete rubbish.'

'I know,' he said, 'it's almost as though you never have to leave. Speaking of, I'm staying at yours tonight, don't forget.'

Tressa felt her stomach flip. She looked down at her feet on the dusty path.

'I haven't forgotten,' she said. Not even for a moment, she thought. Dan in her house for a night. How long had it been since she had a lover? It seemed too long ago. Not that Dan was her lover but a girl could dream couldn't she?

24

Penny had already set up chats with Marcel and Pamela at the pub, and Rosemary March would walk along the esplanade and pretend to bump into Penny and chat about having known each other all their lives.

'Is there anyone younger?' asked the producer woman with a clipboard and an earpiece constantly in place.

Penny thought. 'There's Tressa,' she said, 'she's an artist.'

'That sounds great – let's go and interview her.'

Penny, a cameraman, the interviewer, and the lady with the clipboard walked down through the village, stopping and chatting to the people she had organised to speak to. They talked about the village and a little about Penny's story. They waved at people on the pier and they filmed Penny with bare feet walking in the sea foam, while she tried to not grimace at how cold it was. For someone who'd once been crowned Miss Crab, she didn't really have an affinity with the ocean.

As she put her shoes back on up on the pathway, Tressa and Dan were approaching, with Richie the dog ambling beside them.

'Hello,' she called out and waved them over.

'Hi,' said Tressa, looking curiously at the people around Penny.

'This is Tressa,' Penny said.

The man with the camera was circling them, and the interviewer stepped in. 'Penny says you're an artist, and you live in Port Lowdy. What is it like for a young person to live here?'

Richie jumped over the wall and started to chase seagulls and Dan whistled at him and called out his name.

The interviewer turned to him, the camera following. 'And aren't you Dan Byrne? The columnist? I remember when I interviewed someone you wrote about. They didn't like you very much. What're you doing here?'

Penny glanced at the interviewer. She had just told him about Dan and now it seemed he was goading him. 'I told you, he's running *The Port Lowdy Occurrence* for us, as the owner's wife is taken poorly.'

'Bit of a step down from opinions in world news and Irish politics. Have you retired early?' The interviewer had a tone in his voice that Penny didn't like and from the look on his face nor did Dan.

'No,' he said, 'just taking some time out.'

'Is that why you wrote the story on Penny but then put it under your girlfriend's name? From corruption to crabs, the illustrious career of Dan Byrne. Never thought you'd move somewhere like here, eh?'

Penny watched Dan's jaw twitch. He crossed his arms. Tressa was scraping the ground with her foot, making a dragging sound that felt like the discomfort this conversation was causing.

'She's not my girlfriend, and I'm not staying, I'll be returning to the news when I have finished here. It's just a stop on the way, not the final destination. I'm thinking of moving to New York actually.'

'New York – ambitious,' said the man and he turned to Tressa. She had folded her arms across her chest as though shielding herself from a non-existent cold wind. What was going on between them all? Penny wondered. It seemed so tense and awkward.

Dan stalked away, and the reporter looked at Tressa.

'So what keeps a beauty like you in a place like this?' he asked smoothly.

'I live here,' said Tressa.

'I hope you don't think Dan Byrne will stay here. I've seen him break hearts from Clonakilty to Donegal. He went out with a friend of my sister's and he strung her along for a story and then dumped her just as she was ready to give him the keys to her house and car. He's a real shite. Would sell his grandmother for a good story.'

Without a word Tressa turned and walked away from them, while Penny wondered what had just happened and if she had missed a memo on what the real story was about.

25

Dan called after Tressa but Richie was still running around the beach, desperately trying to catch a seagull.

'Dammit, Richie, come here,' he bellowed. Penny and that awful prick of a reporter had walked up the hill and Tressa was no longer in sight.

A whistle rang out and Richie stopped in his tracks. Dan turned to see Remi on the wall of the beach.

'You have to teach me how to do that,' he said as Richie came running up to Remi.

Remi smiled and lit a cigarette. 'It's easy enough,' he said and stared into the distance.

Dan looked at Remi and then back towards Tressa's house. That reporter had irked him. He didn't want the news industry to think he had stayed in Port Lowdy because no one else wanted to work with him.

Remi had a story. Tressa knew it, and said it was tragic. Perhaps there was an injustice there? He could write about it and get back into the big papers. That could be his thing: correcting the injustices of the world one person at a time.

'How's the job?' asked Dan. 'Marcel seemed like a good fella.'

'He is nice, so is Pam, very kind.'

Dan paused. 'If you want to talk to me about it, I might be able to help. Or at least listen. I'm a pretty good listener. That's what makes my ears so big.' He waggled them at Remi who smiled a little.

'I hurt someone. I went to prison.'

'Okay,' said Dan slowly.

Remi took a breath and then spoke again. 'I never meant to kill him. Tressa said she understood. It was an accident but no one believed a young kid from the worst part of Paris whose dad sold drugs. I didn't stand a chance. I only pushed him because he had Juliet against a wall, but he hit his head as he fell. That's how he died. They said I meant to push him to kill him, but how can you do that? I didn't know the angle he would fall, I just wanted him to get away from Juliet.' Remi spoke in a rush and Dan listened carefully. It was almost as though all of Remi's thoughts fell out of his mouth at once.

'Oh, Remi, it's terrible, truly,' he said and he thought for a moment. 'Where is Juliet now? Did she speak to you after the court case?'

'She used to try and see me in prison but I didn't want to have a girlfriend who had to wait for me, and so I wrote her a letter after two years and I told her I didn't want to see her anymore. It would have been a waste of her life to wait for me. She doesn't know where I am now. I hope she is happily married with a baby and a man who doesn't have a past.'

'Everyone has a past,' Dan said. 'Even angels.'

'Juliet was my angel,' said Remi and he looked at Dan. 'Don't tell anyone. You promise? I don't want people here to judge me.'

'No, mate, never,' said Dan. 'I have so many secrets that belong to others. I wouldn't tell anyone ever.'

They watched the water for a while.

'I'm here anytime, Remi, please know that.'

Remi nodded and then walked away towards the pier and Dan went slowly back to Tressa's. He felt like he had stepped into a gift of a story but if he wrote it he would be betraying Tressa and Remi both and he just wasn't sure if he could do it.

Tressa's front door was open with a piece of paper stuck to the mantelpiece.

Upstairs painting. You can have the sofa. Blankets in cupboard under stairs. Make your own dinner or order from the pub. I'm not eating. Don't disturb me.

Dan read the note and then screwed it up into a ball and threw it from where he stood, towards the sink, but it bounced off the edge and onto the floor.

Tressa had been so friendly with him on the cliff and now she didn't want to hear from him. He understood she was working but there was a tone in the note that wasn't familiar.

He ran over what he'd said from the cliffs to meeting Penny and the reporter. What would Tressa care if he went to New York? She wasn't interested in him, was she?

He settled Richie in his bed and walked upstairs. He stood outside her studio and softly knocked on the door.

'Tressa, have I upset you?'

'Go away. I'm working.'

'Was it because I said I wasn't staying, that I was thinking about New York?'

'I don't care where you stay or go. New York sounds like your style,' he heard through the door, and he realised she was standing on the other side, close to him.

'You could just open the door,' he said.

'I don't want to.'

He smiled at the petulance in her voice.

'Tressie, please,' he said and then the door flew open.

'Don't call me Tressie. Only people who love me call me Tressie. You haven't earned the right to call me that.' She was yelling but he saw tears in her eyes.

'Jesus, what have I done? Why are you so angry with me?' He had stepped back from her so he was backed against the wall.

'You're so ignorant and unaware, Dan. You have no idea what you say and how it affects people.'

'What did I say?'

Tressa shook her head and slammed the door in his face. 'Go away.'

Dan opened the door, and saw her leaning against the windowsill. The window was open and the sea breeze floated in to meet him.

'Is it because of New York?' he pushed again.

'It's because of everything,' she said, and burst into tears. 'You can't let my parents think we're together and then say we aren't to the Mr Fancies Himself telly man. You don't get to say what we are to anyone. And stop using me as a pawn in your mind games.'

'Oh God, don't cry,' he said. He moved to her and tried

to put his arm around her. 'I'm an eejit sometimes, probably all the time. I was wrong to say that – I see that now. How can I fix this?'

Tressa wept. Then she looked up at him. 'You're going to leave and I like you. I like you a lot and you think my world is small and silly and I am just a stupid, anxious girl who can't say boo to anyone, especially my parents. You think I'm just wasting my life in Port Lowdy. And I get why you would leave. Who would want to stay here when you're you? I mean you're right. I am wasting my life here, hiding from the world.'

She took a breath and Dan started to speak but she continued.

'I would never have seen that gallery if it wasn't for you, and then you stood up to my parents and took me out of that house that I hate so much, and now you tell me you are going to go, which is your right – you don't need to stay here. It's not for you but I like you and I'm upset that I thought you would stay. I don't know why.'

Dan crossed his arms. 'You could have done those things for yourself. You didn't need me to do them.'

Tressa shook her head, and he held back a desire to move the curls away so he could see her face.

But she was right: he wasn't going to stay in Port Lowdy. He wanted to be back writing about things that mattered, things that changed lives.

'I like you too, Tressa,' he said in a low voice. 'I like you a lot but I won't stay here. It's not the life I can see for myself.'

They stood in silence for a while.

'Do you want me to leave?' he asked. 'I understand if you do.'

'No, I don't,' she said and she put her hand out and took his. 'I don't want you to leave.'

Dan couldn't help it, he leaned over and kissed her. A slow, soft kiss, and he could taste the salt of her tears as she leaned into him.

Her mouth felt like home and with the smell of the paints and the sound and scent of the sea outside, the gulls celebrating their connection, he wondered why he thought he could leave.

He pulled Tressa upright from leaning on the sill and her arms went around his neck, her face nestled in his neck.

'You do know I am falling in love with you,' he stated bravely. 'And I have never been in love before, so I am clearly rubbish at it, with my stupid words and stupid ideas.'

Tressa kissed his neck and he felt a shiver of pleasure run down his body.

'You are terrible at it but so am I.'

She kissed his mouth as he pulled her so close to him, she was standing between his knees and she leaned against him.

God, he wanted her but he would wait. She didn't seem like she wanted to rush things.

As though reading his mind, she stepped back and held his hand and looked at him for a long time.

He smiled at her.

'Well, are you taking me to bed or what?' she asked and he laughed, never happier to be wrong.

'But I said I can't stay here,' he said meeting her gaze.

'At my house? For the night?'

'I mean in Port Lowdy. Do you want to pursue something when we don't know how it will end?'

'How does anything end?' She shrugged. 'I'm just tired of being afraid.'

He loved her – he did – but could he love Port Lowdy? Could she travel with him? How could it work? Her kiss hushed his worries and he stood up, kissing her in return as he took her hand and led her from the room.

'You are a mystery, Tressa Buckland, and I can't wait to uncover you,' and he took her to bed.

Dan ran his fingers up and down Tressa's arm as they lay together in her bed.

'Tell me about your sister.'

He felt her body tense. 'What?'

'You mentioned her when we first spoke on the phone. You said you were the third. Mentioned you had a sister.'

They lay in silence.

'You don't have to,' Dan said after a while. He didn't want to scare her away but he was genuinely curious. He wanted to know everything about her and more. 'I shouldn't have asked. It's none of my business.'

Tressa was quiet and he closed his eyes.

'Cancer,' she said in a soft voice. 'A brain tumour.'

'That's shite. I'm so sorry.'

And he was sorry, because no child should die or have a brain tumour. He couldn't fathom the pain her parents must have felt.

'Then you must be a gift to them,' he said.

Tressa laughed, almost meanly, he thought.

'I think they thought they were getting my sister back but

instead they got me. I wasn't what they thought they were getting and my parents, well, we aren't close.'

Dan kept tracing patterns on her arm with his finger. 'I understand that. Sometimes people expect children to heal something inside them – a broken marriage, a broken heart, even a broken soul.'

'How did you know that?' She leaned up onto her elbows, her curls falling over her face.

He moved them out of the way so he could see her beauty. 'Know what?' he asked.

'That I was supposed to heal them, fix the pain after Rosewyn died.'

Dan sighed. 'I've seen it myself. I was in and out of foster homes. They either wanted me for the extra benefits or they thought they could fix me with God and punishment.'

'I'm sorry,' Tressa said and he knew she meant it.

'It's fine. I mean, I'm fine now. I had one good one. You know they say that's all a kid needs. One functioning adult who can show you what it is to be normal, to be a role model. I had that and more with Maureen. She kept me on the straight and narrow. Curbed my anger and resentment to a point I could make a career out it, for a while.'

Tressa lay down again. 'I think Caro was mine. She encouraged me to use my imagination when my mother told me I was daydreaming and wasting my time with art. Caro told me to paint what I saw when I closed my eyes.'

'She sounds terrific.' Dan kissed the top of her head. 'I love your curls,' he said.

'Why, thank you,' she said and he heard her voice soften. He moved so they were facing each other.

'I used to hate them. I have learned to love them, along

with no sugar in my coffee and a cold shower for ten seconds every morning.'

Dan laughed. 'Remind me not to have a shower with you.'

'It's only ten seconds. It reminds your immune system to turn on. Mum made us do it as kids. I think she worried we would get cancer, so she would shower me for ten seconds in cold water and then turn it hot. It was supposed to teach my body that I can withstand something difficult and that I will get warm again.'

'That sounds horrendous,' said Dan. 'Like something from a Dickens novel.'

'I don't think so. I rarely get a cold and the cold water wakes me up. My brother and Dad do it. It's a Buckland thing.'

'I like warm baths and a whisky; that's a Byrne thing.'

He kissed her slowly, lingering. 'And I like being in bed with a girl with curls and paint under her fingernails.'

'Oh?' asked Tressa. 'And what else do you like?'

'I like this,' He kissed her shoulder and moved down to her breasts. 'And these, I like very much.'

Tressa giggled as he kissed her stomach.

'You're gorgeous.' He looked up at her. The light came through the window and crossed the pillows. A coloured light scattered on the bed and over Tressa's face. 'You look like a kaleidoscope.'

'It's the sun-catcher,' she said, looking at the window.

He turned to see a crystal prism hanging on a white satin ribbon, spinning in the sun.

'That's lovely,' he said, watching the spinning crystal scattering light.

'You're lovely,' he heard Tressa say and his stomach flipped with desire.

He hadn't felt like this in a long time, he thought as he kissed Tressa passionately. Perhaps he had never felt like this before. He wasn't sure but it felt like the light had changed since he met Tressa and he didn't want it to ever go dark again.

26

The sound of the phone ringing interrupted Wendy's meditation and chanting session. She had been diving deep into a spiritual expansion lately and David told her she was falling for snake oil salesmen but it did make her feel better, less anxious; thinking more about life and death, more about little Rosewyn than ever before.

Maybe it was because she was turning sixty that the memories were coming thick and fast, or maybe it was the meditation, disturbing the mud they had so long lain buried in. Wendy had been told by her family doctor to keep busy, have another baby, life goes on, and not to think about Rosewyn so much, so she had.

But every moment of Tressa's life, until she passed seven, the age when Rosewyn had died, Wendy was on edge, waiting for the bruises on the skin, the tiredness, the headaches, which was how Rosewyn's illness showed itself at the start.

Tressa passed seven without incident and then ten and onwards but Wendy never stopped worrying about her and then she'd had the breakdown at art school. Wendy had wanted to tell her she understood what it was like, that she had hidden in the broom cupboard at the wake for Rosewyn until David had sent everyone home.

But she was clumsy with her support for Tressa and clumsy in her love. She was so worried about losing her daughter she had driven her away to Port Lowdy. Wendy never understood why Tressa loved the place so much but if they didn't go there, Tressa would cry and Wendy hated to see her cry. They could have gone to Spain or France or even Greece but little Port Lowdy was the only place Wendy had seen Tressa truly happy, until she saw her with Daniel Byrne. He was abrasive and rude and rightly or wrongly found her and David wanting as parents. Perhaps they were. If she had her time again she would have been a different mother, more like the one she'd been to Rosewyn before she became sick. Once Wendy had played with her daughter and son, had read them books and put on silly voices and let them be imperfect, and then Rosewyn died and that mothering part of her died along with her.

The phone rang and she picked it up and answered.

'Wendy? It's Barbara from St Ives Gallery. I had your daughter in here – we are going to show some of her work. You didn't tell me she was so special! What a talent.'

Wendy panicked. Why hadn't she told Barbara about Tressa's work? Probably because she would be accused of interfering or told that the gallery wasn't good enough or was too good. Wendy always got things wrong around Tressa, especially to do with her art.

'Why hasn't she had a show before?'

'Don't tell her we know each other,' Wendy said. 'She will think I've arranged it or something.'

'Of course not, but she had some wonderful pieces. I would like to push her towards a show later in the year.'

She almost said something to Barbara about Tressa's only show and its outcome. But she stopped herself. That was the past.

'Can I pop down and see what pieces you have?' Wendy asked.

'Of course. I'm not hanging them until Friday, in time for the tourists, so come and see.'

Wendy finished the call and sat on the sofa, thinking about Tressa. It had always been hard with Tressa and she felt intimidated by her daughter, simply because she didn't need Wendy the way she wanted to be needed.

Rosewyn had needed her that way. Tressa never did. Wendy loved her dearly but they didn't have a connection, nothing to keep them close. Caro was more Tressa's mother than she had ever been; perhaps that's why she had gone back to Port Lowdy to live. But now Caro was ill, touch and go George said, and for the first time Wendy put aside her insecurity about Caro and wondered what Tressa would do if she lost Caro. Deep down, Wendy knew what Caro had given her daughter. Caro lived wholly and with complete and open joy. She mucked in and was not afraid of what people thought. That was as foreign to Wendy as wearing exercise gear to a social event.

She stared ahead at the lifeless artworks on the wall and realised how much she hated them. As though in a daze, she walked upstairs.

Everything felt different as she carried the paintings downstairs. One of dark emerald sea and the light coming from the clouds. Another of the cliffs at Port Lowdy, the beach below with small figures on the sand, seagulls overhead.

Wendy looked closely at the figures and saw a woman in a pink dress, her hand holding the hand of a little girl in a sunhat, and a man behind them in a deckchair, reading a paper. A boy was to the side, lying on a towel reading a book. Such tiny details she had never noticed before and she picked up her glasses and looked at the sea and she could just make out the figure in the water, under the sea. The outline of a little mermaid, with a name was etched into the scales of her fin: *Rosewyn*.

Wendy turned the painting over to read the date it was painted. The year Tressa started art school.

She looked closely at the other painting of the sea. She wasn't sure what she was looking for but then she saw it: the outline of the mermaid in the bottom left-hand corner. It was so light she wasn't sure what it was except for the name again, written on the tail.

Wendy grabbed her car keys, rushed out of the house, and drove to the gallery. As she pushed open the door, Barbara walked out and smiled.

'Hello, that was quick.'

'Where are they?' she asked.

'In the back,' Barbara said and Wendy went into the back area where the art was lined against the walls, on the tables and hanging on the walls.

'Tressa's are here,' she said, gesturing.

There were several small sketches of Port Lowdy and some bigger canvases of the sea.

Wendy carried them to the table and laid them out and

saw a magnifying glass on Barbara's desk. She moved it over each piece while peering closely.

There was Rosewyn in the sea again, under the pier, peering through the window of the shop in the sketch of Port Lowdy, her name on the side of the fishing boat and on the name of one of the terrace houses.

Rosewyn was everywhere in Tressa's art and Wendy had never seen it before until now.

Rosewyn had never visited Port Lowdy. That was a place they went to after Tressa was born, so why would she place her there?

And then she realised: it was she who had taken Rosewyn everywhere with them. She never stopped talking about her because she wanted her to matter, and to mean something to Tressa. Or perhaps she was just afraid of forgetting her over time. But Tressa never did. Wendy felt herself slump. It was though she was winded from the realisation.

All this even though Tressa had never met her sister, or perhaps Wendy had never let her forget.

Part Two

27

Dan and Tressa slipped into a routine that was easy and familiar but still with excitement and passion. For a week they barely left Mermaid Terrace because everything they needed was inside.

There were moments when Tressa was painting and Dan was lying on the sofa, reading a book, or sitting at her kitchen table, attempting to start the book he had in his head, when he felt contentment and a sense of peace that was foreign to him. It was almost too much to bear, like being tickled until you gasp for the tickler to stop but still wanting them to go on and on forever.

Dan realised he had been on edge his whole life, waiting for the sword to fall. The next foster family, the next social worker, the next angry policeman when he had run away again. The only time he hadn't run away was when he was placed at Maureen Dow's house.

Lovely Maureen who put a hot water bottle in his bed and taught him how to brush his teeth properly, and who loved Lionel Richie.

They would sing his greatest hits while cooking a roast after church on Sunday, and when they washed the windows once a month in the autumn. That year he had the only enjoyable Christmas he'd ever had. Maureen gave him a typewriter she'd found at a charity shop in Rathmines. It came with a stack of paper and a new ribbon and he spent the holidays typing letters to the editors of the papers, letters to local council, and to the Minister of State for Children where he wrote a detailed report on every foster parent who had been shite.

It was a comprehensive list and he remembered when Maureen read the letter, she cried and then told him he was a brave soul who would change the world.

But how could he change the world living in Port Lowdy?

He felt more at home at Mermaid Terrace than he had felt anywhere. Even Maureen's house. He thought about his flat in Dublin, with the sharp architectural edges and white tiles and metal staircase. Why had he been so upset about letting it go when he could be held in the soft curves of this house, with the sound of the gulls outside and Tressa humming along to Lionel Richie as she made them a niçoise salad for lunch before she went back to her studio to paint?

Then Tressa would come downstairs, paint on her hands, wearing her flannel shirt, and she would sit on his lap and kiss him until they couldn't catch their breath and they would spend the afternoon in bed until the sun set and he wondered why they would ever need to leave Mermaid Terrace.

The next edition of the paper was looming and they walked Richie to the office, where they saw Remi and Marcel having coffee outside in the beer garden of the pub, which was yet to open.

'Morning,' called Dan, wondering what they were in deep conversation about. He'd been planning to catch up with Remi, and then Tressa and him had happened and everything had been put on hold, including the paper.

As they walked up the hill to the office, Penny came rushing by. 'My TV show is on tonight – don't forget,' she called as she bustled down the street.

Tressa and Dan exchanged a look. 'Her TV show? Is she flippin' Kirsty Wark now?'

'Don't be mean – she's proud of it.' Tressa smiled and he kissed her for reminding him to be nice.

Tressa made him want to be a nicer person, or maybe he was always a nice person with a defensive shield from so many years of being on alert. Foster care will do that to you, a social worker had once told him. Always having to look out for the next thing he might have done wrong or the next smack to the back of the head from an angry adult made a person ready to fight against anyone and for anything.

But Tressa soothed him with words, kisses, her laughter when he was so far up on his high horse she asked him if he needed a ladder to get down. One morning, after he'd been reading the paper aloud and expressing outrage about a current politician, she had said to him: *You can still be cross about the state of the world without having to be cross at everyone else around you.*

And he realised that, in fact, he was angry with the world – not just for the state of it but also for allowing a small child into the homes of strangers who abused him, a boy no one cared about until Maureen.

It was as though she knew his pain, because she saw it in her own life. They shared stories, little snapshots of each other's lives.

Dan told Tressa about being unfairly punished for stealing

money from the church when he was nine. 'I was whacked with a wooden spoon by the woman who was supposed to be caring for me. I refused to say I'd stolen the feckin' money because I hadn't stolen it. The priest had blamed me because I was hanging around the vestry as I wanted some of the chocolate I knew he had in his desk and the money was gone. I'm pretty sure it was Allan Mullen who took it but I got the blame because I was the poor foster boy.'

'That's awful,' Tressa had said. 'I hate that you were blamed.'

'It's easy to blame things on the poor because they have less to fight back with. And they're tired. Tired of being blamed for everything wrong with the world.'

They walked along the beach in the mornings, sharing stories and watching Richie chase the seagulls. One morning, Tressa told him about being a disappointment because she wasn't a reincarnation of Rosewyn. 'I think they wished I was her. It's not the same as being blamed for stealing something and being beaten for a crime you didn't commit but it hurt not to be seen by them for who I am. They only see me for what they want me to be, so I'm a failure in their eyes.'

Dan held her hand as they wandered.

'It is the same – sort of. Being blamed for something you're not or didn't do. It wears you down. I think that's why I went into journalism. Trying to right wrongs through the media.'

Tressa squeezed his hand. 'And you have changed people's lives, even here. Look at Penny. It's amazing how you've helped her.'

Richie was paddling in the water, bobbing his head up

and down, trying to get the tennis ball that Dan had thrown for him.

Tressa paused. 'I need to apologise to you for being difficult about that story on Penny and me saying it wasn't worth publishing. I was wrong.'

Dan pulled her into a hug. 'Thank you, Tressie, you're a sweetheart but I went over your head anyway, which wasn't very respectful, so I'm sorry for being an eejit. I'm trying to learn how to be less defensive. It's as normal to me as is breathing.'

Tressa kissed him. 'You can lower the defences now. I'm not planning on blaming you for anything other than stealing the covers at night.'

'Earth to Dan,' he heard Tressa say and he looked up at her holding two cups of tea and smiling. 'George rang. Caro is refusing chemo. I am going to call her later. She's being so pig-headed about this whole thing. She's convinced she's dying.'

'Maybe she is,' said Dan.

'The doctors said they can treat it. It's like she doesn't want to fight.'

Dan shook his head. 'I don't understand the fighting cancer thing. It's a stupid analogy. It's not a game to be won or lost. It's a shitty illness that ravages the body.'

He thought about his final days with Maureen before he was moved to the next foster home. She was rail-thin and coughing until she couldn't catch her breath, but she still insisted on ironing his school shirts.

'If someone "loses the battle", that implies blame that

they didn't fight hard enough. But cancer is a random cluster of cells and there are no rules. It's not a military campaign.'

'You're right,' she said. 'I am going to tell Caro that and claim all of that thinking as my own.'

Dan laughed. 'What's mine is yours, darling.'

'We'd better get this edition to bed,' Tressa said.

'I would rather take you to bed,' he said and he saw her blush. He liked making her blush; it was so sexy when she gave that little sigh after he kissed her.

'Come here,' he said.

'No, we have to do the paper,' she said and put the tea down on the desk.

'I'd rather do you,' he said grumpily as he opened his computer.

Tressa looked over her shoulder at him. 'Finish your work and you can have your way with me.'

Dan pretended to type furiously and Tressa burst out laughing. This was his third favourite thing about her after the little sigh and the way she called out his name when they were in bed.

They worked the day, buoyed by the energy of each other and there were moments when Dan thought this could be the life he wanted. Then, when he wrote a small article on the new line painting on the esplanade and the traffic changes expected, he remembered that staying at *The Port Lowdy Occurrence* wasn't sustainable. It was Tressa who sustained him right now.

'Shall we get something from the pub for dinner and watch the show at home?' she asked.

'Sounds great,' said Dan, as he typed.

'Did you get a picture of *Lady Penny*, the new boat?' he asked, searching through the files.

'Ah, shit sticks. Better pop down to the pier and take it now,' said Tressa, standing up and picking up her camera bag.

'Want me to come with you?' he asked.

'No, won't be long. Give me an hour at most,' she said and as she leaned over and kissed him, he pulled her onto his lap.

'Don't fall in love with a handsome sailor,' he murmured in her ear.

'How can I when I spend my days and nights with an Irish muckraker?' she said.

'Go take photos before I become too invested in you being here,' he said and Tressa laughed and walked to the door.

'Oh hey, Remi,' she said. 'You after me or Dan?'

'Dan,' he said and he walked into the office.

Tressa waved at them and Dan gestured at the seat opposite.

Remi looked tired and drawn and Dan knew it was more than working chef's hours.

'You all right?' Dan was never a fan of small talk and he had the feeling Remi needed an ear.

Remi rubbed his face with his hands, and then he ran them through his hair.

'I don't know, Dan, but I think I need some advice.'

Dan sat back in his chair and nodded. 'I can do my best. Talk to me.'

He watched Remi think, start to open his mouth to speak and then stop again.

Dan knew that silence was the best way for Remi to feel comfortable. He wasn't going to make false promises or false reassurances. It wasn't his way. Instead he sat quietly, while Richie snored gently under the desk.

Finally Remi spoke. 'I need to tell my story.'

28

Penny was sitting on her chair while Primrose played with Tegan's dollhouse that Penny had saved for exactly this moment. The dollhouse belonged to Penny as a child and she had saved it for Tegan; now it was with Primmy.

The decor of the dollhouse was old-fashioned, Victorian-style, not that Penny or had Tegan had minded as children. There was a mother doll and a baby doll but the father had gone missing before Tegan ever played with it, something that Penny now thought was a harbinger of her own experience as a mother and then Tegan as a single mother also. Although Primrose's father was very involved in her life, and he and Tegan got along well, it wasn't a serious relationship, Tegan told Penny when she announced she was pregnant and keeping the baby.

'But it's so hard,' Penny had said, feeling her heart drop at the news.

'You did it,' Tegan had replied. 'And I never wished for my father – you did such a wonderful job.'

Penny had cried that night for many reasons but Tegan had more possibilities than she'd had at the time. Tegan had a university education, she had her own money and she had left Port Lowdy. Society didn't think twice about single parents now, and there were so many resources available compared to when she had Tegan so many years ago. The idea of Penny leaving home and raising her daughter alone was never even an option. She was stuck in the post office from the moment she told her parents she was keeping Tegan and not putting her up for adoption.

Tegan turned on the television and sat in the other chair and Penny watched as the theme music played and then there was Port Lowdy. They had used something called a drone to film Port Lowdy from above and it looked wonderful.

'This is going to do a lot for tourism,' said Tegan but Penny didn't answer as the drone was filming coming up the hill to the post office and – there was her home.

The interviewer started to talk about Port Lowdy using words like charming, and timeless, and simple, and then they were inside the post office, and there was the photo of Penny as Miss Crab.

'I feel sick,' she said to Tegan.

'It'll be fine, Mum, I promise,' said Tegan.

And it was fine; it was better than fine. Penny's phone rang so often with text messages, she had to turn it off so she could hear the interview and the talking. Penny laughed as Primmy ran on the beach and smiled when they interviewed Marcel and Pamela about Port Lowdy, and Rosemary March talked about what a good friend Penny had always been.

There was an odd part with Dan Byrne being shown off and a bit where the interviewer said that Port Lowdy was a place where people hid from their futures but she ignored that; she didn't want anything to spoil her night. Dan could be a grump sometimes but she knew he was just covering up whatever was irking him.

Tegan brought her a glass of wine midway through and it was very nice, sipping the cold liquid as she watched her life on screen.

When the end credits finished she raised her glass to her daughter. 'To Port Lowdy,' she said and Tegan raised her glass in return.

'And to the last Miss Crab of Port Lowdy! You deserve the world, Mum, and I love you very much.'

Penny sat in happy silence, the programme running over in her memory. She did matter and so did the village. They might be considered old-fashioned and out of touch but there was more love and support in this village than she realised and for that, she was grateful beyond measure.

'It all worked out in the end,' she said to herself. 'Funny how that happens.'

At Mermaid Terrace Dan was fuming. 'What a feckin' insult. I should sue him. I should sue the network.'

From the sofa Tressa watched him pace the small living room. Richie was lying on the floor so Dan had to keep stepping over him, thus the pacing had a slight goose step in the middle but she didn't want to bring it up.

'He said this is where people went to hide from the world. How fecking rude is he? I knew when he stopped us he was trying to get an angle. He's a television hack now; he hates serious journos.'

Tressa said nothing as she watched Dan wrestle with

his ego. The TV interviewer had definitely had a dig at Port Lowdy, and Tressa had every right to be insulted but she wasn't because she knew it simply wasn't true. Port Lowdy wasn't a place to hide; it was a place to escape.

'I'll show him,' said Dan, walking into the kitchen and taking a glass. He poured himself a large whisky from the bottle he'd bought a few days ago. Tressa noticed the bottle was nearly half empty and she wondered if he was drinking when she was painting. He had seemed fine, but now she wasn't sure.

He sipped his drink and sat in the chair instead of back where he had been sitting next to her on the sofa.

Tressa turned off the television and looked at him. 'What is it that upset you so much?' she asked him. 'The personal dig, or is it that you think you're hiding here?'

Dan crossed his legs. 'I don't know. Am I hiding here?'

Tressa shrugged. 'I don't know. Are you? You took a job to get away from something stressful. You've helped George and the paper. The last edition sold double what it normally would. And you're holding my hand, so I am glad you're here – many of us are.'

Dan said nothing.

Tressa got up and walked to the back door and called Richie to let him out.

'He doesn't want to go out,' snapped Dan as Richie dutifully got up and walked outside.

'Seems like he does,' said Tressa peaceably. She looked at him sitting in her chair like an angry statue.

'I'm going to bed,' she said, picking up their plates from dinner and putting them in the sink and running hot water on them. 'These can wait till morning.'

Dan said nothing as Richie wandered back inside.

From the top of the refrigerator Ginger Pickles sat watching them like a spectator at a tennis match.

Tressa locked the back door and walked into the lounge room. She stood by the stairs.

'So, you coming to bed?' she said with a smile, but Dan didn't get the hint or if he did, he ignored her.

'Goodnight,' she said and paused.

'Night,' said Dan and she felt her eyes sting as she turned and walked up the stairs to bed.

She had lost him at some point tonight. She knew it, and she wondered why she had thought she or Port Lowdy would ever be enough to make a man like Dan stay.

29

After the television show aired the tourists were arriving in their droves. Penny had Rosemary March working behind the counter as she greeted those who came to see the post office and have their photo taken with her at the front.

Everywhere was booked out and the pub was full for dinner every night – not that Tressa and Dan would have gone. Dan was working ferociously on a story and Tressa was labouring on the paintings the gallery had requested.

Someone had bought all the works she had given the gallery and now they wanted her to put on an exhibition.

'Who bought them?' she asked Barbara from the gallery. But Barbara said the person wished to remain anonymous. It was a private collector; that was all she could say.

Tressa's mind ran over who would have bought them. Dan? He didn't have any money.

Caro and George? They already had many of her works and they had bigger things to worry about right now.

Her family? She scoffed at the thought.

Tressa wished she had Caro to talk to. But Caro was still in hospital. The surgery had gone well but she was struggling to regain her strength enough to start chemotherapy.

George had called her the previous evening.

'We won't be home for months,' he'd told her. He had sounded so worn.

'Oh God, it's so exhausting for you.' Tressa wished she could fix it all for them.

'She'll have to have the treatment here. No idea how long that'll be. Especially with complications, which could happen.'

'We have to remain optimistic,' Tressa had said, but her heart wasn't in it.

'The thing is…' George had paused. 'I think we might sell the house.'

Tressa had gasped at the thought. Caro's house was her pride and joy. Why wouldn't it be? With sweeping views over the village and the bay, it was a true sea captain's house with a history to match.

'So many ghosts,' Caro used to say, shaking her head as she looked in some corner of the room where Tressa could see nothing but reality.

But in her own way, Tressa knew about ghosts. Rosewyn was the ghost who followed Tressa around from the moment she knew who her sister was. Of course, Wendy had told Tressa early about sister, older but forever a baby, and how special she had been. It was natural that Tressa would be curious. She must have been five or six when she found the boxes packed away in the storeroom. All of Rosewyn's toys and clothes, her books and her school reports. She was smaller, but Tressa could still wear some of her clothes, like the red hooded coat that reminded her of Little Red Riding Hood. It was of thick wool and had a royal blue satin lining that made Tressa happy to look at it, and it felt cool to touch.

But it was the smaller box that thrilled her so much, as she wore the coat and explored the contents. So many mermaids of all sizes and types. Fabric mermaids with knitted hair and delicate china mermaids painted in jewel tones, a mermaid with a silver tail. There was a mermaid family, a merfather, mermother and little children. Only two, of course. She turned them upside down and saw 'Jago' and 'Rosewyn' written by a child's hand in marker pen underneath the figurines.

Tressa had taken them out and lined them up along the window ledge in the storeroom and played with them, singing songs and making them dance through the imaginary sea. Until Wendy had burst in, looking for Tressa.

Tressa would never forget the look of horror on her mother's face as she turned around with the coat on, hood pulled over her curls, the china mermaid of Rosewyn in hand.

Wendy had screamed and lunged at her.

Tressa had dropped the mermaid, the figurine's head breaking from the body at her feet.

She remembered her father had come running to pull Wendy off her. She'd had the coat yanked from her body and she was smacked and sent upstairs to her room. She didn't leave her room for the day or night and no one came to check on her.

Late in the evening, the door handle to her bedroom turned and Tressa had jumped down and hid under her bed. Was it her mother? No, it was Jago. He'd given her some toffees and a can of lemonade.

'Don't worry about it,' he'd said, standing in the doorway of her room. 'They're just sad. Rosewyn really liked mermaids. She said she wanted to be one when she grew up.'

Tressa had mulled over this insight into her dead sister. Perhaps that was what happened when you died, she thought. You became a mermaid and swam with the fish and ate oysters for dinner and rode whales to school. It sounded perfectly lovely – better than being here.

And so that summer, when they were in Port Lowdy, she looked out for mermaids.

Walking ahead of her father and brother, she stopped when she asaw an odd-shaped piece of seaweed. It was a square, with a tail from two corners.

She poked at it with her foot when a woman walking with no shoes on passed her. 'Found a mermaid's purse? You're in luck then.' She was looking at the item at Tressa's feet.

Tressa leaned over and peered closely at the object. 'A mermaid's purse?' she asked the woman, who was smiling at her.

The woman leaned over and picked it up and Tressa was impressed at how brave she was. 'Yes, this is where the mermaid keeps her money.' She opened the top of the purse. 'Do you know what mermaids use for money?'

Tressa shook her head, trying to think what it would be.

'Shells,' she heard. 'The limpet shells are 10p. Cowries are 20p. The cockle shells are 50p. A pink queen scallop is a pound and a great scallop is two pound.'

Tressa listened carefully, committing the underwater currency to memory, and they walked the beach together, picking up shells and putting them into the purse.

'You have quite a good fortune there for a lucky mermaid,' said the woman.

'How do I get it to her?' asked Tressa. She liked the feeling of the purse in her hand. It wasn't as slimy as it looked and the weight of the shells they had been collecting in the purse gave it a sense of importance.

'The rock pools, my dear,' said the woman. 'You have to throw them into the rock pools around the bend and when the tides come in, so do the mermaids and they take the purses and head to the sea markets.'

Maybe Rosewyn was one of the mermaids now. She wanted to pay for the china figurine she had broken by accident. Her mother hadn't spoken to her for a week after it happened and when Tressa went downstairs again she found there was a lock on the storeroom door. She wanted to try and glue the mermaid's head back on, but the locked door stopped that plan. But now the mermaid's purse filled with coins might help assuage her feeling of shame.

David and Jago caught up with them then and her father looked at the purse in her hand. 'A spotted ray capsule,' he said to Jago. 'It's where the embryo of the ray is stored, very unique, like an amniotic sac.'

Jago made a face as he looked at it, and Tressa had a sense she shouldn't tell them the real meaning of what she was holding, since her mother and father had had such a bad reaction to her playing with Rosewyn's mermaids.

Instead she pocketed the purse while her father introduced himself to the woman.

'David Buckland – and this is Tressa and my son Jago. We're on holiday here,' he said, holding out his hand.

The woman looked at Tressa and smiled. 'Hello, Tressa, I'm Caroline, or Caro to my friends.'

Tressa felt shy. She wasn't used to being singled out by

anyone, especially when her family were around – but this woman had a happy face and eyes so green they looked like the sea.

They all walked to the rock pools together and when Jago and David were discussing the crabs or lack thereof, Caro whispered, 'A penny for the mermaids means a wish for the giver. Make a wish.' Tressa closed her eyes, squeezing them tight to give the wish more power.

I wish my mother loved me like she loved Rosewyn, she repeated in her head. It was the same wish she made every time she blew out candles on a cake or someone found an eyelash on her cheek and held it under her chin; when she blew a dandelion or saw the occasional shooting star.

But over the years, Rosewyn was the prize that had her mother's heart and Tressa was merely the booby prize.

30

The memories felt heavy to hold. Tressa watched Dan typing on his laptop at the kitchen table. He had been writing for two days, and every time she asked him what he was working on, he said nothing. But it mustn't have been nothing because he closed the laptop when he was finished each time, not letting her see the topic, or the words.

She hoped it was his book but he was on the phone a lot, pacing the back garden, while Ginger Pickles and Richie watched him from their respective sunbathing positions on the brickwork.

It had been a week since the television show about Port Lowdy and they were due to start the next edition but Dan hadn't mentioned any of the story ideas she had sent him, and he only grunted when she brought them up at dinner.

She was tired of him in her space giving her nothing, so she went next door to see Janet and Ivy.

'She's doing beautifully,' said Janet, showing Tressa the box where the kitten lay on a towel next to a warm wheat bag. The kitten was looking better and stronger but its eyes were still closed.

'I have to take her to the vet next week but I'm not concerned. She's a strong little thing,' Janet said proudly.

Tressa noticed Janet wasn't in her dressing gown, which was a change. Janet said she was planning on driving to Plymouth to see Caro. 'Why don't you come along?'

She jumped at the chance, not just to see Caro but to get away from Dan for the day.

'Let me go and get changed,' Tressa said. She rushed back to Mermaid Terrace where Dan was pacing outside again, all the while talking on the phone.

Dressed and with her hair pulled into a bun, she ran downstairs to find him sitting at the table. He closed the laptop as she entered the kitchen.

Secrets were not part of the deal, she thought, knowing she would have to talk to him when she returned from Plymouth.

'I'm going to Plymouth to see Caro. Janet's driving.' Her voice sounded cold to her ears and Dan must have heard it also.

He turned to her. 'I would have driven you,' he said.

Tressa shrugged. 'You seem to be busy with whatever you're working on, so I will leave you to it.'

Dan pulled her to him but she stayed strong before him. 'Are you upset with me?' he asked and she paused, trying to see how she felt.

'No, I'm not upset but I don't understand you yet,' she said at last, being as honest as she could.

'I know. I have been a spectacular shit this week but I promise it will be worth it. I just don't want to show you until it's done. I'm sorry for being an idiot.'

Tressa felt herself breathe out a sigh of relief. 'Okay, well you have really been awful, so thank you for saying that. I'll be back this afternoon. Can you please look at the story ideas I sent you? For the paper?'

Dan managed to pull her to him now and he put his arms around her while he was still seated and pressed his face against her stomach.

'I adore you, Tressa. Have some faith in me, please.' He spoke softly and she kissed the top of his head.

'I'm trying but you're trying,' she said, half-jokingly, and she pulled herself away and grabbed her bag and left him with his secrets.

Caro lay in the narrow hospital bed, her face as white as the sheet, while George sat napping next to her in an uncomfortable-looking armchair.

'Perhaps we should go,' whispered Tressa to Janet.

'Don't you dare,' they heard Caro say from the bed as she opened one eye.

Tressa and Janet edged towards her as George let out an enormous snore that woke him up.

'Goodness,' he said as he saw them both on the other side of the bed.

'Goodness indeed,' said Janet sternly.

Caro laughed and then grimaced in pain.

'I won't ask how you are, as it's evident,' said Janet and Tressa was grateful for Janet's sensible words and her presence. Seeing Caro so vulnerable on the bed made her heart ache and she wished for a moment it was her mother who was ill, not Caro. It felt terrible to think it.

Caro pressed a button on a remote she was holding and her bed lifted her to a sitting position.

'Come here,' she told Tressa, who approached the side of the bed.

'Janet, take George for a cup of tea and something to eat. He hasn't left my bedside since last night.'

Janet whisked George away with an efficiency that Tressa hadn't seen in her before and Caro gestured Tressa to come closer still.

'You're in love,' she stated.

Tressa nodded. 'But he won't stay. He's too important for Port Lowdy and for me, but that's okay,' she said. Her voice betrayed her and her eyes stung with tears.

Caro put her hand out for Tressa to hold.

'No one is too important for anyone,' she said. 'But this isn't just about him. What else?'

Tressa shook her head. 'I didn't come to talk about my life, I came to check on yours. Good to see you're still with us.'

Caro sighed and moved her head restlessly on the pillow. 'It's not over yet. I'm having that bloody chemo. That would kill anyone.'

'It's meant to keep you alive actually. I mean I don't know much about it...' Tressa heard her sentence lose momentum. Little Rosewyn had been given chemotherapy, and it hadn't kept her alive.

She let go of Caro's hand. 'Look, I'm tired of you saying you're going to die. It's stupid and hard for those around you to hear. I wish you would stop it, because your predictions are more often wrong than right. You're just guessing. I could guess anything and claim it was a prophecy.

I understand you're upset at this whole awful situation but playing the victim won't help you.'

Caro turned her nose up at her. 'And you're not playing the victim? He's too important for me? Who says that? Tell him to be honest with you and not have secrets about important things that affect you both. That's a one-sided relationship.'

Tressa and Caro stared at each other and then both burst out laughing.

'I miss you,' said Tressa, a tear falling down her cheek.

'I miss you too,' said Caro. She smoothed down her bed hair and straightened her nightgown. 'I'll make you a deal,' she said to Tressa.

'Okay?'

'You remind yourself you're important and worthwhile regardless of anyone else's opinion – and I will keep going with this whole chemo thing and promise not to be the Mistress of Doom.'

Tressa smiled at her friend and put out her hand. 'Deal.'

They were sitting chatting about Port Lowdy and the television show when Janet and George returned.

Janet thought it was silly but George thought it would be good for the paper, while Tressa sat next to Caro and listened to their chatter.

Caro was right. She needed to tell Dan to step up and not have secrets and discuss their future. She was resolved from the hospital to the front door of Mermaid Terrace, right up until the moment Janet waved and left her to go and feed Ivy.

Dan was asleep on the sofa, his laptop open at a precarious angle. The bottle of whisky was on the coffee table, empty.

Tressa quietly walked into the room and took the laptop from him and walked it to the kitchen table. She knew she shouldn't look at what he was writing, but she did. *For* The Guardian *submission*, read the top line. Then the headline told her all she needed to know.

A Murderer in Port Lowdy

Young chef Remi Durand might seem like a blow-in but that is only because he is not wanted in his own country. Durand served seven years of a ten-year sentence for manslaughter.

Tressa closed the laptop and sat at the table. Dan was going to betray Remi. He had told Tressa and Dan his story, but he hadn't wanted it to go any further. Dan Byrne was a user, a nasty lying prick, who was living in her house and writing stories about vulnerable people behind everyone's back.

That was it. He had to go from Port Lowdy and as soon as possible.

31

'Fifty first-class stamps please,' Penny heard the customer ask and she looked up at the sound of his accent.

'Hello, Penny,' the man said and Penny promptly fainted.

When she came to, she was lying on the floor behind the counter and there was a flurry of people around her, all suggesting ideas for her recovery, from ambulances to a strong glass of brandy.

But Penny wanted neither. She sat up and looked to the man in front of her. He was still handsome, albeit with less hair, but those eyes still twinkled when he smiled at her, as he was doing now.

She slapped him.

She slapped him for all the lies he'd told her and all the times she had waited for him to return and for the sleepless nights worrying about how she was going to raise a child and for the days he missed out on in Tegan's life.

'Mum,' Penny heard. She looked past him and saw Tegan holding Primmy, her face shocked at her mother's behaviour.

'It's all right,' he said, 'I deserved it.' Penny started to get up, but her head felt dizzy again and she lay down.

'Close the shop and everyone out,' said Tegan, putting

Primmy down. The child went and lay next to her grandmother, thinking it was a game.

Once everyone else had left the post office, Penny finally sat up and leaned against the counter.

'You knew about this?' she accused Tegan.

'Paul contacted me after the television show was on. They showed it in Australia. Isn't that amazing?'

'Thrilling,' Penny sneered.

'I flew out the next day,' said Paul, now sitting on the floor with Penny and Primrose. 'I didn't know, Penny – about Tegan or anything. I would have come back but I had to leave suddenly because my mum got sick. I wrote to you.'

Penny scoffed. 'You never did.'

Paul reached into the pocket of his jacket and pulled out an old notebook. He let it open where it fell.

'Here are the dates I posted you letters and rang you and sent you telegrams. I tried for a year.'

Penny took the book and looked at his notes. Each one had a stamp next to it of the date the contact was made. She felt her eyes sting and she started to make a gulping sound.

'Hiccups,' said Primmy to Paul and she imitated her grandmother's noises while Penny's gulps turned into sobs.

'Why? Why didn't I get the letters?' she stammered. 'I live in a post office. It doesn't make sense.' She thrust the notebook back at him as though it burned.

Paul shook his head. 'I don't know, Penny. Did your parents ever mention them to you?'

'No,' Penny said. 'Never.'

But inside she knew something wasn't right. Not that Paul was lying but as though the veil had been pulled back on something bigger.

'I went back because my mother was diagnosed with MS. I wrote to you and told you I could come back, or you could come to Brisbane. When I didn't hear from you I assumed you didn't want to be with someone who was caring for their sick mum. After a year I stopped contacting you, because... I thought you would have written back, Penny.'

Penny couldn't speak. She was crying so violently that her chest hurt.

'Do you think it was Pa?' Tegan asked. 'I know you don't want to think about him that way but there's no other explanation.'

Penny knew Tegan's words were true but she didn't want to hear it. 'Don't speak about your grandfather that way,' she snapped at her daughter.

Why was she being so loyal to him when he'd taken her future from her?

'I have never seen any letters, and I know every inch of this house and shop,' she said.

'Why would he keep them, Mum? He would have got rid of them, or maybe Granny did.'

Penny shook her head. 'My mother never did anything without Dad's approval.'

Perhaps her father didn't want her to leave him as he aged. If her father had destroyed the letters, she realised now, she had never been given a choice in her own life. Maybe that was why he'd been more understanding than she'd expected when she announced her pregnancy: because it made her even more reliant on him and she had to stay.

'You missed out on so much,' she said to Paul. Her throat burned from the bile in her throat.

'I'm here now,' Paul answered and behind him Penny saw Tegan wipe her eyes.

'Come on, you three, off the floor. Let's go upstairs and have a cup of tea and then we'll all head to the pub later for dinner. Pamela has a table for us.'

Upstairs, Paul showed them the photos of his grandchildren, who were older than Primmy. He told Tegan about her half-sisters, Julie and Claire, and that his wife had passed away from cancer when she was in her forties.

Penny looked at the photo of his wife and thought she looked like a happy sort, who probably would have made him laugh and who could have organised an army and a dinner for six all at the same time.

Paul had become a camera salesman. Then he'd moved into hospital X-ray equipment. It had taken him all over the world, he told her. Until his wife died.

While he talked, he held Primmy, or touched Tegan's arm and shoulder. His daughter smiled at him. He was as tall and as handsome as he'd ever been and Penny remembered how it felt to be in his arms those nights so long ago.

'How did you come across the TV programme?' she asked him.

'It was my daughter Julie, actually. She knew I had been to Cornwall and said that she thought I might like it. I nearly fainted, like you, when I saw you all.'

He paused. 'And then I was just so sad that I wasn't here to know you all.'

There was silence in the room as the sun started to set. A lovely orange light came in and circled Penny on her chair.

'If I had known...' he said. 'I would have...'

Penny put up her hand. 'I know, you are a good person. I see that now.'

Tegan stood up and picked up Primrose. 'Dad is staying at the pub, so we can head down if you like?'

'Dad?' It sounded so foreign to Penny. It was too soon, she was about to say – and then reminded herself that this wasn't just about her.

Tegan deserved a dad. Primmy deserved a grandfather.

'Let's go,' she said and she grabbed her coat and bag and they headed down to the Black Swan.

Being out in public felt nicer than Penny had expected. People even took photos of them posing together and Penny remembered what it felt like to have Paul's arm around her shoulders.

They ate in the dining room, until Primrose became overtired and Tegan took her back to the post office.

'I'll see you later, Mum,' she said and kissed her cheek. She whispered in her ear, 'You have lovely taste in men.'

Then she kissed Paul goodnight and he stood up and gave her such a long hug that when Tegan pulled away, her cheeks were wet from tears.

Finally it was just Penny and Paul at their corner table.

'She's wonderful,' said Paul. 'She's a real credit to you.'

Penny sipped her glass of white wine. 'She is partly you, also.'

'She looks like her sisters a little,' he said and Penny felt a sting. She would have liked more children, but she had never even had another lover since Paul.

Pamela came to the table. 'Dessert?' she asked, holding two menus.

Penny looked at Paul, who shrugged. 'Why not?' he said, and she was glad he wanted to stay on longer.

'Tell me about your mother?' she asked.

'She had MS, as I mentioned. It's a horrible disease – so unfair.'

Penny nodded, not because she knew about the disease but because she knew about unfairness.

'How long did she live with it?'

'Ten years. I was her carer for most of it. Dad couldn't cope and my brother was in Papua New Guinea working… so it just ended up being me and Mum.'

Pamela came back and Penny quickly glanced through the menu.

'The lemon tart for me,' she said and Paul ordered the chocolate pudding.

'We can share,' he said hopefully and Penny smiled.

'I would love that,' she said, and she meant it. It had been a long time since anyone asked her to share anything and she couldn't think of anyone better to do it with.

32

When Dan woke as the sun set, he rubbed his eyes and saw Tressa sitting opposite him.

'How long was I asleep?' he asked. The sun certainly seemed lower, and the room was uncomfortably warm.

'The rest of the bottle long,' Tressa said and he remembered the whisky and groaned.

'I think I'm going to give up drinking for a while,' he said. 'I promise.'

He sat up. Richie was lying at Tressa's feet and Ginger Pickles was on the back of her chair: a female Francis of Assisi.

He stretched loudly. 'What time is it? I'm supposed to meet—'

'I don't care what you do,' she said. 'Your things are packed and in your car. You can stay at the office until the next edition is finished and then you can go. I will be replacing you.'

'What?'

Dan wasn't sure if it was the light or the whisky, but Tressa looked beatific and his heart skipped a beat.

'Tressa, darling, what's wrong?'

'I read your story on Remi,' she said and before he could explain, she went on. 'You betrayed him by writing that story, just so you can get your big career back. Do you even like me? You're just using me, like you used Remi. You're an awful person. That reporter was right about you. He told me how you use people to get ahead in life. You're such a liar. Come to think of it, you probably did steal that money when you were nine.'

Dan sat in shock but Tressa hadn't finished.

'You don't think about anyone but you. No wonder you were fired – you have no ethics, you're unscrupulous. You ruin people's lives; you're a ruiner. You ruin everything.'

Dan took a long breath and then stood up. 'I'll be going then,' he said.

'Good,' she replied.

He looked at his things neatly piled by the front door.

'You've been busy,' he said, leaning down to pick up Richie's lead.

Tressa said nothing.

'Richie, come on,' he said but Richie sat by Tressa's side.

'Richie,' he said again and but Richie put his head on his paws and looked away.

'Can you blame him?' said Tressa, looking smug. 'He knows character and yours has been found wanting.

'And you say your mother is judgemental,' he said.

'Leave my mother out of this.'

'Your bloody mother is in everything you do, Tressa. You're so busy wanting her love you let other love pass you by.'

Tressa said nothing but she crossed her arms.

'Richie,' he hollered, but Richie didn't move.

'Have you drugged him?' he snapped at Tressa. His head was hurting now and so was his heart.

Tressa laughed unkindly. 'No, but it's obvious, he doesn't like you any more than I do.'

Dan stood in the doorway, his head reeling.

'You won't be able to drive,' she said. 'So you're going to have to sleep in your car. Shut the door after you leave.'

'Tressa,' he said, but she put up her hand.

'Save it, Dan, just go. I'll call Remi and tell him what you're planning to do and see if I can't protect him somehow.'

Dan shook his head. 'Yes, you should call him and tell him about protecting himself from me – the worst person in the world. The evil journalist, the user and liar.' He threw Richie's lead onto the floor. 'Keep him then, since he loves you so much.' He picked up the bags Tressa had packed and opened the door.

As he did, Remi walked up the path. 'Oh look, here comes the very man I betrayed – how wonderful, Tressa. You want to tell him I threw him under the bus to get ahead in my career?'

Remi stood looking at Tressa and then at Dan. 'What's happening?' he asked.

'I am being kicked out because apparently I betrayed you by writing your story.'

Dan watched Tressa's face as Remi gasped.

'No, no. I asked him to write it. I want people to know how unfair it was and how corrupt, and how hard it is for me to have a life in England, knowing no one and how kind people have been to me here.'

Tressa was shaking her head, as though trying to

understand. 'What? Wait. Oh God, I didn't know. Dan, I'm sorry. Really I am.'

'You told me what you thought of me, Tressa. You've made yourself clear.'

'I don't… I mean I know I said that. But I didn't realise.' She tried to touch his arm but Dan pulled it away.

'You didn't ask me,' he corrected her. 'You assumed. You listened to other people's opinions of me and then judged me. I have spent my life being judged, always found wanting, but it hurts being accused by you, when you told me to let my defences down.'

Tressa's eyes filled with tears but he was too angry to console her.

'So say you're sorry and Dan will tell you he's sorry and we will all be happy, *non*?' Remi leaned in awkwardly, spreading his hands. But neither of them heard him.

'I should have asked. Just like you should have asked about taking photos of my artwork and I forgave you.'

'And I was sorry for that. But I didn't bring up your past to prove my point like you did with the story I told you about the money at the church.'

'And I'm sorry – I am. That was a shitty thing to say.'

Dan nodded. 'It was but at least I know what you think of me, deep down.'

'But I don't,' said Tressa, wishing she could turn back the clock to minutes before.

Remi looked down at the floor. Richie was anxious now and moved to the calmest person in the room, sitting on Remi's feet.

'Christ on a bike, Richie, you're the most traitorous of all.'

So this was what Tressa thought of him. Was that what everyone thought of him in Port Lowdy?

Perhaps he didn't always think before he did things, but he did believe he had some sort of moral code.

Dan looked out to his car and back at Tressa, Remi, and Richie. Everyone thought he was a joke, even his own dog. The air in the room was tense and he breathed out slowly and turned to Remi.

'I'll put these in the car and walk with you back to the pub, see if Pamela has any rooms now the TV people have left.'

He looked at Tressa. 'I will come back for him when I have somewhere that will take dogs.'

'Dan…' she said but Dan shook his head.

'No, you made yourself clear,' he said and he walked out of the house and put his things in the car and waited for Remi. Then they walked into Port Lowdy, Dan without his two great loves.

33

Tressa ran to the front door after Dan had left with Remi but Richie whimpered at the back door and scratched it with his paw, wanting to go out.

'Shit sticks,' sobbed Tressa. She let Richie out and leaned against the door, trying to quell the tears.

Richie sniffed about the back garden, seemingly unbothered by Dan's departure. Tressa hoped this was a sign he would return and she could tell him she was sorry.

But why had Remi wanted Dan to write the story about his life? He had sworn her to secrecy – then suddenly he wanted his life story published in a national paper?

It made no sense.

Leaving the back door open for the dog, Tressa went inside and lay down on the sofa where Dan had lain. Her head was in the indentation of the feather pillow where he slept and she could smell the whisky and his aftershave.

The sound of her phone ringing made her jump up and run to where it was lying on the kitchen table. It wasn't him. It was her mother.

'Mum. Hi.'

'Darling, can you come to St Ives tomorrow? I want to chat to you about something.'

Tressa rolled her eyes, knowing it would be about the house and her moving home and the usual pressure.

'I can't, Mum, sorry.'

'What's wrong? You sound like you've been crying.'

'No. I've been outside in the garden. Allergies maybe.'

'You never had any allergies when you were little. Late-onset hay fever isn't normal. You should be checked by a doctor.'

'I'll be fine, Mum. Anyway, I'm looking after Dan's dog and he can't be alone. He's very destructive,' she lied as she watched Richie stroll inside and plonk down under the kitchen table.

'Of course – he left a terrible surprise in our garden. Dan really should have picked it up,' Wendy said, and Tressa could imagine the turned-up nose as she spoke.

'That's fine about not coming here,' her mother went on. 'I'll come to you. Shall we say midday for lunch? Don't go to any trouble,' she said and before Tressa could answer, her mother had rung off and Tressa was left holding the phone.

She had assumed, she had accused, she had judged, and she had failed. And she realised she had sounded like her mother the whole time. Not letting him speak or be heard was something her mother had taught her.

Why be so quick to judge?

'Double shit sticks,' she said. And without warning Ginger Pickles launched herself from the top of the refrigerator, tearing a clump of her hair in her claw on the way down.

'Seriously?' Tressa yelped, but it seemed the world was very serious and in the space of half an hour she had lost her love, her mother was coming for lunch, and most likely she now had a bald patch on her head. She filled Ginger

Pickles's bowl with food but the package slipped and the contents went everywhere, the sound of dry cat food scattering from one end of the kitchen to another. Tressa sat on the floor and wept, while Ginger Pickles and Richie cleaned up the mess around her.

For three hours Tressa stared at the canvas she was working on. Nothing seemed right. The colours were dull and the perspective was all wrong. She was sure it had been fine yesterday and now it seemed like someone had come and taken the painting she had been working on and replaced it with some inferior one.

Who was she kidding thinking she could paint? She picked up her sketchbook and started to draw. Sometimes it helped her refocus and get her head back into the space but right now all she could think about was Dan and the curve of his mouth before he kissed her and the scar under his eyebrow and his hands. God, he could do mysterious things with his hands, she thought as she drew his face, and when she looked down at the sketch she burst into tears. She had made a huge mistake and she needed to say sorry.

She ran down the stairs and picked up her phone to see she had three missed calls from George.

'Oh God,' she said aloud as she called back.

'Please don't be dead, please don't be dead' she pleaded with Caro as the phone rang and then George answered.

'What the hell has happened?' he demanded as soon as he answered.

'I don't know – you tell me. Is Caro all right?'

'She's fine. She's eating a chocolate pudding in bed, but

Dan Byrne has resigned, as soon as the next edition is done. Said it was a hostile workplace and he couldn't continue to write under those conditions.

Tressa could hardly believe her ears. 'Hostile? He's the one who's hostile,' she said. 'God, no wonder he got fired from his last job. He's unbelievable. The arrogance. I should have fired him.'

'Not your paper to fire people, Tressie,' said George but he sounded amused. 'But if he was being a problem at the paper, then I would have fired him for you. Was he a problem?'

Tressa was quiet. 'Not at work, no.'

'Sort it out, Tressie – the paper needs you both.'

Tressa ended the call and texted Dan.

You resigned? That's ridiculous. Let's sort this out, please.

She pressed send and sat waiting for a reply. She stalked around the house, tidying up the kitchen with jerky movements. She fed the animals, even though Ginger Pickles didn't deserve any food or love, because that cat was disloyal like her mother and Dan – but Richie was happy to be fed. She glanced at the time. Nearly six, enough time to take Richie for a walk but she wouldn't walk him into town, in case they ran into Dan. Dan, Dan, Dan. Damn. Clipping on Richie's leash, she headed out the back door and locked it behind her and then they went through the back gate and up around the cliffs.

They would go around the bend to the rock pools.

Perhaps she could find a mermaid's purse and send it off for some luck. God knows she needed it.

The wind had picked up but it wasn't cold. Tressa stood and looked out over the sea as the sun began to set. It was a perfect sunset, the sort she would have painted: but the desire just wasn't there. She felt nothing but exhaustion as she watched it lowering in the sky. She never tired of this view but now, for the first time, she wondered if Port Lowdy was the place she was meant to be forever, especially if forever meant being alone.

34

Wendy parked the car outside Tressa's aqua home and checked her lipstick in the rear-view mirror. She was nervous to speak to Tressa about the mermaids but she knew they needed to talk.

She stepped out of the car and looked out over the seaside. On days like today, she could understand why Tressa chose to live here. She just couldn't understand why Tressa chose to be so far away from her and David and Jago. Her children were the light of her life and she wished Tressa would experience that joy. Tressa would be a wonderful mother, she and David often said. She was creative, kind, and patient, things that Wendy knew she was often lacking as a parent. Perhaps if Rosewyn hadn't died? She often told herself that but she couldn't remember parenting Rosewyn before she became ill. It felt like a dream that she could see snippets off but not fully recall.

As Wendy crossed the road, Tressa's neighbour stepped out of her front door, holding what looked to be a cat carrier.

'Hello, Mrs Buckland, I haven't seen you down here for a long while.'

Wendy chose to ignore what she thought was a dig at her for not visiting her daughter.

'A new cat?' She peered at the carrier.

'Yes. Ivy. Tressa found her on the road coming back from St Ives, and she asked me to foster her but I think I like her so much, I might keep her. She's become quite attached to me.'

Wendy smiled and raised her eyebrows. 'It is good to have something to care for when you're alone and older,' she said as punishment for the woman judging her for not visiting Tressa.

But the woman, Janet – that was her name, Wendy remembered – didn't take offence at her comment. Instead she nodded vigorously in agreement.

'You're right, you know. Tressa told me she had been worrying about me for a long time. I was a bit lost after I retired from teaching and my old cat had died. This little mite brought all sorts of reasons back into my small world. Just like what Tressa did for Penny – well, that was Dan also writing the story but she's a gem, that girl. It's funny how Tressa always knows what people need. She must have got that gift from you.'

Wendy was taken aback, mostly because Tressa had inherited nothing from her as far as she knew and because Tressa seemed to do more good than she realised.

'I'm off to the vet to get this one microchipped, and have some injections. Then tomorrow I'm heading to Porthleven to see about volunteering at the shelter there. They need people who understand cats apparently.'

Wendy thought of something pithy and perhaps bitchy and then caught herself. Why did she feel the need to always have the upper hand?

The spiritual podcast she had listened to during the drive

on the way down told her it was because she had too much ego due to feeling insecure underneath. She had nearly turned it off because it was so wrong and offensive but then she realised it was uncomfortable because there was truth in the statement. She did feel insecure, especially around Tressa.

The child had never needed her from the day she was born. Tressa came into the world en caul, still in the sac, perfect and peaceful, with a head of dark curls.

'A little water baby,' the Irish midwife had said, as the baby moved and the sac pulled away from her body. 'Born in a mermaid's purse, the old wives' tales say.'

Had Wendy ever told Tressa that? She couldn't remember. It was the sort of thing Tressa would have liked to know. She was always asking what she was like as a baby and when she was little but Wendy didn't always have the answers.

'Have a nice visit,' said Janet as she opened the gate and walked away.

'Good luck with Ivy,' Wendy called out, and Janet turned back and gave her a genuine smile.

'Thank you,' she called back in return.

She knocked on Tressa's door and Dan's dog barked. Wendy had never been one for pets, but Tressa had rescued a kitten as soon as she moved from home. The orange cat was a menace, and had once clawed Wendy's good Max Mara pants, causing a pull that was difficult to fix.

Tressa opened the door and Wendy noticed she looked tired, drawn.

'You feeling well, darling?' she asked, kissing her daughter on the cheek.

'Yep, fine,' said Tressa and Wendy knew the tone. Something was wrong but Tressa wouldn't tell her unless she dragged it out of her and then nothing Wendy said after that would be helpful.

'Something smells lovely,' she said, meaning it.

'It's just a quiche heating in the oven. I didn't make it before you get all enthusiastic. I got it from the bakery. Spinach and goat cheese.'

Dan's dog kept nosing Wendy's bottom until she turned and pushed him away.

'Stop it. You must learn manners. Now go and sit quietly and think about being more respectful.'

To her surprise the dog let out something that sounded like a sneeze and went and jumped up onto the sofa and lay on his back, legs in the air.

'Is he allowed on the furniture?' she asked.

'Yes, I guess so. He won't be here for long, so I don't care,' Tressa said with a shrug.

Wendy sat at the kitchen table, far away from the dog hair that could cover her black linen pants.

The cat sneered at her from the top of the fridge and Wendy felt she was being judged and found wanting.

'Did you want to come up for Easter with Dan?' Wendy asked. 'We are having a Sunday lunch and Jago and Kelly and the twins are coming.'

'I can't, I have to work, lots of Easter things to photograph.'

Wendy noticed that Tressa didn't mention Dan.

'How is Dan?' she asked carefully.

Tressa shrugged again. 'I have no idea. We're not talking. He's resigned.'

Wendy sat in shock. 'What? You can't be serious? That very unprofessional.'

'No, it's okay, I'm holding his dog hostage. He will come back and apologise. He's filled with hot air and nothing else, and since the dog is the only thing in the world that loves him, he won't be so ready to part from him.'

Wendy watched her daughter's face as she spoke and saw she was lying – but she was surprised Tressa was so forthcoming with her about Dan. It was clear from the state of her that she loved Dan and whatever had happened between them was causing her enormous pain.

'How is the painting going?' she asked, now treading more carefully than a tightrope-walker without a net. Any sudden slips and she would lose this tenuous connection with Tressa.

'Terribly. I can't seem to get anything to work,' Tressa said and she emptied a bag of ready-made salad mix into a bowl and then covered it in balsamic vinegar and olive oil. Wendy held her tongue about making a proper vinaigrette because Tressa's tone was vinegary enough without her adding to the mix.

'I am sure it will come back – perhaps it's just the thing with Dan and being unsettled.'

Tressa sawed at a baguette so violently, Wendy almost felt sorry for the bread. She had never seen Tressa this upset before. She had seen her sad and anxious and paranoid but she hadn't been angry. Perhaps being angry wasn't such a bad thing sometimes; it reminded you of your worth and what you wanted in life.

'I went to the gallery and looked at your paintings,' said Wendy, keeping her tone light.

'Oh.' Tressa dumped the bread into a bowl and put it on the table with some force and then pulled out a chair and sat opposite her.

'The paintings are incredible, Tressie, really beautiful.'

Tressa sat and stared at her for a long time until Wendy felt uncomfortable.

'And?' Tressa put her hands up, as though gesturing for Wendy to go on.

'And what? They're stunning. I really think you should do an exhibition. They're collectors' items, truly.'

Tressa narrowed her eyes at her as though mistrusting.

'What I loved about them also – and it's something I had never seen before – are the tiny mermaids in each one. It's sort of like your signature, it seemed. I can't believe I hadn't noticed before.'

Tressa looked down at her hands while Wendy was speaking.

'Is it because of Rosewyn you liked the mermaids so much?'

Tressa lifted her head and glared at Wendy.

'No? I saw her name but I had forgotten that Rosewyn liked mermaids. No, I was thinking instead, did I ever tell you about when you were born?'

Tressa shook her head.

'When you were born, you came out in the amniotic sac. It's a very rare thing – I think close to one in a million babies are born like that. I remember because you sort of slipped out and into the world, while still tucked away from the world.'

Tressa was listening to her intently. 'And the midwife, a lovely Irish woman from Dublin actually, told me that you were born in a mermaid's purse – that's what the old wives' tales call it – and that you would be very lucky in life, have visions, and would never drown. So perhaps while Rosewyn liked mermaids, you were the little mermaid. I think you two would have been terrific friends.'

As she spoke, she felt her eyes sting with tears. Why hadn't she ever told her that story?

Tressa's eyes were bright with tears.

'Do you think she would have liked me?'

Wendy nodded, gathering her words. 'I always wanted a third child, which is why we named you Tressa. I was going to name you Elowyn but your grandmother wanted Tressa, after some great-aunt who was supposed to be one of the last Cornish witches or some rubbish. She was sent to the Launceston gaol for drawing politicians in unfavourable ways, which doesn't sound very terrible now but then it was supposed to be a huge drama. Some old family secrets or something that I try not to think about.'

Tressa shook her head. 'Why are you telling me this now, Mum?'

Wendy paused. 'Because I saw your paintings and I worried you thought I loved Rosewyn more than you.'

Tressa burst into what sounded like mean laughter. 'But you did love her more than me. That's all I ever heard about growing up – how Rosewyn was good at this or that or how gorgeous she was or how special. It's quite a cloud to be born under.'

Wendy said nothing, because Tressa was right in a way. She had focused too much on Rosewyn.

'I just didn't want to forget her,' she said, looking at Tressa.

'You didn't let anyone forget her – not that we would have, Mum – but you were so hard on me because I wasn't her.'

'That's not fair. I was proud of you. I pushed you because I saw your talent.'

'So much that you only hung one of my works in your home? So much that you sounded surprised when I told you the gallery called me? I bet you didn't think I could do that again after my breakdown at college.'

Wendy felt her defences rise as Tressa spoke, because she knew what she was saying was the truth but she couldn't say it to her daughter because then what sort of a mother did that make her?

'That's not true. I went and saw Barbara Crawford. I know her, you know, and I bought everything you painted. I want to replace everything in the house with your work.'

Tressa gasped and for a moment Wendy thought it was through excitement but then she slammed her hand on the table, causing a piece of the butchered baguette to fall off the top of the pile into the bowl.

'You made Barbara Crawford call me, didn't you? I didn't earn that; you made it happen and you bought all of my art. God, that's so embarrassing. Jesus, she must think I am some spoiled brat whose mummy still has to make her feel she has contributed to the world somehow.'

Tressa was yelling now and out of her chair and Wendy knew nothing she said would be heard in the face of this rage..

Tressa was leaning against the kitchen cupboards, shaking her head. 'Do you know what Caro once said about you?'

Wendy felt her hackles rise at the mention of Caro talking

about her to Tressa. She knew Tressa felt closer to Caro than her, and Wendy wondered if Tressa wished Caro was her mother instead of herself.

'No, I don't know what Caro said about me but I am assuming it's not flattering since you have decided to bring it up in this context.'

Wendy clasped her hands in her lap, trying to keep her composure.

'She said you stayed in grief with Rosewyn and never let yourself love me. The loss was bigger than anything I could replace, and you were angry, so you pointed out all the ways I wasn't Rosewyn. All the ways I wasn't what you wanted.'

Wendy was silent, trying to think of something to say, something she could use to defend herself, or something to explain but there was nothing there.

Instead she looked up at Tressa, her mind blank. 'I think the quiche is burning,' she said.

Tressa shook her head slowly and then sighed. 'Fuck the quiche, Wendy, it's done. Now go home and let me live my life alone.'

35

Easter in Port Lowdy had always been something that the village excelled at. Port Lowdians were not particularly religious in the main – but the decorations and colours matched the village.

There was an Easter service at St Cuthbert's, which some residents only went to as an excuse to then attend the Seaside Easter Egg Hunt. There was no end of activities for the tourists, which Tressa was supposed to photograph with Dan. But he wasn't anywhere to be found.

She tried the pub, but Pamela said he had checked out. He wasn't at Penny's and he wasn't at Janet's. She asked her casually over the fence.

'Oh no,' Janet said, 'he hasn't been here, but I did hear from Rosemary March when she picked up old Walter from the bus stop that Dan was driving towards Plymouth, and he looked very determined.'

'I bet he did,' Tressa said. And she jumped on her bike and tied Richie's leash to the handlebars and went riding away along the esplanade.

'Determined to get away from me,' she muttered as she pedalled. 'And leaving me with his giant, crotch-sniffing, farting dog.' Richie seemed to have not missed Dan at all, which was both pleasing and concerning.

It had been a week since she'd had the fight with Wendy and paired with the break-up with Dan, she felt desolate. If her childhood with Wendy had taught her anything, it was to continue as though nothing had happened and as though everything was normal.

Penny was adamant she hadn't seen Dan. But Tressa was sure she knew more than she let on. Marcel said Remi was with Dan and he didn't know where or when Remi would be back.

Tressa had texted Dan so often she thought she might soon receive a cease and desist letter.

Maybe he would be back at the office, she thought as she rode along the esplanade, Richie loping joyfully beside her. As they came around the bend, the expanse of the beach came into view and seagulls flew off the stone wall as Tressa and Richie approached. And then he lurched.

He lurched so hard at the birds, his leash still attached to the bike, that Tressa flew over the handlebars, while Richie leapt clean over the wall, dragging the bike clattering behind him.

Tressa heard herself scream, then she felt herself flying through the air, about to land on the road. The last thing she thought was, 'I'm going to break my arm.' And she did.

Dan drove back from Plymouth with Remi. They had photographed Remi leaning against the pier where the ferry had come over from France. And then a short video, with Dan asking questions about his time in prison, his life before prison, the pain he felt for the family of the man who died and how he never had a chance in hell of a fair trial against the power of the victim's family.

Dan had listened carefully and made many notes as Remi spoke.

This was a new form of journalism for Dan and one that meant he didn't need to be the angriest man in Ireland, or the United Kingdom. He would write the facts and allow the reader to get angry on Remi's behalf.

He wondered what he would do if anyone ever tried to attack Tressa. He couldn't bear thinking about it, nor the thought that she now hated him so much. He had been receiving her texts and calls but he just couldn't speak to her yet.

But he had told George he would be finishing up after this edition of the paper and somehow, he had to get through Easter with Tressa, writing about bonnets and egg hunts and chocolate displays at the bakery. Easter was so sweet it made his teeth stand on edge; and all for a God he didn't believe in.

Remi was quiet as they drove home.

'You okay?' Dan asked him.

'I don't know, I think I am. At least people will know now. I cannot live my life here in hiding, running away from what happened. Port Lowdy is nice and Marcel is kind but it is not where I can be forever. I want something, someone to be with and they aren't there.'

'You mean Juliet?'

'I don't know. She would have a boyfriend now, maybe a husband,' said Remi. 'Maybe even kids.'

Dan was silent.

Remi spoke. 'I just don't want to be alone all my life; life is meant to be shared. Everything is meant to be shared. Food, laughter, problems, love.'

Dan drove, looking ahead as the Cornish coast passed him by. He'd had that with Tressa, and then he didn't. She had been unfair to him and he hadn't trusted her. Perhaps they were just for a moment, not forever – but why did he miss her so much?

He'd left Richie there so he had an excuse to keep in contact, but that wasn't enough of a reason. Why couldn't he talk to her and tell her why he was the way he was?

They drove around the esplanade and he glanced at Mermaid Terrace but it was quiet and the front door was closed.

'You need to speak to her.'

'I know,' he said. 'Soon.'

As the village came into view, he saw a crowd of people standing around a mangled pink bike. Penny was holding Richie's leash. Richie was sitting on the footpath looking bereft.

In the distance an ambulance was driving away, with lights and sirens on.

Dan slammed on the brakes and, not bothering to park, just jumped from the car, the engine still running, and ran towards Penny.

'What happened? Where's Tressa?'

Penny's eyes filled with tears, and she reached out and touched Dan's arm.

'She came off her bike. Richie jumped at some birds apparently and she went over the handlebars and right into the path of an oncoming car.'

'Oh my God, oh my God,' said Dan. Penny kept her hand on his arm but he couldn't feel her.

'She's knocked unconscious and she has done something to her arm; that's all I know. They're taking her to St Ives.'

Dan thought he might be sick. Or start crying. Or both. He looked at Richie, who put his head down on his paws. He knew what he had done. There was nothing Dan could say right now to assuage Richie's or his own guilt. Or the horror. If he hadn't left Richie with Tressa, this wouldn't have happened.

'Can you take him? I have to go to St Ives.'

Penny nodded. 'Of course. Maybe call her mum and dad also. I have their number – I'll text it to you.'

Penny told him where the hospital was and how to get there. 'You need to drive slowly. We don't need two accidents.'

Remi was by his side. 'I will drive,' he said. 'It's okay.'

'Do you even have a licence?' Dan asked and then he threw his hands up. 'I don't care, just get me there.'

They ran back to the car and Remi got into the driver's seat.

'You make the calls and I will drive and chase the ambulance,' said Remi.

As they drove carefully around the accident scene, Dan saw a tall, older man picking up Tressa's bicycle. He was talking to Penny, and he wondered briefly who it was.

Tressa, oh Tressa. He needed to call her parents. He needed to tell George. Most of all he needed her to be all right.

36

Richie was quiet on the walk back to the post office, ignoring the seagulls on the wall and occasionally glancing at Paul carrying the broken bicycle.

'He knows what he's done,' said Penny to Paul as they walked back to the post office.

'He does look pretty guilty,' answered Paul.

They had been going for a walk, after Penny stopped by the pub. They went to the bakery and ate warm slices of quiche and drank coffee under the apple trees in the garden. They talked easily about everything.

Tegan had been down again with Primmy, who adored him. But Paul said he would be returning soon to Brisbane. Penny didn't know what to say to him.

She didn't want him to go but she also saw there was no reason for him to stay. He had met Tegan and Primmy; he had offered for them to come to Brisbane and meet his children. He said he would be back again but when? Just to visit his daughter and granddaughter, or to see Penny?

She didn't know where she stood with Paul and she wasn't sure where he stood with her. When they'd set out on that walk she was on the point of asking. Her stomach was nervous as they walked and then Tressa went flying into the path of a tourist's rental car and everything else was forgotten.

Paul stayed calm, which made Penny feel calm too. He told her to stay with Tressa and call the ambulance while he ran after Richie. The last thing they needed was Richie to run onto the road and get hit also.

Even though Tressa was wearing a bicycle helmet, she was out cold and there was a bone sticking out of her forearm. Blood ran from the wound.

'You're okay, Tressa,' she said gently to the girl but Tressa didn't respond and the driver of the car was pacing and kept asking if she was dead.

'Not dead but a little broken,' she said.

Tressa's eyelids fluttered.

'Tressa,' she said, 'open your eyes. It's Penny. You fell off your bike.'

But Tressa's eyes didn't open and Penny called for the ambulance again. She was told one was on its way.

When the ambulance arrived, they pushed Penny out of the way, so she stood by Paul's side and watched, her heart beating fast as she felt sick for Tressa. They took off her helmet with infinite care and put a neck brace on. Even when they put her arm in a cast she didn't flinch, and Penny knew that was a bad sign.

'Oh it's awful,' she said to Paul, her voice breaking. 'She is so loved. Tressa really is Port Lowdy. She's just the most wonderful person.'

Paul reached down to take her hand, and he squeezed it. She hung on to him for dear life as the team loaded Tressa up into the ambulance.

'Where are you taking her?' she asked the paramedics.

'St Ives General,' they said and as they drove away, Dan came up the road.

Penny didn't think she had ever seen anyone so distressed as Dan in that moment when she explained what had happened. And when Remi drove away with Dan in the direction of the ambulance, she had wept a little for the love between Dan and Tressa and the hope they would not lose it as she and Paul had.

The post office came into view and Paul stopped.

'Penny, I think we need to talk about a few things.'

Now the moment of truth was here and Penny found she didn't want to hear what he had to say.

'Can it wait until we get upstairs and I make some tea?' She was stalling for time now. Richie stood patiently beside her. Paul rested the bicycle on the path.

'I have to go back to Brisbane,' he said.

'When?'

'In two days.'

Penny was silent.

'But I want you to come with me.'

'Come with you? Why?'

She couldn't process what he was saying.

Paul sighed. 'Because I love you. I have always loved you. I loved my wife too but now I see you again, I realised I don't want to be without you. You're still that beautiful girl with the gold crab claw crown that I fell in love with, and our daughter and Primmy are the icing on that cake. But I have a life in Brisbane and I want you to see it. Meet my children and see my home.'

Penny was silent, trying to think, as the tourists passed on the street, eating ice creams and laughing.

'Brisbane?' she asked. 'But what about the post office?'

'I don't know. We can sort something out, surely?'

Penny looked at Paul. His hair was almost gone and his skin was sun-damaged, but his eyes were still bright blue and he still threw his head back when he laughed, and his hand in hers felt like she had come home to herself again.

'And in what capacity would I come to Brisbane? Your ex fling who had your baby and who you never followed up with?'

'That's not fair,' he said. 'I did try and contact you; I wrote letters.'

'Did you? I haven't seen them. My parents never spoke about them. How do I even know that you tried to contact me?'

Paul looked at her for a long time. 'All I can give you is my word.'

'Like you did twenty-seven years ago.'

Paul turned and began walking on, towards the post office. 'I suppose that's a bad idea to you,' he said quietly, and Penny and Richie followed him.

All her life she had wanted to leave Port Lowdy and now she had the chance to go to Australia and she was stopping herself. She hated that she couldn't say why she was afraid.

At the post office Paul took the bicycle to the back of the garden and then walked back round to the road.

'Will I see you again before I go?' he asked as Penny let Richie off the leash into the garden and then closed the gate.

'If you want to,' she said.

'I want to see you every day, all the time, but I can understand your distrust of me and if I could change it

I would. But I can't. And if I changed what happened, I wouldn't have my children at home, whom I love dearly.'

Penny knew he was right. But she couldn't let go of the past to allow herself to move forward. 'I understand, Paul. But I have been alone for so long, I don't know what you want or need or even why you're really here. Twenty-seven years is a long time to not be in contact. It's a long time being lonely and afraid.'

His eyes brightened with tears. 'I'm so sorry, Penny. I can't convince you to go with me, and I can't convince you of anything except I love you. I love being with you again and seeing your kindness and your concern for others. That incredible daughter you raised alone. That is… it's amazing. I'm in awe of you. You run a business, you support so many in this place and I wonder if anyone supports you the way I want to. The way I could if you let me.'

Penny felt tears forming but she didn't want him to see her cry. She had never felt more seen in her life.

When she looked at Paul, he had tears on his cheeks. 'I just love you, Penny Stanhope. Always have, always will.'

And he wiped the tears away and walked down the road towards the Black Swan, his broad shoulders slumped and his head down.

37

'Wendy? Dan Byrne,' Dan barked on the phone when Wendy answered the number Penny had forwarded to him.

'Hello, Dan,' said Wendy in a cool and formal tone. 'I have no idea why you're ringing me but you should know Tressa threw me out of her house and used very strong language about a quiche that I did not appreciate hearing, so if you're trying to broker peace between us you can't.'

'I don't give a fuck about your quiche, Wendy. Tressa's been hit by a car. She's on her way to St Ives. Can you meet me there?'

'Oh my God, is all right?'

'I don't know, Wendy. That's why I'm asking you to meet me there. They said she was unconscious,' Dan said, trying not to scream at her. God she was the most self-righteous woman and her bloody daughter was unconscious.

'I will meet you there.' Her tone had changed, and she hung up immediately.

Dan rang George who, thankfully, answered.

'Tressie's been hit by a car. I am going to the hospital now so I will let you know what happens.'

'What? Jesus. Do you want me to come?' George asked.

'No, Wendy and David are heading there and I will be there in an hour.'

'What's her condition?'

'Penny said she's broken her arm and hit her head. That's all I know.' Dan looked at his phone. 'Wendy is calling. I have to go. I'll call as soon as I know anything.'

'Yes, yes. Of course, keep us informed,' George said.

Wendy called to tell him where to park but really she wanted to talk about Tressa.

'Was she upset when she left the house? How did the dog pull her off her bike? Which arm is broken?'

He couldn't answer any of her questions because he hadn't been there. He'd failed Wendy and he had failed Tressa.

Remi drove fast, within the speed limit, but they didn't catch up to the ambulance and Dan felt sick as they drove. He wanted to tell his friend to drive faster, much faster, overtake the other cars; he wanted to scream at them to get out of the way.

Finally they arrived and Remi pulled up at the entrance. Dan jumped from the car and ran inside. He found Accident and Emergency and saw Wendy sitting in the waiting room and David pacing. Dan ignored them and went straight to the desk.

'Tressa Buckland, how is she?'

The nurse looked up at him. 'Tressa is being seen by the doctors now. Who are you?'

He paused. Who was he to Tressa? 'I'm her boyfriend,' he said, feeling stupid using a teenage word. 'I'm her partner,' he corrected himself. He could feel bravado in his tone. She would think he was lying.

'The doctors will let you know how she is as soon as they can,' was all the nurse said, and she answered a phone call.

Dan felt his temper rising and he went and sat next to Wendy.

'Were you with her?' Wendy asked, not looking at him.

'No, I wasn't. I arrived just after she was taken by the ambulance.'

Wendy said nothing but the judgement and blame from her flowed over him like hot tar.

Dan watched people coming and going, nurses and doctors calling people's names but no one called him or Tressa's parents.

'One of the paramedics said a dog had pulled her off her bicycle and she then went over the handlebars and onto the bonnet of a car.' Again Wendy spoke while staring straight ahead.

Dan bit his lip, thinking of many, many things he could say. 'Yes, that was Richie. Tressa was looking after him for me.'

'Because you resigned?'

Before he could answer, a doctor walked through the double doors and called out for the family of Buckland. Wendy jumped up and David pushed forward to the doctor's side. Dan sat, unsure if he was included or not. Wendy walked through the door and then looked at Dan.

'Are you coming?' she asked and Dan rushed in behind them.

A nurse walked them through the emergency department and stopped outside a room with a glass sliding door. The curtain behind it was drawn.

'Tressa suffered a significant arm fracture. She will need

surgery,' the doctor said and Dan closed his eyes, knowing what that would do to Tressa and her painting.

'But she has suffered some bad bruising to the brain. We have done an MRI and there were contusions, which will clear… but she may be confused and suffer some headaches and tiredness for a while. She may not be safe to leave alone for a few weeks and she will need to be watched.'

The doctor opened the door to the room and pulled back the curtain. Tressa lay on the bed, an oxygen mask fitted to her face, her arm in a splint, and her eyes closed.

Dan let Wendy and David be with Tressa first, while he stood outside the room, watching them. Wendy moved Tressa's hair away from her cheeks and tucked it behind her ears, adjusting the mask oxygen mask so it sat straight.

David picked up the chart at the end of the bed, seemingly immersed in the information and then checking the monitor reporting her blood pressure and oxygen levels.

Wendy fiddled nervously with the blanket over Tressa's legs, smoothing out every wrinkle, and then tucked it under her feet. Neither of them spoke to her.

David looked up from the chart. 'Everything looks in order. No concerns from me.' But his voice betrayed him and Dan knew he was petrified.

Dan walked into the room and to the clear side of the bed and kissed her forehead.

'Darling Tressie, it's Dan. I'm so sorry. I'm so sorry about Richie. He and I will have words later but right now I'm here for you.'

Tressa blinked a few times. She opened her eyes and looked at Dan and then looked at Wendy.

'Who's that?' she asked her mother and Dan felt his heart sink.

'It's Dan, Tressa, he came up to see you. He's been worried.'

Dan was grateful she was being kind but Tressa looked at him and shook her head.

'Oh, Dan,' she said sounding disappointed, and closed her eyes again.

Dan stepped back from the side of the bed while Wendy leaned over her daughter.

'Dan called us to tell us about what happened.'

'I should go,' said Dan. 'She doesn't want me here. I am glad you're here though. She needs her family.'

'You can stay,' said Wendy but Dan shook his head.

'No, it's all right. I should go and get Richie from Penny anyway.' He stepped forward and looked at Tressa, whose eyes were closed.

'I hope you feel better soon,' he said, feeling stupid at the formality but also embarrassed.

'I'll call you,' said Wendy. 'After the operation.'

Tressa opened her eyes and looked at her mother. 'An operation? On what?'

Wendy didn't answer her, instead she patted Tressa's arm.

'Shhh, Tressa, I'm talking to Dan.'

Tressa closed her eyes and then opened them just as quickly and sat up in bed. 'You.' She pointed at him.

'Me?' he said, pointing at his chest.

'You broke my heart.'

'Oh, Tressie,' he said, feeling like he might cry.

'He likes Lionel Richie,' she said to Wendy.

'Oh, I love Lionel Richie,' said Wendy. 'Dancing on the ceiling,' she said and did a little dance. Even in these moments, she was awkward.

'I do,' he said, to Tressa. 'I love him, actually.' But then the nurse pushed in behind him and began checking the numbers on the monitors.

'Okay,' Tressa said, and she lay down again on the bed.

The nurse looked at them all. 'We have to take Tressa to the theatre now, so give her a kiss.'

Wendy leaned down and kissed Tressa's forehead in a surprisingly tender way, smoothing back her hair and leaning against her for a time.

'Come on, Wends,' said David and he leaned over and kissed his daughter's cheek. 'See you when you come out, Tressie,' he said casually, but Dan heard his voice break a little and he was gazing down at the floor.

The nurse unplugged a few cables attached to Tressa and put her monitor on the foot of the bed. A porter came in and kicked up the brakes.

'And now we're off,' he said to Tressa, who didn't open her eyes as the bed started to move. Dan stepped back to let the nurse and the porter push the bed through the doorway but as Tressa passed, she opened her eyes and put out her unbroken hand towards him.

He took her hand and she looked right at him. 'I know you didn't steal the money,' she said. 'And I'm sorry I was so awful.'

'I know,' he answered, 'and I'm sorry I didn't tell you about the story.'

Tressa smiled, and he let go of her hand as she was wheeled away with Wendy and David following her.

What if he could fix this? he wondered. Maybe time would help, maybe if he did everything he could to make her life better in Port Lowdy and get the paper out and take care of Ginger Pickles and Mermaid Terrace then she might forgive him.

It wasn't the worst idea he'd ever had and it gave him hope, which was enough for now.

38

Port Lowdy was in a tizz. With news of Tressa's accident and then the article on Remi coming out in *The Guardian*, there was quite a lot of chat at the post office, in the bar at the Black Swan, on the corner near the bakery, and on the pier amongst the boats. A video of Remi being interviewed by Dan was front page of *The Guardian*'s website. Villagers looked at him in a new way now that he'd revealed everything online, but Remi didn't care. He felt free with people knowing what happened to him, and what he did, and that he'd served his time. Perhaps he might have given some hope to other people leaving prison, perhaps his story would make those in the legal system in France fight harder for fairer sentences.

Marcel and Pamela had been supportive of the story when he told them he had asked Dan to write it and even when people came into the restaurant to ask about Remi, they protected him and said he was hard at work in the kitchen, which he was. They had never been busier.

Port Lowdy was having its moment and Remi was enjoying himself. He had been talking to Marcel about looking for another job, perhaps in London, once his parole period was over and Marcel promised to introduce him to a few people he knew, when he was ready.

People spoke to him in the street. Rosemary March gave him a few jars of her new rose petal jam and lavender jelly, which was a deadly shade of purple but tasted better than it looked.

On Easter Sunday, he was in the kitchen. The restaurant was booked out and he and Marcel worked quickly and without conversation other than about the food.

Melon was humming along to what sounded like Broadway showtunes on his headphones and Remi was carving pork belly when Pamela put her head through the pass.

'Remi, there's someone to see you,' she called.

'He can't go now – he's with the pork belly,' Marcel said, but Pamela shook her head.

'No, Remi, you need to come now.'

Remi put down the knife and wiped his hands on his apron. He walked out of the kitchen and into the dining room... and there she stood. Juliet.

'Hello,' she said and he felt his stomach flip. She was as beautiful as he remembered, perhaps more so, the way women who aren't afraid to grow into themselves are. Her hair was shorter but chic, her face was smiling, and her eyes looked older but wiser, as though she had seen more than she'd expected in life so far. He knew that feeling.

He couldn't speak. He nodded at her.

This whole time he had dreamed of this moment but he assumed she would be in France. He had believed he would never see her again.

He tried to find words but nothing would suffice.

'I saw the article,' she said.

'Okay,' Remi answered. Pamela walked past behind him carrying two plates of pork belly. 'Are you here for a while? I can see you after I finish work?'

He sent a prayer up to a God he didn't believe in to make Juliet stay for a while.

To his relief, she smiled. 'I will wait for you,' she said. 'What's another few hours?'

Remi felt his heart leap and his eyes stung with tears.

'Go finish your shift. I will sit here and drink some wine and eat some delicious food and think about all the things we have to talk about.'

Remi stood still, unsure of what to do next, until Juliet showed him – she walked to him and hugged him. His arms wrapped around her and she leaned into his chest.

'You saved me,' she said, pulling away and looking up at him.

He gazed down into her so familiar long-ago eyes. Had he saved her? Yes, he had, there was no doubt about that but it was what any man would have done.

'I am glad you're okay,' he said. His arms were still around her and she hugged him again, tightly, and kissed his cheek.

God, she smelled incredible. He sighed.

He didn't know why she was here, other than to say thank you. He reminded himself seven years was a long time in her life. She might be engaged or married. She could have children.

'I will come back,' he said and she reached out and took his hand.

'I'll be here,' she said.

Remi rushed back to the kitchen, where Marcel looked at him and narrowed his eyes.

'Who is that? Your Juliet?'

Remi nodded. He was trembling. He tried to read the new orders coming in, clipped on the pass.

'Then what are you doing here?' said Marcel.

'I have to finish,' said Remi.

'I can manage, said Marcel gruffly and he flapped a tea towel at him. '*Allez, allez.*'

Remi undid his apron and hung it up on the hook.

He walked out to the restaurant and watched Juliet for a moment. She was sipping her wine and eating some of the parmesan chips he had made earlier in the day.

As though she could feel him looking at her, she turned and smiled at him and he died a little inside. He still loved her; he had always loved her. He was going to have his heart broken again and there was nothing he could do about it.

He sat on a bar stool next to her.

'Want a drink?' she asked.

He shook his head no. He didn't need anything to dull his memory of this moment. It would be replayed in his mind for years to come after she had gone. This was her closure but he didn't need closure. Juliet would never be someone he could close his mental door to; he would always leave it open to let the memories drift in and out.

She drained her wine and then she leaned over and kissed him on the mouth.

At the touch of her lips, he gasped. He could taste the wine and the parmesan and he wanted more of her.

She was standing now and she kissed him more passionately.

'What are you doing?' he asked, confused.

'Kissing you.'

'Why?' He glanced around the restaurant and noticed a few people looking at them.

'We should go,' he said. 'We should talk.'

'We should do everything,' she said and she smiled again.

Remi knew what he wanted. He held her hand and walked her through the kitchen door and then into the back hallway and up the stairs to the guest rooms.

His body was tingling with her hand in his and the taste of her kiss on his mouth.

He found the key in his pocket and opened the door to his room, and he and Juliet walked inside.

She went to kiss him again but he stopped her.

'Why are you here?' he asked. 'It's been seven years since everything happened.'

Juliet sat on the bed. 'You wouldn't let me see you in prison, even though I tried, and you didn't want my letters. You wrote that one time where you said to forget you but how could I forget you?'

'You should have,' said Remi. He sat down next to her on the bed. 'I am not someone who you would want to be with.'

'Why?' Her dark hair was falling over her face and she pushed it away angrily.

'Because I have been in prison,' he said. 'Because I can't go back to France, because I am just a cook.'

Juliet frowned. 'I loved you before you protected me. I loved you when we talked at work every day, every minute we could. I loved the way you made me feel and laugh and the way you looked out for me. I had already decided you were the one for me before this happened. I just hadn't told you yet. So I waited for you.'

Remi started to cry; he couldn't help himself. Of every single scenario he had imagined, this wasn't the one he thought would come true. He hadn't even dreamed this would be how Juliet came into his life again.

Juliet held him as he sobbed.

'I am so sorry,' she repeated. 'I am so sorry.'

When his body stopped heaving with sobs, he lay on the bed, exhausted.

'It wasn't your fault,' he said as they faced each other on the bed.

'It felt like my fault. But I couldn't stop him. I wasn't strong enough to push him off,' Juliet said and she started to cry. It was his turn to hold her.

Tenderly, he moved the hair from her face and wiped her tears from her cheeks.

'Your fingers smell of garlic,' she said.

'Sorry,' he said but she held them to her nose.

'I like it.'

He closed his eyes while she kissed the back of his hand.

'I have always loved you, Juliet,' he told her. Tiredness was sweeping over him. He wasn't sure if he said it aloud or not. He wasn't even sure if she was really here. He didn't want to open his eyes to find out.

39

Tressa sat on her parents' couch, looking out the window at the road. She missed her sea views and she missed her cat and she missed Dan. Of course, she'd known perfectly well who he was. She just wanted to hurt him the way he'd hurt her.

She read the article on Remi again.

It was a wonderful piece of writing, telling Remi's story factually and without bias so the inescapable truth shone through. There were personal details she hadn't known about Remi and his life, how he grew up poor, how no one came to see him in prison, how he watched men be beaten and berated until they lost their minds and even their lives, and how he managed to survive, thinking about Juliet.

Not that he expected to see her again, but she was his north star, his *étoile polaire*.

She wondered if Dan was her north star. She hadn't heard from him since she had been released from hospital. But then why would she? She had pretended she didn't even know who he was, though she hadn't been able to keep up the farce.

Easter had come and gone, and she was worrying about the next edition of *The Port Lowdy Occurrence*. George told her it was all in hand, then said he was sorry for the ill-thought-out words – since she had broken her arm.

Even Caro had been on the phone, sounding tired and weak, but she told Tressa to rest up and take as much time as she need to heal at her parents' house.

And that was the other thing that was worrying her: being back with her parents. Janet rang to say she had Ginger Pickles and that she was happily teaching Ivy the ways of being a cat.

Meanwhile in St Ives Wendy had replaced everything hanging on the walls in the house with Tressa's paintings. It felt like an exhibition plonked into a *House and Garden* magazine article. Somehow it was very disconcerting to be surrounded by her own paintings. She had now been here ten days, and counting. Wendy had rushed Tressa around the house when she was released from hospital, wanting to show her all the paintings, and each time she did she touched the mermaid in it and said, 'And there's Rosewyn.' It was weird but sweet – but mostly weird.

Tressa's headaches were lessened now and her arm wasn't aching as much as it had when she had first come out of surgery. She barely needed the pain tablets. Yes, it was time to go home.

She knew her parents would want to drive her home but she didn't want to go through the pageantry of her mother helping her, offering to escort her. Wendy had become more helpful – but still she never did anything without expecting a parade at the end.

And since the argument at Mermaid Terrace, and the

accident, Wendy and Tressa were still tiptoeing around each other. Tressa hated herself for having been so nasty, and wished she had been more mature. But also she wished her mother understood her.

Only Dan understood her, and Caro. She called Caro, who was still in Plymouth.

'Hello, Tressie.'

'How are you feeling?'

'Oh fine, I mean awful but not worse awful. The nurses seem to have a pill for everything. Being sick, not being sick, constipation, the runs, sore bones, aching feet – it's remarkable. Now, how are you? How are things with Dan?'

Tressa paused. 'He's fine, I think. I haven't seen him,' she said. Even if she did see him, what would she say? *Sorry for being exactly like everything I hate, like my mother? Please bear with me while I work out how to be a kind, trusting, less defensive person? I don't know when that will be but stick around and let's hope for the best?*

'I said some terrible things to him,' she admitted to Caro.

'So go home and work it out.' Caro made it sound so simple.

A text from Janet interrupted her thoughts with pictures of Ginger Pickles and Ivy cosying up on a paisley comforter. Caro was right. And it was time to go home. She tried to work out how to break the news to her parents.

Just then, Dan's red car pulled up to the front of the house.

'Shit sticks,' she said, as Wendy came to her side and looked out the window.

'Isn't that nice? He's come to see you. Now no nasty words please,' said Wendy.

'Did you know he was coming over?' Tressa demanded to know. She wanted this reconnection on her own terms.

'Yes, I asked him to take you home. I think you're ready now and if you stay here too long you will become dependent on us.'

Wendy went to open the door for Dan.

Dan walked in and Tressa wished she were wearing something that wasn't flannel pyjama pants of her father's and a T-shirt of her mother's that read *This is what 50 & Fabulous Looks Like*.

Not that she had ever seen her mother wearing anything remotely like this, which was why it had been offered to her. Always a cast-off for Tressa.

'You look nice,' said Dan with a grin and she couldn't help it, she burst out laughing.

'I do not,' she said. 'I look like I've given up on life.'

Dan sat opposite her. 'How's the arm?'

'Healing.'

God, he looked good. He had some colour in his face and looked less drawn than when he had arrived in Port Lowdy.

'How are you?' she asked.

'Fine.' They sat in silence. Tressa was trying to think of something to say, to apologise, to pretend she didn't remember him, anything.

'Are you ready to head home?' he finally asked.

'Oh sure, I will need to get my things,' Tressa said but Wendy was in the doorway, swinging a pink Cath Kidston bag.

'All here, just a few things. Personal items and some hair ties,' she said. 'Turn around and I'll put your hair up.'

Tressa groaned. 'Leave it, Mum. The only person my hair annoys when it's down is you.'

Wendy handed the bag to Dan and then kissed Tressa on the cheek.

'Safe trip, darling, and Dad will call you tonight after work.'

Before Tressa could say a word, Wendy almost pushed her and Dan out the door and shut it behind them.

She adjusted the sling holding her wounded arm and walked down the steps slowly in the slip-on massage slippers her mother had given her, which had the word 'Sheraton' embroidered on the front.

Dan helped her into the car and then leaned over her to put on her seatbelt, like the day she had Ivy the kitten on her lap.

She tried not to breathe in the scent from his skin but failed, taking a gasp of Dan's force field in the air. 'You all right?' He looked at her, concerned, his face so close she could see the flecks in his eyes.

'Fine,' she said.

'It sounded as though you're gasping for air. Are you in pain?'

'No,' snapped Tressa and Dan ran around the front of the car and jumped into the driver's side.

'I would like us to start again,' he said. 'I'm Dan Byrne, angriest man in Ireland and most awful man in Cornwall.' He put out his hand.

Tressa looked at him and saw the twinkle in his eye.

She took his hand.

'I'm Tressa Buckland. A painter who likes to jump to conclusions when not jumping in front of cars.'

'Oh, this is perfect then. We're going to get along just fine.' He turned the car around and drove towards home.

40

Dan wasn't sure what to think when Wendy called him and asked him to pick Tressa up and take her back to Mermaid Cottage.

'She barely remembers me,' he said, but Wendy scoffed.

'Tressa is my daughter so I can say this about her; she creates drama sometimes, so just ignore it and look after her for us. She wants to be home and she's moping around here like an egg with no yolk.'

Dan wasn't sure what that meant. He missed Tressa so much his heart ached. He had even been to the local doctor, who told him he was as fit as a fiddle and to get some sun. So Dan had walked Richie every day to the seaside and sat on the beach after lunch.

During the two weeks Tressa had been away, he'd pulled the next edition of the paper together by himself and he had taken the photos. They weren't as good as Tressa's pictures, but they would do.

He went to the Easter Bonnet Parade run by St Cuthbert's and had interviewed the winner, Mrs Duncleaver, who had been working on her hat's 'concept' for six months. It was a top hat made of chocolate with a white chocolate rabbit bursting through the top, complete with a pink satin ribbon and tiny sugar iced eggs around the brim.

He had to photograph this creation rather swiftly. There had been a delay in the running of the parade, due to the vicar being caught up in judging the jam competition. Naturally Rosemary March won with her passionfruit butter but by the time the vicar arrived back, Mrs Duncleaver's hat had started to melt onto her forehead. Dan took a few quick photos of its good side and then some of the other hats. Everyone around him was asking about Tressa.

He said the same thing over and over, that she was all right. She'd had surgery. She was staying with her parents until she felt up to being back in Port Lowdy.

He went to the Easter egg hunt, where he took photos of little Primmy Stanhope sitting on a chamomile lawn, her fat fist hanging on to a little basket with eggs inside.

There were so many events, he was rushing from one to another, recording interviews onto his phone, so he could write up the stories later.

Then he was down to the crab-catching competition at the harbour and onto the naming ceremony for the new fishing boat. They named it the *Lady Caro*, at which everyone clapped when the captain smashed a bottle of Cornish Knocker ale against the bow.

And everywhere he went, people wished him *Pask Lowen*. He finally worked out this meant Happy Easter in Cornish when the eighth person had passed him and smiled as they said it; so he returned the phrase, feeling happy to be a part of something.

That Easter Sunday he dined at the pub with Remi, Juliet, Marcel, and Pamela, as well as a young fellow called Melon. What a name! Dan asked him about it. Turned out the young skivvy was called Marlon but Marcel had mispronounced his name and it stuck.

He watched Remi and Juliet, feeling sad they had missed so much time together, but noticing how they never stopped touching. Remi had changed. He looked five years younger, and Juliet was everything Remi had said she was. Beautiful, kind, engaging, and clever. She was living in London, working for a large fashion brand and living with some work friends.

But she and Remi talked about her coming down every other weekend, and him going to see her. There wasn't even a moment of doubt they would make it work.

Now with Tressa sitting next to him in the car, he wondered if they would be as determined.

He didn't want to rush her. Tressa stared out the window, and he knew her well enough to know she was stewing about something.

'Are you shitty your mam kicked you out?'

'It would have been nice to have discussed it but she probably needs to get back to her Zumba and her wine club. Anyway I had already decided to leave when you turned up.'

'That's lucky then that I arrived when I did,' he said with a smile and a quick glance at her.

They drove in silence for a while.

'I'm sorry about Richie,' he said. 'Did I tell you about the time he chased the gulls and Remi called him in for me? He seems to have an abnormal attraction to them.'

'Remi or Richie?' she asked and he laughed.

'Remi's Juliet came to find him,' he said.

Tressa bounced out of her dull mood and twisted towards him. 'Really? That's amazing! Is she amazing? Are they amazing together?'

Dan laughed. 'They are amazingly amazing.'

Tressa gave a big sigh. 'That makes me so happy. Amazingly happy, in fact.'

Dan felt pleased to bring her such good news. 'Also Penny's Paul came from Australia. They have been spending time together.'

'So much love in Port Lowdy – it's finally living up to its name,' Tressa said.

'What does Lowdy mean? Is it a word? I always thought it was just a name.'

They turned onto the coastal road that would take them all the way home to Port Lowdy and Tressa pushed the button for the window to go down. She put her head out the window like Richie the dog, her hair flying back in a mess of black curls.

'I missed the smell of the sea,' she said. 'Mum's house smells like potpourri and disappointment in me.'

Dan roared laughter. 'You are terrible. Now tell me about Port Lowdy.'

Tressa wound the window up a little, and then turned to him.

'Lowdy – it means Love Day.'

'That sounds nice, but what is it?' he asked.

'A love day is a single day during medieval times, where any argument could be resolved outside a court and decided by an arbiter or arbitration committee. It could resolve anything at all, unlike the court, but the whole time the two parties were presenting their arguments, they had to hold hands.'

'Really?'

'Yes, and the reference to "day" meant they had a day to sort their argument out. And at the end they had to remember they were bound by the bonds of love to resolve their arguments and then they had to seal their pact with a kiss.'

'Oh, how I wish they had a Love Day in Dublin. I would still have my flat, and a kiss for my troubles.'

'But the Love Day has to be witnessed by the people in the court, or village, and they have to add their blessing. It's like a marriage, I guess. So Port Lowdy was the place for these disputes to be resolved and that's where it got its name.'

'That's the loveliest story I have heard in a long time,' he said, and Tressa smiled at him.

'Just another reason why I love Port Lowdy.'

And another reason why I love you so much, thought Dan as they drove into Port Love Day.

41

Juliet yelled at Remi across the beach. She was standing knee-deep in the water. 'You said you would walk to the other side of the world for me. But the water is too cold? *Une poule mouillée.*'

Remi took up her challenge and strode into the water, shoes and all. When he reached her he kissed her and she melted into his arms.

They had spent the morning in bed, and then emerged for lunch. The first time it had been rushed and fast. He was clumsy. He felt like a virgin again. He apologised into her shoulder but she kissed his neck and held him until they moved together again. This time it was what he thought it would be, but better. And then the third time, he thought he would die of pleasure and love.

They had spent a few days together but she would be heading back this afternoon and he already missed her. Still, they had a plan, and it felt like something to hang on to.

He had to stay in Port Lowdy for a year before he could move on, and he wanted to be in London with Juliet.

'It will be like reconnecting over and over again,' she had said when he worried it would be too much for her.

Now she walked up the beach towards him, her dress

tied up around her thighs. He wanted her again and as she came close to him, he saw she wanted him too.

'Let's go back to bed,' she said as she kissed his mouth and he pulled her close.

'Juliet Lassez, marry me.'

'But of course,' she said, as though he had asked to borrow her pen.

'You aren't surprised?' He shook his head at her.

The sun was shining on her dark hair and she lifted up her red-framed sunglasses and smiled, showing the gapped teeth he loved so much.

'It has been a seven-year engagement, Remi; of course we will be married. That's that.'

'That's that,' he repeated.

They held hands on their walk back to the Black Swan and Remi wondered if people passing took them for tourists. He felt like a tourist in a new world. One he never thought he would visit – but now he was living in it. Juliet stopped to gaze into the window of a shop that sold candles and oils and handmade gifts.

'These are pretty,' she said.

'Which one do you want? I will buy it for you,' he said, his hand on the door of the shop.

Juliet pulled him away. 'I don't need anything. I was just saying they're pretty.'

'I want to buy you everything,' he said, and it was true. 'I can't afford an engagement ring yet though. I will save.'

She put her hand back in his and they walked up the hill until they reached the top at the pub and could look down across the bay. The sun sparkled on the water and the bunting left over from Easter swayed in the breeze across the cobbled streets down to the esplanade.

'I don't want a ring, Remi. I just want you.'

'Juliet!'

'I missed you every day,' she said. 'Sometimes I would drive to the prison and sit out the front in my car and try and tell you I loved you, to hold on, to wait for this moment. I have been saving money, working for us. You saved my life and now it's my turn to help you build a life. I want to be with you every moment of the future.'

Remi closed his eyes for a moment and then opened them again quickly. He needed to see if he was dreaming but no, she was still by his side. There was Dan walking his dog; there was the old man who tried to get into the bar most days for a drink, whom Pamela set up with a ginger ale in the garden, an umbrella in it as though it were a cocktail. There was the lady from the post office who Pamela said was a famous crab. Or something.

'We can marry here,' she said.

'But your family?'

'They can come if they're nice,' she said and Remi wondered if perhaps they hadn't wanted her to wait for him. He doubted anyone had ever won an argument with Juliet once she had made her mind up.

'Okay,' he said. 'That is a very good idea.'

'I know,' she said, and she leaned up and kissed him. 'I love you, Remi Durand.'

'Let's start our life together in Port Lowdy and see where it takes us.'

42

Penny straightened up the postcards of Port Lowdy and rearranged the jams by the front door, putting Rosemary's winning passionfruit butter at the front, its gold sticker displayed proudly on the jars.

Actually Penny herself had put the stickers on. It was just a round one from a pack of fifty that she had in the shop. She liked Rosemary and thought she deserved a sticker, not just for her jams but for her friendship.

Paul had gone back to Brisbane and Penny couldn't stop thinking about him. Sometimes she wondered if she had done the wrong thing by not going with him. And other times she had a terrible urge to tell him that she loved him. But it was too late now, she told herself.

Paul had left the next day after Tressa's accident and she had said goodbye to him in a stiff and formal way. She hadn't returned his hug the way he hugged her. She hadn't been with a man since Paul all those years before and his arms around her felt almost foreign. She felt disconnected from him in a way that made her sad. She realised she had so much anger and pain, for all those years alone, that she wasn't sure where to put it all. But now – she regretted it. Petty Stanhope, she thought her new name should be.

Tegan had told her she would be heading to Brisbane next month to meet her half siblings. Penny felt betrayed by her daughter but couldn't bring herself to admit she had made a mistake.

The young Frenchman Dan wrote about walked into the post office carrying a bag. Penny didn't associate with criminals as a rule, but she had read the article on him and had even cried a little for his loss.

'*Bonjour*,' she said, trying to let him know she didn't judge him for what happened.

'Hello,' he said and his shyness made her like him even more.

'It's not easy being in the papers, is it? I know because of the article Dan wrote about me. Once you're in the public eye, everything changes,' she said knowingly.

Remi looked confused.

'I didn't see your article,' he admitted.

Penny stepped behind the counter and pulled a copy out from under the bench and handed it to him.

'That's me,' she said pointing to the photo of her as Miss Crab and then the photo of Tegan and Primmy.

'I fell in love and had my daughter… but the man and I were separated, sadly.' She did feel sad as she spoke. The whole thing was sad and the thing was – although she was trying – she couldn't forgive her father for being so selfish, just to keep her to himself.

'Ah yes,' he said, 'Pamela told me. I remember now. But your friend came here from Australia, yes?'

Penny paused. 'Yes… he came to meet our daughter and to see me again. He saw the show.'

'And so now you are happily ever after like Juliet and me.' He smiled as he spoke.

'Did Juliet come and find you?' she asked.

'Yes, she waited for me and I waited for her. An *acte de foi*.'

Penny wasn't sure what that meant. Remi caught her look and shrugged. 'How you say? A leap of faith.'

Remi went across to the area where the postal bags and boxes were and measured the bag against them for size. Was Paul coming to see her a leap of faith? Why was she so angry still?

'Remi?' she called, and he turned to her.

'*Oui?*' She liked the way he said yes in his language. She smiled at him.

'Do you ever get angry about all the time you lost in prison? Angry with the man attacking Juliet and you losing so much?'

He picked up a large postal bag and came to the counter.

'I always focused on getting out. But I didn't know I would be in Port Lowdy. Sometimes, though, the prison can be your mind.'

Remi put the items, all carefully wrapped, into the post bag and wrote on the front. He handed it back to Penny to weigh.

'For Juliet,' she said, reading the front.

'She is back in London, so I send her some little things she likes. It is nice to have a surprise sometimes, *non?*'

Penny nodded, her heart racing as she handed Remi his change for the post.

'I have to go for my shift. *À bientôt*,' he said, with a wave. Penny waved back.

It was hard to try and reconcile that her parents had interfered with her life, based on what Paul had said about the letters. She had searched the house again and her father's old papers but there was nothing that showed any reference to Paul.

The post office phone rang and she picked it up.

'Port Lowdy Post Office, can I assist you?'

'Mum. Why don't you ever answer your mobile phone?'

'I'm working. It's upstairs,' she said, flicking some dust from the top of the register with a tissue.

'I emailed you something. You need to see it. I'm sending it to the office email account. Can you open it?'

Penny clicked on the post office computer and opened her email. An email from Tegan was flashing in the inbox.

She opened the email. 'Read the attachment, Mum,' Tegan said.

Penny double clicked it and saw handwriting that made her heart sink.

It was a scanned image of a notebook page, with her father's handwriting.

To Paul Murphy,
Please stop writing to my daughter Penelope. She is not interested in hearing from you or pursuing any sort of connection. She has instructed me to write to you to tell you such and furthermore...

'What is this?' she asked Tegan, trying to make sense of what was on the screen.

'I remembered all the boxes of old writing paper that you had when you cleaned out Pa's papers. Boxes of it and I kept it because there were stamps and old envelopes and ribbons and all sorts of treasures that a girl wanted. There were a few half-written letters. I never read them till now because I didn't go through all of them. The papers have just been in the box on top of my wardrobe but then I went through them and there it was. He did write to you, Mum. Your dad lied to you.'

Penny didn't say anything to Tegan. She just hung up the phone and then dialled Rosemary March.

'Rosemary, man the fort. I'm off to Australia.'

She put down the phone and clapped her hands.

Little Miss Crab was finally coming out of her shell!

43

Ginger Pickles was gazing at Tressa with disdain from her vantage point on the top of the fridge.

'What?' Tressa asked of the cat, but was ignored for her troubles. Ginger was decidedly disappointed with Tressa's time away from her and having to put up with the small cat next door and Janet, who seemed to be less willing now to feed her five times a day.

Dan walked into the house balancing a box of groceries, a paper under his arm, and a bunch of daffodils, which he waved at her. Richie trotted in behind him.

'These are from the woman at the gift shop. She sends her best wishes for healing.'

Tressa nodded. 'That's nice. She's lovely.'

'I picked up Richie from Penny. She's going to Australia. Isn't that lovely? To see her fella.'

Richie came and sat at her feet, looking forlorn.

'Richie is very sorry, he wants you to know,' said Dan.

'I can tell,' she said and reached out and patted his big solid head. 'Seagulls and you are a deep and real issue. You need therapy.'

Dan laughed as he unpacked the groceries. She lay

sprawled on the sofa. Her mind wanted her to help but she felt so tired, she thought she might be sick.

Coming home wasn't as exciting as she'd thought it would be. The house didn't feel like it normally did, as though the arguments between her and Wendy, and her and Dan, had settled in all the corners and were judging her.

'How about a cup of tea? I have some nice treats from the bakery that will put the colour back in your cheeks.'

He was so kind and she was so awful, she thought. She didn't deserve anyone like Dan – no wonder her mother struggled to love her. She burst into tears.

'Oh no, what's happened? You don't want tea? I could get you a whisky but I drank it all, which is why we had a big fight and also because I was being a total eejit but, Tressie, my darling, don't cry.'

Which of course made her cry more.

'I want a shower and I want to go to bed,' she said and cradled her arm in its cast. 'But I left the thing at Mum's to put around my cast to stop it getting wet. She kicked me out because she hates me.'

Dan was sitting next to her on the sofa now and he put his arm around her.

'She doesn't hate you, she's just not good at showing you how she feels. She's complicated, like her daughter. And as for the shower, she put the things in the bag – you just didn't look. So I can help you wrap up your arm and then run you a lovely shower. I will change your sheets and have the bed all ready for you when you get out, okay?'

Tressa nodded, feeling like a child. She so desperately needing to be looked after.

'You don't have to do this for me,' she whispered.

'I do. It was my bloody dog that caused this mess, and besides, I want to do it.'

Later when Tressa had managed to shower – washing her hair with one hand, which was harder than she'd thought it would be – she put on a soft fresh clean nightgown and slipped into the clean sheets that Dan had put on the bed.

Dan came into the bedroom, a cup of tea in hand and a little plate of biscuits.

'Something to soothe you,' he said. Then he pulled the paper from under his arm and put it on her lap. 'And the latest edition of *The Port Lowdy Occurrence*.'

'Oh God, I thought you would have just missed an edition with everything going on.' She picked up the paper and looked at the front page.

'Mrs Duncleaver did it again, I see.' She gazed at the photo of the chocolate hat on the round-faced woman.

'Yes, but I had to take the photo quickly or she would have looked like Augustus Gloop when he is covered in chocolate. The photos aren't good like yours but they get the job done.'

Tressa laughed. 'Last year she wore the crucifixion on her head, made out of polymer clay. The vicar wasn't impressed and she didn't place. Clearly she has taken the feedback on board and turned it into something more palatable, as it were.'

'A crucifixion? On her head?' Dan roared with laughter.

'Yes, on top of the hill of Golgotha, which was very detailed.'

'Golgotha – is that the name for it?' He was crying with laughter.

'You're a good Irish Catholic. I thought you would know that.'

'Oh, I didn't go to church as much as you would think and no Sunday school either. I am a bad Catholic.' He wiped his eyes, standing at the foot of the bed.

Tressa turned the page. 'Oh, look at Primmy at the egg hunt. She's a doll.' Flicking through the pages, she saw the boat named *Lady Caro* and touched the photo. 'This is perfect.'

Looking up at Dan, she smiled. 'You must have worked so hard to do all this by yourself, how did you do it all? Writing, editing, designing, photos, and all the ads?'

'It kept me busy and my mind off worrying about you,' he said, and she looked down at the paper again.

'I'm okay,' she said.

'Now, but you weren't and it's my right to worry.'

He was right. They were silent for a moment. 'Well, I should push off and let you rest. I've fed Ginger and topped up her water.'

'Where are you going?' she asked, worrying about him now.

'I'll sleep at the office,' he said cheerfully. 'Then I can have Richie with me.'

'The office,' Tressa heard herself almost screech. 'You're not staying in the office. You can sleep on the sofa – it's very comfortable – and Richie can stay in his bed in the kitchen.'

'Tressa, I can't stay here.' He made a face at her that made her want to kiss him.

'I need help; you need a place to stay. We can be grown-ups about this – can't we? Whatever happened between us happened and now we can just move on and be adults.'

Dan sat at the foot of the bed. 'I don't know how to fix this, Tressa. I don't think I can. But I will stay until you're well, and George is back.'

'Perhaps we were too fast with everything. I mean we want different things, don't we?' she said carefully.

Dan looked ahead to the window. 'Oh, I don't know about that. I don't know what I want, really. I'm a bit of a mess.'

Tressa didn't look at him. He didn't want her – that much was clear.

'I'm tired,' she said.

'Okay, sorry. I'll be here when you wake up.' He closed the door behind him and Tressa lay in the bed looking at the ceiling.

She realised that neither of them knew what they wanted and sometimes love just wasn't enough.

44

The plane landed smoothly and Penny breathed out very slowly. Surely she hadn't been holding her breath for the last twenty-four hours? But it wasn't the flying that caused her to hold her breath so tightly inside; it was the idea of seeing Paul. A thousand scenarios ran through her head.

What if he was lying to her and his wife was still alive? What if his children hated her? What if she didn't like Brisbane? So many what-ifs, her mind could barely keep up.

'You okay, Mum?' Primmy was asleep between them and Penny turned to her daughter, filled with gratitude that she had a travel companion.

'Whatever happens, Mum, and whatever the outcome with Paul, we can still see some of Australia and show Primmy some of the wildlife and the beaches there. I mean that's pretty great, and we have never had a holiday together – so that's something.'

Thinking back, Penny realised it was true. She never took time off from the post office, even though she could have if she had wanted to. She told herself that the post needed her but really she needed the post. It gave her a sense of purpose, especially after Tegan left for university.

'Welcome to Brisbane, where it is a balmy twenty-seven degrees today,' said the captain.

'Twenty-seven degrees? That's hot,' said Penny. 'I hope I cope in the heat.'

'You'll be fine, Mum,' said Tegan as the plane gently rolled to a stop and the seatbelt light went off.

They let the other passengers leave the plane first, while Primmy slept soundly, her round face relaxed in a way that made Penny wonder if she herself had ever slept that peacefully.

Finally, the aisle had cleared, and Tegan gently lifted her daughter up and onto her shoulder. Penny took the hand luggage from above their heads and they walked off the plane and into a busy terminal.

'We have to get our luggage first, and hopefully Primmy's pushchair hasn't broken. She's heavy,' said Tegan. They joined a queue to have their passports checked.

The wait wasn't too long and still Primmy slept on her mother's shoulder.

Eventually, they had their luggage on a cart. Primmy was awake and in her pushchair, drinking from her bottle of water and looking around sleepily, and they walked out the doors into the arrivals area. It was so humid Penny felt like she had stepped into a sauna. People were everywhere. Talking, laughing, walking with their little cases on wheels. It was exciting to be somewhere so new and she felt butterflies in her stomach.

Tegan was pushing Primmy. They spotted a huge homemade sign high above the people waiting to greet the new arrivals.

Welcome to Penny, Tegan, and Primmy.

It was Paul and his daughters. They were all in summer clothes of bright colours and were waving madly. Paul was in white shorts and a pink polo top and he had sunglasses hanging from his neck. He seemed more handsome and as tall as ever. Penny felt silly in her navy pants and prim white blouse and laced-up shoes. She wanted to wear pink and orange and sandals and sunglasses and throw all her old clothes away.

'Tegan! Did you tell them we were coming?'

Tegan grinned. 'He was so excited when I told him.'

Penny looked at Tegan and then at Paul. She hesitated, frozen. 'Go, Mum, go – he wants you.'

And then Penny ran forward and threw herself into his arms, crying and laughing, while he kissed her head and held her tight.

'Penny, my Penny,' he kept repeating. When they pulled apart Tegan was hugging her half-sisters and Primmy was out of the pushchair and in her Aunt Julie's arms, playing with her necklace.

'Penny, I would like you to meet my daughters, Julie and Claire, who are the light of my lives and beautiful like their mother and smart like her too.'

Penny loved him all the more for including his wife in the introduction. She wanted these women to know that she respected their mother and her part in his life.

Hugs all round. His daughter Claire said, 'Thank God you're here. Dad's been a nightmare since he came back. All he does is carry on like a pork chop about you all. Now we can all get on with it.'

'Exactly,' said Julie. 'Let's head back to mine and you can meet our other halves and the kids. We both have one each:

a boy and girl. I have Patrick who is ten months and Claire has little Violet, who is about Primmy's age, yes? Isn't that nice? A Primrose and a Violet. If we have more girls, we could have a whole bouquet.'

They strolled in the direction of the exit, still carrying the sign, Primmy back in her pushchair. Penny and Paul hung back and watched them for a moment.

'I couldn't believe it when Tegan told me you were all coming,' he said, taking her hand.

'I couldn't believe it when I saw the sign.' She laughed.

'You look wonderful,' he said.

'Then wonderful must look happy, because that's all that's changed about me since you saw me last.'

'So the trick is to keep you happy,' he said, and he leaned down and kissed her. A proper kiss. A kiss like the ones they had shared when they first met so many years ago.

If Penny thought that desire was gone, or that she was too old for a lover or too out of practice, it all dissipated in that kiss. Her arms went around his neck and she kissed him back passionately until they were both out of breath.

'I am sorry it took me so long to get here,' she said.

'Yeah, it's a long flight,' he agreed.

'I mean – to kiss you, to be with you like this,' she explained.

'You're here now, and you have all the time to world to make it up to me.' He was teasing. It felt good to be teased.

'Me? Make it up to you? Oh, Paul Murphy, you have some making up of lost time to get on with.'

'Then let's make it up together,' he said and they kissed again, just for good luck.

45

Dan put down the phone and stared out the window across the sea.

He had been offered a job. A proper journalist's role for the largest paper in Britain – based on the story on Remi.

The editor wanted him to profile people and he could write from anywhere. He just had to interview people of his choice, and the interviews should be between ten thousand and fifteen thousand words. That was a lot of words. But in the past he'd felt fenced in by the strict limit of fifteen hundred words on his column. Now he could explore the story, unravel the situation – the person. 'You can profile whoever you like. But they have to be interesting and they have to sell papers.' The editor had laughed, but he wasn't joking. 'People you might think are one thing but end up being something else. There has to be a twist in some way.'

Dan would have to be curious, but he could give a sense of place and tell the story the way the subject deserved.

He was supposed to deliver one profile every six weeks, which was plenty of time – but he could stretch it to eight weeks if the subject needed more exploration. And there would be a video component, like they had done for the article on Remi.

'An immersive experience,' the editor had said.

He had said he would need time to decide, which was a lie, but he wanted Tressa's opinion first.

As though reading his mind, Tressa came downstairs in her familiar red and orange flannel shirt. 'What are you looking out at?' she asked him, coming to stand by his side.

'Just the weather,' he said. 'Can I make you some lunch?'

'Lunch? It's ten in the morning,' she said and patted Richie as she passed him. The dog was sleeping on an armchair with Ginger Pickles perched on the back of the same chair, looking at Richie as though he were a nuisance, but a bearable one.

'I'm going to try and paint,' said Tressa.

'With your left hand?'

'No, if I hold the brush a certain way and peel back the cast from my thumb, I can manage.'

Dan frowned. 'I don't think you're supposed to do that.'

'I don't think you're my doctor,' said Tressa, but she wasn't smiling as she spoke.

'Okay, no – I'm not your doctor but if it hurts, please don't do it,' he said.

Tressa turned away and switched on the kettle.

'Did you sleep okay?' he asked.

'Fine. How was the sofa?' Again there was a tone.

'What's wrong?' he asked her.

'I'm sick of this cast,' she said. 'It's heavy and it aches and it's itchy and everything else that goes with it.'

Dan nodded. 'I remember when my leg was broken how itchy it was. Maddening. You need a knitting needle to poke down and scratch it.'

'I don't knit,' she said.

'The end of a paintbrush then.'

She poured them both tea. 'Want me to carry yours upstairs?' he offered.

They were treading so carefully around each other and they still hadn't spoken about Remi or the terrible fight.

'No, it's okay.' She went away upstairs.

Dan sat down at the table and Richie came and sat at his feet. Ginger Pickles leapt down to check her bowl and complained with a rattling meow.

How long could he stay in the same house with her and not tell her how he felt? That he had made a mistake? That he wanted to be here and take the job? That they could have the world, if only they could trust each other?

He walked upstairs and knocked on her studio door.

'Yes? Come in.'

'Hi, um…' She was by the window, mixing paints onto a palette. She looked up and then back at the palette, moving it to the sunlight.

'I just wanted to say, I mean when we had our fight, I said terrible things.' God, he was completely shite at apologies, he thought – but he'd never really given any in all his life until he met Tressa.

'Ah, shit sticks,' said Tressa.

'Do you want me to stop talking?'

'No, my mum is here. Why didn't she call?' She pushed past him and went down the stairs, leaving him alone in the studio.

He stood alone in the empty room, which smelt of paint. 'Shit sticks,' he muttered.

He could hear her talking to Wendy, feigning surprise and politeness. Now wasn't the time. He went downstairs.

'Hello, Wendy,' he said, 'you're looking well.'

'Oh thank you, Dan; I wanted to come and see you both. I have shopping bags in the car. Can you pop out and be the porter for me?' She dangled the keys and Dan bowed to her.

'Of course, m'lady,' he said. She laughed, but he thought she was secretly pleased. If he'd believed in past lives, he would have said Wendy was the Queen of Sheba.

Wendy seemed to have bought up most of Waitrose. Dan loaded up, determined to carry back all ten bags in one trip.

'Mum, what on earth?' Tressa cried.

'You two need sustenance and there were so many delicious things, I just couldn't help myself.'

Tressa was peering into a bag. 'Three pomegranates, a whole stilton and oysters. Give me a skull and I can paint a Flemish still life.'

Dan laughed and Wendy shrugged. 'You love oysters and there is goat cheese for a salad and you can add some pomegranate jewels to it – just delicious.'

'Wow, well this is too much, Mum,' Tressa said.

'Dan, be a dear and put it all away. Tressa and I are going for a walk.'

'I was about to paint,' Tressa started to say but Wendy flapped a hand at her. 'Your paintings can wait. I cannot. Pop your shoes on and let's go. And take that flannel shirt off. You'll die of the heat in that thing.'

Tressa sighed and gave Dan a look that made him turn away so Wendy didn't see his laughter.

At least they still had Wendy holding them together.

46

Wendy and Tressa crossed the esplanade and walked down the few steps to the sand.

'Shouldn't you have your sling on?' asked Wendy.

'No, it's not so bad now,' said Tressa. 'Which way do you want to go?'

'You decide, I don't mind,' Wendy said. She was wearing a pink sun visor and pink pants and a pink T-shirt.

'You look like a flamingo,' Tressa told her mother.

'A glamourous old bird,' said Wendy and Tressa laughed. Perhaps her mother was getting a sense of humour in her later years.

'Pink suits you,' she said, and she meant it. Wendy looked great in bright colours. 'You should wear more of those sorts of shades.'

'I should,' said Wendy. 'I should do a lot of things.' She laughed.

They walked along the shoreline, towards the rock pools in the distance.

'There is one of those things you used to collect as a child.' Wendy's toe touched an egg case on the sand.

'A mermaid's purse,' said Tressa, leaning down to pick it up.

Wendy peered at it with a frown. 'They're not very pretty, are they? For mermaids.'

Tressa looked her mother's pink outfit up and down. 'I wonder why they have to be pretty though. Is that the siren thing? Luring sailors to their death?'

Wendy shrugged. 'I suppose you're right.'

'Actually… I used to spend hours filling these with pretty things then dropping them in the deepest rock pool as a type of offering to the mermaids. It's supposed to be good luck.'

She opened the top of the egg case so Wendy could see where you could stow things inside.

'What did you put in them?'

'Little shells, sea glass, sometimes bits of broken crockery from shipwrecks that came to the shoreline. Just little things,' Tressa said.

'Let's fill one together,' said Wendy, taking the purse from Tressa's hand. And she set off down the shore, looking down at her feet. 'Ooh, a periwinkle,' she said and put it into the case.

Tressa looked around to see if she was being filmed for a comedy show. Her mother in pink from head to toe, picking up shells and putting them into a sting ray egg case was something she never thought she would see. Whenever Tressa was out as a child, usually playing at the Foxes' house, she would come back to their holiday house and Wendy would have thrown all of them away.

She spotted a shard of green glass on the sand and picked it up. 'Here you go,' she said to Wendy, who inspected the glass first, then put it into the case.

'Good find,' she told Tressa, as though she were the expert on the subject of mermaid purses.

'Thanks, Mum,' said Tressa sarcastically, but Wendy didn't hear her tone.

Tressa wondered if she was having a post-accident brain infarction. Was she really with her pink-clad mother, beachcombing for sea jewels to put into a stingray case?

'It's funny that you told me I was born in a mermaid's purse and that I always collected these as a kid,' said Tressa, trying not to put too much weight on the coincidence. She didn't want to remind Wendy too much of their fight, and ruin the moment. But the parallel was not lost on her. Wendy didn't answer. She was picking up shells and inspecting them like avocados, throwing them back into the ocean if they didn't meet her standards.

Tressa wanted to tell her mother she had wanted to do this with her every summer until she was eighteen. But she said nothing. It didn't matter now. Wendy was on the beach with her and doing something Tressa loved.

They came closer to the rock pools and Tressa pointed out a brown crab waddling across the rocks. Wendy began to climb and Tressa followed.

'Which rock pool is the best one?' asked Wendy. Tressa smiled at her mother. She always expected quality, even in a rock pool.

'This one is fine,' she said, looking down at the crab who was sitting still at the bottom of the clear pool. Little rocks and sea lettuce created shelter for the snails who sat patiently, waiting for the tide to roll back in later in the day. Small fish darted about and a starfish sat on a rock, sunning itself.

They sat down gingerly and Wendy slipped off her shoes and dipped her feet in the water.

'Good Lord, that's cold,' she said but put her feet in further and closed her eyes as her body became used to the temperature.

'He'd better be quick or a gull will grab him and turn him into a bisque,' Tressa said and Wendy watched in wonder as the crab disappeared under a rock.

'So what do I do with it?' Wendy held up the purse.

'You can drop it in and say a little something to the mermaid who you hope finds it.' Tressa smiled at her mother, who looked nervous. 'Or if it's Rosewyn you want to have it, then say something to her, leave her the gift. I have. For years.'

Wendy turned to Tressa. 'You did this for Rosewyn?'

Tressa paused. She didn't want to upset her mother but she also wanted her to know that she cared.

'Every day of every holiday. I didn't want her to miss out, so I would drop little things in the rock pools. Sometimes I even dropped in the sea salt fudge from the bakery because I thought she would like it, because of the sea salt.'

Wendy started to cry. 'You're a lovely younger sister, aren't you? So kind – you have always been kind, Tressie, always.'

Looking down at the rock pool, Tressa swallowed. The starfish had gone, probably hiding from the family drama emerging above.

'So you drop the purse into the rock pool and say what to Rosewyn?' Wendy asked, and Tressa thought she looked so uncertain and worried.

'I said hello or I'd tell her about my day or about life if it was the start of the holidays. I don't know, just kid stuff.' She shrugged. 'Nothing major.' But that was a lie because she used to tell Rosewyn everything and she would ask her sister why Wendy didn't think she was good enough.

Wendy held up the purse in both hands, like Circe offering the cup to Ulysses.

'Hello, Rosewyn, it's Mummy, with Tressie. We made you a lovely purse filled with pretty things.' She paused and looked at Tressa, who nodded encouragingly.

'I miss you but I have lovely Tressie and Jago, who has twins! They are so much fun. And Tressa is a famous artist. She paints so beautifully, it is remarkable. I am always so impressed but I don't know much about art so sometimes I think she must think she was born into the wrong family.'

Tressa looked down at the pool. She realised this was Wendy's way of saying what she felt and although it was clumsy, it was authentic.

'But I am very proud of her. I adore her and when she broke her arm, I thought I would die at the thought of losing her after I had lost you. A mother cannot lose two children in her life.'

The breeze blew up through Tressa's hair and Wendy's visor flew off her head but Wendy didn't run after it; she sat still, holding the purse in front of her.

'But, Rosewyn, I have to focus on Tressa and Jago now. I know you've passed and are wherever you are now. Energy has to go somewhere so I hope it has gone to something wonderful because you always had so much energy, my little love.'

Tressa held her breath as Wendy continued.

'I came here today to tell Tressa I am sorry for always talking about you to her. You would have hated it, I know.

Now I know Tressa kept you around in all her paintings, so you were always there, I just didn't look hard enough.'

Tressa blinked away tears as Wendy held up the purse and dropped it into the rock pool with a hollow splash.

'Goodbye, Rosewyn, my sweet.'

Tressa started to cry in earnest, as did Wendy, who held her close.

'Oh, Tressie, you were right here all this time and I was so silly to not see it. I'm sorry.'

'It's okay, I'm sorry she died. It's utter shit sticks.'

'Absolute shit sticks,' said Wendy and Tressa giggled into her mother's shoulder.

'You are a fairy tale, Tressa Buckland, and I couldn't wish for a better and more magical daughter.'

Tressa kissed her mother's cheek and pressed against her, smelling the Dior perfume Wendy always wore.

'Now where's my visor? I bought that in Provence; it's very good quality. I don't want to lose it.'

And Wendy Buckland was back in action.

47

Dan woke and checked his phone; it was two in the morning. Nothing good happened at two in the morning.

He sat up and stretched. It was warm and he was hot on the sofa. He kneeled up and opened the window to let the sea air inside.

Richie whimpered in his sleep – probably chasing seagulls, Dan thought.

A creak on the stairs made him look up and there was Tressa in her nightgown.

'Sorry. Did I wake you?' she asked.

'No, I was a bit hot, so I opened the window,' he said, suddenly aware he was bare-chested.

'Yes, it's warm. I couldn't sleep so I thought I would sit outside for a while.'

'Sounds like a good idea,' he said and Tressa walked to the front door.

'Come sit outside then,' she said, and he stood up and followed her out. Richie twitched in his sleep, on the floor.

They crossed the road in the dark and sat on the sea wall, the moon high above them.

The breeze touched his skin and he felt electric. Or was

that because of Tressa sitting so close in a white cotton gown that barely covered her thighs?

'Your mum was good the other day,' he said but she put her hand on his bare knee in his shorts.

'Shh,' she whispered. 'Listen.'

Dan listened, unsure what he was listening for but he tried hard.

'Isn't it wonderful?' Tressa whispered.

'What?' he asked.

'The silence.'

And he listened again and it was wonderful. Just the water lapping at the shore like a rhythmic lullaby.

'Tressa,' he whispered.

'Yes?'

'I'm sorry for being awful. I'm an immature idiot.'

'I know,' she said.

They were quiet for a while.

'I'm sorry I assumed the worst of you and that you were using Remi to get a job and run away from me.'

Dan thought it best he not tell her he had a job yet, since this was the best progress they had made since the fight.

'We make each other's lives complicated, I think,' she said, and he felt his heart sink.

'Was your life better before me?' he asked.

'It was easier.' She laughed, and Dan joined in, though he felt like crying. So she didn't love him. She was talking about them. Her life had been easier without his love.

'I'm a bit cold,' he said, 'I should go back in.' He swung his legs back over the wall and stood on the footpath.

'Did I upset you?'

'No, why?'

'I didn't mean it was better because it was easier, because easy isn't always better. I was hiding from a lot, and you have helped me be braver about some things.'

Dan nodded. 'That's good. So all of this wasn't wasted, then.'

'Wasted? Not at all, it was the opposite. It was wonderful. It was spectacular.'

Dan felt he was being broken up with and knew his defences were rising up.

'I was going to tell you tomorrow but I've been offered a job, in London, writing for a really great paper, so as soon as George is back, I will be off, but I really appreciate you putting me up at Mermaid Terrace.'

Tressa was silent. He saw her jaw drop.

He looked at her intently as he spoke. 'What? Did you think we would be able to just move through this? I think so much has been said that we can't move on from.'

Dan started to pace again but she was very still.

'Neither of us behaved very well,' she said. 'I am sorry about that. I wanted to hurt you.'

'Well, you did.' He said.

'So you have to do the job in London? You can't stay here and try and work on this with me?'

He shook his head. 'Not a viable option, unfortunately.'

'Me or the job?' she asked, but he didn't answer.

'I love you, Dan,' she said and Dan reached for her. They heard a car coming around the bend and then a bark.

'Richie, sit!' he yelled, but Richie came bounding out the front door, which Dan was sure he had closed behind him but obviously he hadn't. Richie jumped the low stone fence and ran across the road. The sound of him being hit was sickening. But not as awful as the sound he made as he was thrown to the ground.

'Richie!' Dan ran to his dog and held him as he whimpered. Tressa ran up to him.

'I'll call a vet,' she said, but Dan was holding Richie on his lap and he shook his head.

'It's too late,' he said, and Tressa sat next to him and stroked Richie's nose as he whimpered in Dan's arms.

'Shhh, it's okay, fella, you can go now, chase all those seagulls in the sky, sniff every crotch you can.'

Tressa cried and laughed at the same time.

Richie wagged his tail once and then gave a huge sigh and died in Dan's arms.

The sound of Dan's sobbing broke her heart and she touched his arm.

'Bring him inside, Dan.'

The driver of the car was standing by the side of the road. 'I'm so sorry, I didn't see him,' he said.

'It's not your fault. He liked to chase seagulls,' said Dan, as he carried Richie inside.

Tressa followed Dan inside. Carefully, he placed Richie on the sofa.

'What can I do?' she asked.

'Nothing,' he said. 'I just want to be with him.'

He didn't hear Tressa leave. He wept until he felt dehydrated. It was dark by the time he wrapped Richie in a blanket from the sofa.

'Goodnight, old friend,' he said to Richie and he kissed his nose for the last time.

48

After Richie died Dan didn't mention him once. It was as though he had never existed, but the more emotional of Lionel Richie's ballads were being played constantly while she was upstairs painting.

Tressa's cast was removed and they delivered the paper to the press with ease, including a lovely profile on old Walter, who had started getting treatment for his alcoholism at the urging of Rosemary March. She had promised he could do the town deliveries for the post office, if he stayed sober.

And he was staying sober, and delivering the mail to the office, so Tressa didn't have to trudge up the hill to pick it up.

'How are you, Walter?' she asked, when he dropped off the letters to the editor.

'Keeping busy,' he said in his gruff voice.

'I can't tell you what a relief it is to have you drop this off. Dan and I have been so busy, so this is a time-saver, I tell you.'

Walter looked very pleased at this news and straightened his shirt collar.

'I best head off. Pamela has her beauty magazines from America, and I know she looks forward to them.'

He left, wheeling his mail trolley, and Tressa closed the office door. 'He's a new man now he has this job.'

Dan looked up from the computer. 'People need a purpose. Before this job he thought his purpose was drinking but now he's actually useful. It helps lift a person's spirit.'

'That will be you soon, with your fancy London job,' she said, trying to sound light-hearted. 'That will lift your spirit.'

But Dan didn't reply and she sat at her desk, scrolling through the advertisements to be placed in the next edition. Her phone rang and she saw it was George.

'Hello, love, how are you?' he asked.

'Great. How's Caro?'

'Doing very well; in fact, they said she can come home soon and have the rest of her treatment at home. They send a nurse around and do the infusions there. They actually think she's going to be okay.'

Tressa could hear the relief in his voice.

'Oh George,' she said. 'Oh, I'm so happy. That's amazing.'

'So I think we will be back in a week, and then you will have me back again. So I'm about to ring Dan and let him know he can head off to London whenever he wants.'

Tressa felt her heart drop. Dan was still sleeping on the sofa but they barely spoke unless it was about work. She didn't want him to go but didn't want to be in a room with Dan, sharing only silence.

George was still talking. 'From what I've heard, you will be happy to see the back of him.'

'I've got to go, George. I'm so happy about the news. Please give Caro a big hug from me,' Tressa said and she put down the phone. She turned to Dan. 'George is going to call you. He will be back in a week, so you can get ready to move on.'

Tressa went upstairs to her studio and slammed the door as hard as she could.

49

All morning, George Fox had been receiving texts from various residents of Port Lowdy.

First there was Dan saying he would be gone by the time he came back and everything for the next edition of the paper was ready for him; and though things with Tressa didn't work out the way he had hoped, he thought it best he move on as he had lost the two great loves of his life in Port Lowdy. He was going to work at *The Times* writing longer articles and that wouldn't have come to him if he hadn't come to Port Lowdy, and he thanked George for the opportunity.

That was a long text.

Then came an even longer message from Tressa saying she couldn't work at the paper anymore because she was heartbroken about Dan and was thinking she might give up everything including her career as an artist and go on the road, painting portraits for food.

Penny texted from Brisbane, of all places, saying she was coming home to Port Lowdy with a surprise and could they have a lunch – she wanted Dan and Tressa there.

Give them my love, she wrote.

And finally a message from Janet, saying that she had

never seen two sadder people than Dan and Tressa, who were clearly desperately in love and they couldn't get out of their own way. Could he ask Caro what was to be done? She always had the best ideas.

George could have been offended but he knew it was true: Caro did have the best ideas.

He looked over at her, asleep on her bed.

'Tell me. I can hear your phone pinging with all sorts of harried messages. Has Port Lowdy sunk into the sea?'

George laughed. 'You're not asleep after all. But you're tired. This can wait.'

Caro pressed the button next to her bed so she was lifted into a seated position.

'Tell me. I would like something else to think about while I wait to hear the results.'

George looked at her. First she'd said she wanted to die, and refused chemotherapy. Then she'd had the chemo, and the doctors had said her markers were down. Now they were waiting on the result of the PET scan that she'd had that morning.

'Dan is leaving, Tressa is devastated, Dan is devastated, they can't seem to work through their issues. They're as stubborn and as unable to work through their feelings as each other. Meanwhile Dan's been offered what sounds like a terrific job at *The Times*, so he—'

Caro was about to interrupt him when the doctors came into the room.

'Caro,' said the senior oncologist. 'We have excellent news.'

He said Caro was remarkable in her healing ability and that she would be a case to be studied. There were no leftover tumours visible on the PET scan. Caro nodded calmly, as though she was aware of her own gifts in healing.

'I told myself I would be okay – I think I knew that,' she said.

George pushed her earlier pessimism out of his mind. None of that mattered. He shook the doctors' hands and then kissed Caro when they had left.

'You are a contradiction and a mystery, Caro, and this is why I love you so much.'

'Enough of that, and I don't need reminding I told everyone I was dying, which I was at the time, so I don't want to hear your arguments.'

Caro's face was flushed for the first time since she had been diagnosed with cancer and she had the spark back in her eye.

'I'm hungry,' she said. This was certainly good news, since she hadn't been hungry in weeks.

'I can pop down to the cafe.' George jumped up, happy to have a task.

'Yes, I would like a lasagna or a shepherd's pie if they have either, and a custard tart and a lemonade.'

George laughed and set out on his mission. When he returned with both shepherd's pie and lasagna and a custard tart for them both, Caro was on the phone.

'Thanks, Wendy; you're an angel. Love to David.'

'Wendy? Buckland? You can't stand her. Why are you calling her?' he said after she ended the call.

'I can cope with Wendy when she's not trying to impress anyone, and right now she's worried about Tressa. It sounds like they've been doing some connecting, which is wonderful, but Wendy is going to organise a few things for us. Now hand over the shepherd's pie. I need to get well enough to get out for next weekend.'

'What's next weekend?' asked George, utterly confused.

'Let me eat first and then I will tell you the big idea.' Caro peeled back the lid of the container of shepherd's pie. She put her face over the steam rising from the dish then picked up the fork and ate.

50

Tressa walked into town. She should buy a new bike soon. She would have to get Janet to take her to St Ives, or should she get her car licence? She certainly couldn't rely on Dan for lifts anymore.

If she had a car and her licence then she could go to the gallery, or maybe even see her parents more often. She had even suggested that she move back to St Ives, but Wendy had told her that she belonged in Port Lowdy – it was her soulmate.

But Tressa had cried that night alone in her bed. Dan was her soulmate. And he was leaving for London.

The beach was busy with tourists when she walked past. Normally all the bright rich colours would have thrilled her but today they looked dull. Someone had turned down the brightness on the world.

The goodbye lunch for Dan was at the Black Swan.

She had tried to dress cheerfully, in a white lace sundress with tiny straps on her shoulders that she had found online, and with her red sandals that had cherries attached to the top like little fruity buckles. She had on her standard red lipstick and her hair was out and she knew she looked summery, but she felt cold inside.

The lunch had been planned by George, and the only consolation for such a dreadful day was that she knew Caro would be there.

Fake it till you make it, she told herself as she walked towards the pub.

Inside, all the tables were pushed back to the outside of the room, and there was a semicircle of chairs with two chairs facing them in the centre of the room.

'What's going on?' she asked, as Dan walked in behind her.

'No idea,' he said. 'You look lovely.'

She didn't say anything. She didn't trust herself to not beg him to stay.

'Hello, darling,' said Caro, who hugged Tressa tightly.

Caro's hair was gone but her spirit was strong.

'Caro,' said Tressa, returning the hug and trying not to cry.

'This is a bit shit sticks, isn't it?' she said to Tressa, who ignored her question because it was, indeed, shit sticks but she was on edge, feeling like she was ready to run away from everyone just to stop feeling this way.

'You look incredible. Bald suits you – you have a nice-shaped head,' said Tressa.

'Everyone says that when someone goes bald from chemo, but in my case it's not true. I have a head shaped like a cauliflower. I need hair. But this scarf covers the florets of my skull well enough.'

Caro turned to Dan. 'Hello, Dan, I'm Caro.' Tressa could see her assessing him from top to toe and inside and out. He smiled at her.

'Caro, Tressa talks of you constantly.'

'Does she? She talks of you constantly to me. We must get together and compare notes.'

Tressa glared at Caro. Behind them, her parents walked into the pub.

'Why are they here?' she asked Caro.

'Because I asked them.'

'Darling,' said Wendy, hugging Tressa, and David was shaking Dan's hand and Tressa thought she was having an out-of-body experience. Why did her parents need to say goodbye to Dan? What was he to them?

Janet walked into the pub, looking smart in jeans and a pretty yellow blouse. Janet in jeans – the world had really turned upside down. And why would Janet need to say goodbye to Dan?

George was now talking to Marcel through the pass in the kitchen, and then Remi came in through the back with Juliet holding his hand.

Dan and Remi shook hands and laughed. They went into a brief hug. Tressa and Juliet smiled at each other. The four of them were becoming close friends – but now Dan was moving away and it was all such a mess. Tressa felt her throat burn and she turned away to catch her breath. The door to the pub opened and Penny walked in, with a tall man behind her.

'Penny,' Caro called out and clapped her hands.

'Everyone, this is Paul Murphy, my long-lost Australian photographer who I am proud to say is now my husband. We got married in Brizzy, as they call it there. Tegan and Primmy were there and it was just wonderful.'

Pamela came from behind the bar, carrying a tray laden with glasses of champagne, as the room burst into cheers and claps. Pamela handed the glasses around.

'To Penny and Paul,' called George, lifting his glass. Everyone followed and then George turned to face them all. 'Now, friends, let us take our seats.'

Slowly everybody sat down, leaving Dan and Tressa standing side by side.

'Sit, sit,' said George, gesturing to the two chairs facing the rest of the group.

'Oh,' said Dan, 'this is some weird cult thing, yes? You are all in a cult and you're trying to get me into it.' Shaking his head, he stepped back.

'Sit down and be quiet,' said Caro in a stern voice none of them had heard for many months. Dan did as he was told and Tressa sat next to him.

'Now hold hands,' said Penny.

'What?' Tressa was thoroughly confused.

'Tressa, listen to Penny please. Hold Dan's hand,' Wendy ordered, and Tressa took Dan's hand in hers. They were both trembling.

'We are here today to sort you two out,' said George, 'as your kinspeople of Port Lowdy. Both of you have brought so much to everyone in this room and yet you're both getting in your own way of bringing yourselves the love and joy you have brought to all of us.'

Tressa took a gasp. 'Is this a Love Day?'

Dan was looking around the room, as though trying to find something to anchor onto. Tressa felt his hand tightly holding hers.

'We're your closest friends and your family. We're all here

to help you work this problem out. We have a day, where we talk it out and if we can't find a solution, then you two decide that you tried but it didn't work – and you kiss and move on with your life. Right now, you're both unhappy and in pain and need help to work out the way ahead.'

Tressa looked down at her lap. Her eyes blurred.

'I don't really think it's any of your business,' said Dan, crossing his legs and pulling his hand away from Tressa's.

'Hands,' yelled Remi, and he grabbed Tressa's hand again.

'Jesus, calm down.'

Caro leaned forward in her chair, holding her champagne glass, and peered at them.

'So, Dan, you have the new job, and you say you have to move to London. But I know you don't have to. George rang the editor. He said it didn't matter where you live because you will be profiling people from all over anyway. They said you could work from Timbuktu if you wanted to. So why are you going? When I know you want to be here with Tressa?'

Tressa looked at him, frowning her beautiful frown that was almost a squint. She always gave him that look when she knew he was being an eejit.

'Because she doesn't want me here. Port Lowdy is hers and she told me in no uncertain terms that her life was easier without me.'

'That's not fair,' she said. 'That's not what I meant.'

'So what did you mean?' asked her father, and he gave her a look that made her furious. As though she were a child again and he was about to pick apart her argument.

'I meant that before I loved Dan, everything was easier.' Tressa looked down at the scarlet cherries on her sandals.

Caro spoke. 'Everyone in this room has had their life changed because of you two. What you can achieve together is better than anything you have achieved apart – so why do you want to be alone?'

Tressa started to cry and Dan squeezed her hand. 'It's not that, I don't think.'

'So what is it then?' Caro demanded to know.

'I just think Tressa will be fine without me. I'm not good at love. I'm careless – look at Richie.'

The room was silent.

'That's not true,' whispered Tressa, shaking her head.

'What was that?' asked George.

'I said that's not true!' Tressa lifted her head, feeling the tears fall down her cheeks. She turned to Dan. 'You are more capable of love than anyone I know. And Richie was the luckiest dog in the world to have you as his owner.'

A tear fell down Dan's cheek. 'I let him down by being an idiot, like I let you down.'

Tressa took his other hand. 'No! He ran across the road chasing those seagulls and was hit by a car; that was all that was. You didn't cause it. You didn't make him chase the birds. You weren't driving the car. It happened. And you were with him as he passed and I tell you, I would want you holding me with my last breaths. He was one lucky pup.'

Dan had started to cry. 'I miss him.'

'I miss him too. I miss you,' she said, with a sigh.

Dan touched her face. 'Tressie my lovely, you could do better than me. I am a bit broken.'

'Let me fix you, as you've fixed me. Don't run away from us. Let's build a life together. I will go with you to London or Timbuktu or whenever it is you need to work.'

'I don't want to go to Timbuktu. I want to write while you paint and I want to take walks on the beach and find mermaid purses and say good morning to Rosewyn and kiss you every chance I can.'

Janet gave a long, contented sigh.

Tressa started to sob. 'You stupid eejit, why didn't you say so?'

'I told you. I make my life hard for myself. And it seems I make it hard for you also.'

'You make my life better. I wouldn't be showing my paintings without you,' she said.

'And I wouldn't have the new job, without you. I feel like I'm living the life I was supposed to now, without any of the anger but with all of the purpose.'

She kissed him and he kissed her back.

'You're supposed to save your kiss for the end,' Janet called out to them.

'What?' Dan turned to her.

'At the end of the arbitration, you have to seal your decision with a kiss,' Janet said primly, and even George was nodding in agreement.

Dan looked at Tressa. 'I love you, Tressie. I can't believe you know me better than I know myself and you still want to be with me.'

Tressa smiled at him, a damp tearful smile. 'I do love you, Dan. You are so kind. You pretend you don't care but I know you do.'

She leaned over and whispered in his ear. 'And I love you because you calm me and thrill me all at once.'

His hand cupped her knee and she felt her whole body and soul responding to his touch. He leaned forward and Tressa met him halfway and they looked at each other.

'Wait?' she asked. 'What's the date?'

'May the twentieth,' Paul said.

'May the twentieth,' she whispered. 'Our Love Day.' And they kissed each other as though there was no one else in the world.

The Port Lowdy Occurrence

Tressa Buckland's exhibition at The St Ives Gallery was a sell-out, with most of the works sold before the show opened.

Tressa was accompanied to the exhibition by her fiancé, celebrity journalist Dan Byrne who is now living in Cornwall full-time, writing for *The Times* and *The New York Times*.

Dan had their one-year-old dog, a placid Groodle mix named Nora rescued from the RSPCA, who Tressa said was obsessed with drawing and who wasn't interested in chasing seagulls.

Wendy and David Buckland, the artist's proud parents, were in attendance, as were many of her friends from the village of Port Lowdy.

Entrepreneur George Fox and his wife Caro, who was given the all clear from cancer, opened the exhibition and gave a rousing and emotional speech, where there wasn't a dry eye in the gallery.

Dan and Tressa will be married on the beach on May the 20th next year and look forward to sharing their special day with all of Port Lowdy, who have all been invited to a beachside party after the ceremony, catered by the much-respected pub the Black Swan.

Tressa's work is on display for all of September so head down before it closes, and don't forget to look for the little mermaid hidden in all her paintings.

About the Author

KATE FORSTER lives in Melbourne, Australia, with her husband, two children and dogs and can be found nursing a laptop, surrounded by magazines and talking on the phone, usually all at once. She is an avid follower of fashion, fame and all things pop culture and is also an excellent dinner party guest who always brings gossip and champagne.

Hello from Aria

We hope you enjoyed this book! If you did let us know, we'd love to hear from you.

We are Aria, a dynamic digital-first fiction imprint from award-winning independent publishers Head of Zeus. At heart, we're committed to publishing fantastic commercial fiction – from romance and sagas to crime, thrillers and historical fiction. Visit us online and discover a community of like-minded fiction fans!

We're also on the look out for tomorrow's superstar authors. So, if you're a budding writer looking for a publisher, we'd love to hear from you. You can submit your book online at ariafiction.com/we-want-read-your-book

You can find us at:
Email: aria@headofzeus.com
Website: www.ariafiction.com
Submissions: www.ariafiction.com/we-want-read-your-book

- ⓕ @ariafiction
- 🐦 @Aria_Fiction
- ⓘ @ariafiction